Christmas Romance Digest 2024

Love in Other Worlds

Published by Stories Rule Press Inc.
Edmonton, Alberta, Canada.

Registered offices:
#2500, Sun Life Place
10123 – 99 Street NW
Edmonton Alberta T5J 3H1

Edited by Tracy Cooper-Posey
Text design by Tracy Cooper-Posey

FIRST EDITION: November 2024

Fantasy, Romance, Short Stories, Pananormal, Christmas, Holidays

20240901

Praise for previous *Christmas Romance Digest* editions

This is a perfect collection to sit in front of the fireplace on a cold day or curl up on your couch when it's raining outside

I absolutely LOVE this collection!!!

Each author has offered an AMAZING story of holiday love that got me ready for the season!

This compilation of Christmas shorts will hit you in all the feel-goods in all the right ways

CONTENTS

Christmas Romance Digest 2024

Love in Other Worlds

Edited by

TRACY COOPER-POSEY

Stories Rule Press

From Ice Castles to Root Beer Factories

YOU MAY THINK YOU KNOW what fantasy romance is. There has been enormous chatter about fantasy romance in the last few years. Everyone wants to read it. Everyone seems to be writing it. "Romantasy," as it has been dubbed (a sobriquet I resist with every fiber of my being) is Romance + Fantasy. Very simple.

But is it?

I thought I understood fantasy romance until I came to edit this year's edition of *Christmas Romance Digest*. The seven novelettes in this edition span the deep and wide range of fantasy, from ice castles to root beer factories, with styles from dreamy urban fantasy to feisty contemporary fantasy, to softly romantic tales and whimsical dreams.

But all of them are, at their heart, romances entwined with the holidays, with Christmas, Hanukkah or the solstice helping bring lovers together.

Enjoy.

Tracy Cooper-Posey
Edmonton, Alberta
October 2024

Veilbound
by Taylen Carver

1: Reckless, Meet Neatness

I KNEW THE MAN SPRAWLED in my porch rocker, snoring softly. He wasn't the last person I ever wanted to see because he wasn't even on the list.

Kellan Delacroix, himself. And I'd been hoping for a quiet solstice.

I considered creeping right past him and heading inside. I climbed the steps onto the porch. I was tired and stumbled, then thrust my foot out to stay upright, and that killed any chance of ignoring him.

He jerked awake and sat up, rubbing his eyes. Green eyes, dark brown hair, soft stubble, white skin. He was French Canadian, the gossips had explained to me at the last Veilwarden gathering, which had been in Montana this year. Delacroix hadn't been there, of course, even though everyone was expected to turn up. He rarely bothered with Veilwarden business.

"You're littering my porch," I told him, and reached up to retrieve the key from the top of the front railing support post.

"You've been gone hours, Thorn," he muttered.

"It was the solstice. I was doing my job. Why weren't you doing yours?"

"I was." He got to his feet and winced. His left arm stayed bent. He held it stiffly against his side.

"Not sitting here, you weren't." I unlocked my door.

"We're in the middle of nowhere here," Delacroix observed. "You lock your door anyway? I could have waited inside if you hadn't."

"Which explains why I lock my door." I went in and Delacroix followed me, even though I hadn't specifically invited him.

"Woah!" he exhaled, looking around. "You like Christmas, don't you?"

"People decorate at Christmas," I said stiffly. "It's a thing."

"Not like this." He belatedly shut the door.

While he was doing a slow 360, I unchocked the stove door and threw in a log. While I fanned the coals, waiting for the wood to catch, I said, "Where is your car?"

"Not here," he said, looking up. "Is that an actual stuffed owl on the rafter?"

"Then how did you get here?" I demanded. Then I remembered the anomaly. "Helicopter," I said. "I heard it go over about an hour ago." I stared at him. "You rented a *helicopter*? From Edmonton?"

"I rented a jet," he said shortly. "The helicopter got me from the airport at Fort Chipewyan to here."

I pummeled down my resentment and envy. Delacroix's portal was in the Edmonton river valley. He'd built a winery and lounge bar around

12

it and was the social hit of the city. He had more than enough spare cash to... "No, wait." I closed the stove and got to my feet. "The solstice was eight hours ago. Best practice says you're supposed to monitor your portal for six hours before to six hours after the moment of the solstice. It's two hours by air to Fort Chipewyan. There's no way you can be here this fast." I glared at him. "You abandoned your portal? At *the solstice*?"

Delacroix lifted his hand and winced once more. "Rein in the high and mighty, princess. I didn't abandon it."

"Then explain how you're here, now."

"I didn't abandon the portal, because the portal isn't there anymore."

I got my jaw working after a few deep breaths. "Isn't there?" I repeated. Because that sounded intelligent.

"Someone tried to come through. I held it closed. Per regulations," and he glowered at me. "Then something shut it down completely. Threw me across the room."

I laughed. "No one can just shut down a portal. It's impossible."

"Tell that to my arm," Delacroix growled.

I glanced at his stiff left arm once more. "Is it broken?" I asked, with a touch of horror.

"I really hope not," Delacroix replied. "There's too much to do."

"To do? The solstice is over."

He shook his head. "They broke through in Crowsnest Pass." He paused. "Lyra Espenson is dead."

I gasped. "No!" Lyra was...had been one of the best Veilwardens in North America. And she'd had an amazing sense of humor. "What *happened*?"

"They didn't see who came through. Too busy trying to revive Lyra. But whoever came through snatched someone."

"Snatched?" Oh, my inner idiot was shining, this morning. But I was tired. It had been a long, cold night.

"A child."

"A *human*?"

He nodded. "And took her back through to Terranox." He carefully adjusted his arm, resetting it. "I'm tired and I used up a lot of juice last night, holding the portal closed. I need your help, Thorn."

I tried to sit in my chair at the table, but I sort of flopped into it. I rubbed my temple. "You're going in after the child."

"Her name is Chrissy. And yes, we have to get her back."

That was something else the gossips had passed along, behind their hands. It was said that Kellan Delacroix crossed over to Terranox all the time. He spent *days* there.

I couldn't imagine why anyone would want to voluntarily visit Terranox. The place was a nightmare and humans weren't welcome.

The only reason to spend time there had to be self-serving. Scrounging for artefacts, or selling food for Kobold gold, which normal humans couldn't distinguish from ordinary gold... Maybe Delacroix's wine bar wasn't his only source of income.

I felt sick. "You don't need me," I told him.

"I don't like it much either, but I *do* need you. You're a stabilizer, Thorn. A good one."

I refused to feel flattered. "All wardens can stabilize," I pointed out. "There has to be someone else who can help you."

He shook his head. "Not this close, not who can shake off family stuff and jump..." He grimaced.

"While I'm all alone," I said stiffly. "And just waiting for distraction, right?"

He looked around the big main room of my house. "Just how long did it take you to put up all these decorations, anyway?"

I glared at him. "I'm not going with you. You're reckless. You take insane risks."

He swore softly. "I'd forgotten this about you."

"Forgotten *what* about me?"

"Don't you get it, Riva? *Someone* shut down my portal, an hour after Chrissy was abducted."

I drew in a slow, slow breath. "*Chrissy* is a dynamo?"

Delacroix nodded. "Just like Vera Thorn."

My grandmother, who had died in Terranox when my mother was only two years old.

I cleared my throat. Then rubbed my temple once more. Whoever had taken Chrissy must have known she was a dynamo—someone who could create and destroy portals. Dynamos were rare. *Very* rare. Which was why Veilwardens had their jobs; we needed to keep what portals we had stable and impervious.

Whoever had taken her could use Chrissy to reshape the portals. Create too many or shut too many down. That would deregulate the flow of chaos between our two worlds...and that could only be a disaster.

"How old is she?" I asked, with a sigh.

"Six," Delacroix replied. "She'll be scared out of her mind." And *he* sighed.

2: Tick Tock, Tick Tock.

"DO ME A FAVOR," KELLAN Delacroix said, just behind me. He sounded breathless, but I had set a fast pace back to the portal. "When we're over there, don't call it Terranox."

"Why not? That's its name."

"That's the name wardens give it. It's not the name everyone over there uses."

And how do you know that? I wanted to ask. Instead, I said, "Aethryn, right?" I halted by the log I usually sat on.

"They don't like our name for Aethryn," Delacroix said, stopping next to me and peering through the trees.

"It's there, between those two poplars," I said.

"I know. I can feel it."

"Give me a minute to lower the resistance. And build the bridge."

The portal didn't show, not to normal human eyes. And because my portal was right out in the open, it needed a pass-through cloak. A human, a deer, or a buffalo could walk right through the trees and not notice a thing.

I also had to break down the barrier I'd spent all night building up again, once the supreme moment of weakness caused by the solstice had passed. That was why whoever had taken Chrissy had been able to push through the portal at Crowsnest Pass. They must have caught Lyra by surprise...only every warden was absolutely braced for Noxterrans to try to break through on the solstice. So what had happened?

I reached out, embracing the portal in my mind. Encompassing it. My veins hummed; my heart thrummed. Fresh snow coating the branches of trees nearby was shaken loose and drifted to the ground.

Delacroix switched his heavy staff from his right hand to his left, watching the portal. Then he winced and put the staff back in his right hand and tucked the left in his coat pocket.

Then everything grew still. It was done.

"I'll have to rebuild it on the other side," I pointed out.

"Throw a shield over it," Delacroix growled, striding forward.

"That will cut off the energy flow!" Only someone like Delacroix could make such a suggestion. The clear, unimpeded flow of energy was the other function of the portals, and a warden's primary responsibility.

"It won't matter. We're going in and getting out as fast as we can, before whoever has Chrissy talks her into shutting down more portals. Or forces her to it." He didn't even look around at me. He just stepped through and disappeared.

I swore in my mind, took a deep breath and hurried after him.

•

THE WEIRDNESS SET IN THE moment we came through.

I have often peered through the portal, when the pass-through cloak wasn't in place. The view through the portal was of a woodland not unsimilar to the boreal forest that surrounded the portal on this side. A lake glittered not too far away. And sometimes I saw some of the creatures who lived in these woods, but they looked nothing like any animals we had on Terra.

But the land had changed since I'd last studied it. I halted just on the other side of the portal, astonished.

The lake was no longer lying on its bed. It drifted a dozen meters overhead, and through the green water I could see tree tops shimmering. The trunks of those trees were still planted in the ground, beneath the upside-down lake surface.

Icicles hung from the bottom of the lake, swaying softly in an unfelt breeze, tinkling as they knocked together.

The lakebed, which I would have expected to be a soggy, slimy and bare patch of mud, was covered in snow, the rocks that littered the area just white lumps beneath the coating.

I turned and spun the shield up and dropped it over the portal. It made me seethe to be so casual and ignore best practices, but I didn't think Kellan would wait for me.

By the time I was done, I was gasping. It was *hot*. I unzipped my coat, which was designed for northern Alberta winters.

"Best leave it on," Kellan said.

"Are you kidding? In this heat?"

He shrugged. "Okay, then. This way." He headed directly for the icicle forest hanging from beneath the floating lake.

I wanted to protest. What if the lake returned to the surface while we were under it?

He knows his way around, over here, I reminded myself.

Halfway across the lakebed, the air around us became suddenly chilly. Cold enough that my breath blew out as fog.

I fumbled to zip up my coat once more, irritated beyond belief. "Is it always so insane, over here?" I called after him.

"Not as bad as this," he said over his shoulder. "This is chaos boxed up. Chrissy must have shut down more than my portal and this is the consequence."

"This is why you wanted me here? To calm things down?"

"Yes, but not right now." He pointed up at the water with the end of his staff. "Wait until we're out from under this, first."

I rolled my eyes and glared at the back of his wide shoulders. How stupid did he think I was?

We walked for what felt like hours, through a landscape that didn't stop being strange and uncomfortable. We ducked floating logs and floating islands of trees, the soil still clinging to their roots. Water ran uphill, and in one case, ran up into the air as if someone under the ground was pouring it.

The ambient temperature shifted from hot to cold without warning. It wasn't a regular patchwork of hot air pockets, either. Sometimes it took a dozen steps to reach cooler air. Sometimes we walked for long minutes, while sweat gathered under my hair.

After a while, we reached what I called a farmer's track—two parallel runnels worn into the undergrowth, weaving around trees. We followed that, even when the track itself rose in the air, while the trees on either side stayed where they were. The track returned to the normal level a few more paces on.

"No animals," Kellan said. "Nothing but trickling water."

"Do you even know where you are going?" I demanded, for it felt as though we had been walking for days. I pulled my pack off my shoulders, unzipped it and delved inside. I passed one of the energy bars to Kellan. I had to tap his shoulder to get his attention.

He took the bar, amused. "You actually packed food?"

"I always have a go bag packed, just in case." I didn't like the note in my voice, but I was also too hungry to care too much right now. I took an enormous bite of the bar. "It's procedure," I added defensively.

He didn't roll his eyes at me. He just ate. Halfway through the bar, he held it up. "Good idea," he told me.

I nearly tripped over a root that was waving up from the ground, as if the fine tip at the end was seeking more soil, or water.

Not long after that, we reached a crossroad. Kellan looked around, leaning on the staff. Then he looked up. "Ha!"

Floating high above us, hanging upside down, was what I would have called an ancient mile marker, had it been on Terra.

Letters had been carved into the front of this one, but I didn't know Noxterran script. "What does it say?"

"No idea," Kellan said blithely. "But the shapes of the letters are right for the village I want. We're on the right path. This way." He strode off again, moving down the broader road, which was a white bald flat path through what trees still remained in the ground and upright.

Not long after that the village appeared. And it grew colder. Things stopped floating, and the snow grew thicker.

"This is what it *should* be like, here," Kellan said. His voice carried on the crisp air, for there was no breeze to stir the trees. Stillness gripped the land.

"Why would just some areas be affected?" I asked.

"Chaos pouring through fewer portals. It's more concentrated around the portals that are left."

We walked into the village, between houses that crouched right next to the road. I could hear people speaking inside them, which meant the walls were not thick. The walls looked like daub, but the roofs were made of what looked like ochre tiles.

The village had an open square in the middle. Hay had been laid down over the snow, which let us walk without fear of slipping.

All around the square, people were gathered, wrapped in heavy cloaks, and talking together. Rough boxes and crates were being used as deal tables, and in the stalls behind them, stock munched. The creatures looked like large pigs, with deer antlers, and furry tails.

Many of the people were the same height as Kellan and me, but some were half-height, and I knew they were Kobolds. They had humanoid faces, as did the taller people. One of the taller ones had dropped his hood, and I saw long ears beneath his thick hair.

Wood elves or dryads. High elves didn't live in villages. They lived in more remote places, where their high council directed the affairs of lesser folk.

I knew the politics of Terranox, but I'd never seen an elf before.

We were drawing a lot of attention in our human clothes.

Kellan didn't seem to care. He moved around everyone, and over to one of the taller crates, where a woman with pale blonde hair and black eyes was pouring a steaming beverage into cups sitting on the crate.

Three of the taller men, and a kobold stood waiting to take their drinks.

A small handful of coins sat on the crate next to the cups. As the woman finished pouring the beverage, she swept the coins off the crate. I couldn't see what she did with them, but they stayed out of sight.

"*You*," she spat at Kellan.

I knew how she felt.

Kellan held up his hand. "One question, Elysia, then I'm gone."

When we had arrived in the square, everyone had been talking or laughing or calling out to each other.

Now they were silent and watched us. The only sounds were the snuffling of the stock behind the fences.

"No questions!" Elysia cried. "Not for your kind." She spoke with an accent I'd never heard before. "Leave now, or my friends here will *make* you leave! You and your *chaos!* I curse you!"

And she spat. *Actually* spat.

The others crowded up close around us, and the hair on the back of my neck tried to lift beneath my braid. Barely without thought, I sent out a thick blanket of stabilization.

The menacing mood lifted. Everyone standing around us straightened, looking around at each other as if they'd just woken up.

Kellan's jaw worked as he studied Elysia. "I apologize for disturbing you. All of you." He looked around the square and nodded, then said something that I knew was probably the most common language of Terranox. I'd only ever scanned the script. I'd never heard someone speak it before.

"C'mon, Riva," he muttered and headed for the other side of the square from the side we'd entered.

"I don't understand what just happened," I said under my breath.

"I could say the same thing about you. They were ready to lynch us, then suddenly, they weren't." He glanced at me. "That was you, somehow."

We hurried down a narrow, rutted road that led, I presumed, to the other side of the village.

"You said you wanted someone good at stabilization." I shrugged as much as I could while walking fast and carrying a moderately heavy backpack.

Kellan came to a halt so quickly I had to slither to a stop and take two steps back to where he was standing.

"You used a stabilization thrall? On *people*?"

I pulled the straps of the backpack closer together and cleared my throat. "Is there a reason why I shouldn't?" That awful defensive note was back in my voice.

Kellan looked at me. No, he looked *through* me. "Who taught you that you could do that?" he asked softly.

I squeezed the straps. "No one."

"You just decided to try it one day?"

"I…" My cheeks were heating, despite the cold. "I just figured it out, when I was a kid."

23

"What happened when you were a kid?" He used the same light tone, but there was a note in it that made me cautious.

I shrugged. "My uncle...he and my aunt...they fought all the time."

Kellan's gaze didn't shift, but I knew he was now looking at me properly. Measuring me. "He hit you."

I swallowed. "My aunt."

Kellan nodded. "But never after you learned how to cast the thrall, right?"

I nodded. I couldn't have spoken.

Kellan started down the street again. "They were mundanes? Your aunt and uncle?"

"I thought I was merely human, too. That keeping my uncle calm was just wishful thinking, that he'd learned to control himself. But then...."

"Warden at sixteen, the youngest ever recruited," Kellan added.

"Then I found out about my grandmother, and how my mother died." I didn't ask how he came to be recruited because everyone knew the story. He was one of the rare wardens who had no long family history tied up with the portals. He had been in a bar, and utterly drunk. Only the bar was on State Street in Boston, and when Kellan had asked the barman why the mirror on the wall was showing mountains, not the front of the bar, the barman, who was also the warden of the Boston portal, had sobered Kellan up and taken him to meet the wardens.

Maybe that's why Kellan had renovated the warehouse around the Edmonton portal and made it another type of bar.

We reached the edge of town. Fields on either side of the road wore undisturbed carpets of snow.

The trees separating the fields were heavy with the stuff.

Elysia stood between the trees, her hood pulled up over her gleaming light hair, the cloaked wrapped around her. She wasn't scowling any more.

Kellan stopped by her and glanced up and down the road.

"No one followed me," Elysia said. "They're angry. The land is worse than it has ever been, and it is coming closer to the village."

Kellan nodded. "They're afraid, not angry. Where is the child?" His tone was urgent. "Taking her back to Terra will fix this, Elysia. She is creating an imbalance."

Elysia gripped her long-fingered hands together. "Everyone says she will make things better if she stays here." It wasn't a question, but I could hear the doubt in her voice. "If she closes the portals, then no more chaos can come through."

"It doesn't work like that," I said, surprised into speaking. "The portals maintain a balance."

Elysia looked at me for the first time. Her expression was withering. "Balance? Terra sends its chaos and upheaval to us and takes nothing back. We are your...your *stewpot*."

I flinched back from the anger in her voice.

"Aethryn gets all Terra's magic and miracles, too, Elysia." Kallen's tone said he was reminding her of the fact, not informing her. "The portals have to stay open. Look at what is happening with just a few of them shut down. How many farmers have lost their land?"

Elysia chewed her lip, doubt plain in her eyes.

"When we take the girl back to Terra, you will see that everything settles down again, and you'll know I am right," Kellan added. "Tell me where she is."

Elysia wavered. Then she said, "Malachai has her. In the Heart of Aethryn."

"*Malachai*?" I repeated, shocked into it.

"Later," Kellan said flatly, then to Elysia, "Where is the Heart of Aethryn now?"

She pointed across the field behind us. "Head for the afternoon sun. That way."

Kellan spun on his feet and headed for the field.

"Shouldn't we use the road?" I called out after him.

"The fields are safer," Elysia said, her tone grave.

I shivered and hurried after Kallen.

3. The Forest of Echoes

WE HAD CROSSED THE FIRST field, kicking up snow, which clung to my snowpants and jacket, and were through the belt of trees that separated the fields and into the second field before I had the breath to spare to say: "Malachai, Kellan? Are they talking about the same warden who—"

"Yes," Kellan said, cutting me off.

"But...he *died*. Didn't he? He was trapped here by a portal that shut down and died hiking to the next portal. No one knew he was in Terranox, no one even looked for him. I mean, no one ever crossed over into Terranox. They thought the Mexican cartels had taken him." Malachai had been in Mexico when he disappeared. Three years had passed before rumor of a human body found in Terranox explained where he had gone.

"Clearly, he didn't die," Kellan said shortly.

"A human wants the portals shut down? A *warden*? I don't understand."

Kellan was nearly a dozen paces ahead of me, and striding with a full, long-legged swing. But he stopped and glared at me. "You've never heard of anyone going native, Thorn?" His green eyes pinned me to the spot. They were filled with a puzzling fury.

I didn't like that fury aimed at me. I cast about for a way to deflect it. I itched to toss a thrall over him, but that would be rude. I gripped the straps against my shoulders and said the first thing that came to me. "I like it better when you use my first name."

His lips parted. Surprise. The fury in his eyes diminished.

Then he spun and stalked onward.

Just as surprised, I stumbled after him.

•

TWO FIELDS LATER, WE SLIPPED into trees that weren't a thin dividing line between tilled soil.

It was dim under the canopy, but also slightly warmer. Virtually no snow had reached the thick, rich soil between the trees, either.

"Toward the afternoon sun," Kellan muttered, looking back at the long shadows the trees were casting over the white covered field, then aligning himself with them.

"Compasses don't work here?" I asked. It was not a question I had ever thought to ask before. The political structures of Terranox, yes. The types of people and their relationship to each other, too. But I'd never stopped to consider how Noxterrans did something as simple as find their way across the land.

I didn't have a cellphone. My house was well outside any cell tower's range. I guessed that cellphones didn't work here, either, as Kellyn wasn't reaching for his.

"Compasses would just lead you astray, if they did work," Kellan replied. "Things move around, in Aethryn."

I recalled that he had asked where the Heart of Aethryn was now. Not "where is it?", but where it was *now*. "I see," I said diplomatically.

"C'mon," he said impatiently and moved on.

I watched for a hint of the sun ahead to measure if our direction was true, but the trees went on and on. There was nothing but murky darkness as far as I could see.

A crack of dried leaves and twigs made me whirl to face that direction. Kellan halted, too, his staff in both hands.

Silence.

He winced and shook off his arm and put the hand back into his pocket, and we went on once more. "It will be dark, soon," he said over his shoulder. "Best walk close behind me."

I closed the gap. It had been morning when we left the house. "Time moves differently here," I concluded. "Or are the days shorter?"

"I don't know. There are no clocks here, and no cellphone coverage."

Again, the loud crack and crunch of leaf litter sounded. I whirled again, my heart thundering.

From out of the trees, a woman came running toward us. She had bare feet and a simple white gown that fell to her ankles. Her hair was loose and streaming behind her. Black and wavy, like mine. "You *left* me!" she screamed and raised the sword she held up over her head.

"*Mom?*" I threw up my arms defensively. I fell to my knees, my mind scrambling to cope with the fact that my mother was attacking me.

Metal clanged and gave a soft musical note.

I looked up, cringing.

The sword my mother had brought down upon my head had been arrested, a foot above my eyes. Kellan's staff barred it.

The thing that was my mother screamed in protest…and disappeared.

Kellan dropped the foot of the staff to the ground and leaned on it, shaking out his left arm. "Shit, shit, *shit!*" he cried.

"What *was* that?" I scrambled inelegantly to my feet. "It looked like my mother!" I was shaking badly.

"I know," Kellan said. He turned a little to look at me. "This is the Forest of Echoes."

I wrapped my arms around my middle, suddenly colder than I had been even sitting in the dark beside the portal last night. "So *what?*" I nearly shouted it.

"It's called the Forest of Echoes because these bloody trees echo everything back at you. But mostly, they like to throw all the nasty stuff at you. Guilt, shame, embarrassment. All your sins remembered." His tone was withering. "The damned forest has moved, too."

I stayed silent, because if I let my teeth part, they would chatter.

Kellan tilted his head and considered me. I thought that perhaps there was compassion in his eyes, only it was too dark under the canopy to tell for sure. "You and your mother parted when you were young," he guessed.

I nodded. Then, because the guilt wouldn't let me *not* explain it all, I said quickly, "They took me away from her when I was five. I lived with my uncle and aunt after that. I found out later that my mother had been declared unfit. But I thought…"

"You've felt guilty ever since for leaving her."

I nodded. My eyes ached, heralding tears, and I blinked furiously. The last thing I wanted to do was cry in front of him.

He sighed. "*That* is what the forest does to you," he said. "It'll be my turn, next, most likely. Let's get through this place as fast as possible."

"Do you even know where we should go?" I asked, for I had lost all sense of direction.

"I don't care," Kellan growled. "Anywhere beyond these trees is fine by me."

I had to agree with him.

When he broke into a slow jog a few paces later, I only felt relief.

•

THE ATTACK UPON KELLAN CAME without warning. There was no crackle of underbrush, no breaking of twigs. Or perhaps we were crunching enough leaves of our own as we jogged between the trees that we didn't hear it.

Kellan passed the bole of one of the great trees that made up the forest. As he passed a man with thin red hair stepped out, a sword in his hands, held up high.

I moved without thinking. I had impetus on my side, and I was going to run right into the sword, even though it was meant for Kellan. I lunged forward, and shoved Kellan ahead.

Shoving against his back pushed me backward, out of the way of the descending sword. I felt the sharp blade separate the air in front of my face. The man—the real-enough apparition—bent forward as the sword met no resistance. The tip of the blade rammed into the ground, throwing up a fine mist of soil.

I was still moving without thinking. The thing was bent forward, hands low to the ground, presenting an almost horizontal sword.

I jumped on it.

My hiking boots were trail runners, built to grip on any surface including ice. The treads were deep spikes. I landed on the sword with both feet. It should have smashed the sword into at least two pieces.

Instead, the sword disappeared.

So did the red-headed man.

It happened so fast that Kellan was only just starting to spin around.

I reached out to hold myself up against the tree trunk. Kellan did the same.

"Who was that?" I asked between heaving breaths. "He didn't yell at you the way my mother did to me."

"I don't think he had time," Kellan said. "Do you know how dangerous that was, what you did? You could have lost your hands."

"But I didn't." I shrugged with one shoulder. "So, who was he?"

Kellan scrubbed his hand through his hair, as if he was irritated. And perhaps he was. "Malachai," he muttered. "And we shouldn't stand around here. C'mon."

I stayed where I was. "Why would Malachai visit you?"

He turned back with a sigh. "It doesn't matter. It's just the forest trying to manipulate us. Slow us down. It feeds off strong emotions."

I glanced up and around and shivered.

"C'mon, Thorn," he pressed.

"Malachai," I repeated. "Fair's fair."

"This isn't a kid's game, Riva! Those swords can *kill*."

"I know *that*. What I don't know is why the forest thinks showing you the man we're looking for will prod you into shame or whatever." I studied him. It was getting darker in here. His face was mostly a pale blob. "I'm in this, too," I added.

"I need to know what's driving you so I can be braced for the fallout."

He considered me for a moment. "I'm a fully grown adult. I've got buried issues the same as anyone else. It picked one of them. The next could be the first woman I ever stood up—"

"There was more than one?"

"*That's* what you're going to focus on?" He threw his hands up, turned and walked away with heavy steps.

I had no choice but to follow him. I wanted out of this place, too. Preferably before something else from my past showed up wielding a sword. Kellan was right on that point; I could think of plenty of moments in my life that made me squirm to recall them. The last thing I wanted was for some of those people to appear here, where I would have to explain to Kellan Delacroix why they lingered in my memory.

Like Sara Reeseman in my third-grade class. She had broken my green crayon, so I had pushed her on the playground. I'd come up behind her and shoved her—much like I had just shoved Kellan. She had skinned her knees badly enough they had called in her mother to take her to the ER to have them checked out.

An event from when I was eight was powerful enough to make me break out in a guilt-driven sweat.

"You were *mean!*" The childish scream came from behind me, and before I could spin to spot the source, something slammed into my lower back, just beneath the backpack. I cried out and staggered forward, fighting to stay on my feet.

Kellan whirled, the staff up, and ran past me. I heard the clash of wood upon wood and spun to look, but whatever he had confronted had already disappeared.

I felt my back, wondering what had hit me. It hadn't been a sword. My coat was still whole. But my entire back throbbed.

"A girl," Kellan said, grounding the staff. "Maybe seven. Pigtails."

"Sara Reeseman," I breathed. "But it wasn't a sword."

"A cudgel almost as big as she was." Kellan blew out his breath.

"I was just thinking about her..." I looked at him. "The forest taps into our thoughts."

He looked doubtful.

"It's not like we plug in a database of our lives when we come through. It has to get the information from somewhere."

"Our memories," Kellan said, with a *d'uh* note in his voice.

I shook my head. "They're nothing but acid patterns in our brain until we recall them. The forest listens in when we do. It can ramp up the fear and dread with every little attack. They're not meant to be lethal. That would kill off its energy supply."

"You can't know that, Thorn. You just stepped through the portal a few hours ago."

"But I'm right," I said firmly. "The more guilt and fear the forest can make us feel, the more ammunition it has to throw at us, because we start dredging up everything from our past that we feel bad about, wondering what it might use next. It just did that with me."

"And a grade school girl was all it could find for you?" Kellan asked.

I changed the subject because, yeah, I felt guilty about Sara Reeseman and yeah, it was none of his business. "We need to stop thinking about anything negative."

He laughed, not with good humor. "Think happy thoughts?" He turned and walked away.

I caught up with him. "Tell me your happiest moment ever."

"No." His voice was flat with anger.

"If you stay pissed, the forest will use it," I warned him.

He swore. A dozen heavy steps later, he said in a calmer voice, "I can't pick which one is the happiest."

"Think about it," I encouraged him. "Think of all of them and try to figure out which one was the happiest. Rank them."

He remained silent as we passed through the tall trees.

I rifled through my own memories, building a list of happy moments, and trying to rank them. It was an impossible exercise, but simply *trying* to rank them meant I was thinking about them and not negative memories.

I was so busy reaching for every happy moment in my life, and sorting them out, that I barely noticed time ticking on.

"The edge of the forest," Kellan said. Relief tinged his voice.

The darkness seemed to thin out, ahead. We both picked up our pace and hurried toward it.

4: A Litte Chaos, A Lot of Magic

FINALLY, WE STEPPED OUT FROM the trees into a flat grassland devoid of snow. A cool breeze whispered across the stalks, making the grass bend in ripples. A moon shone, overhead, but it was not Earth's moon. It looked larger and none of the markings on the face of it were Luna's.

It was a full moon, which would give us light to see where we were walking.

"Not a single attack, after your happy thoughts order," Kellan said, peering back through the trees.

I looked across the grass plain instead. "Where do we go from here? Where is the Heart of Aethryn? There's no afternoon sun to follow now." I paused. "If there really *is* a Heart of Aethryn."

"Oh, there is. Most people avoid the place."

Joy. "So maybe we should have headed in the opposite direction to the one Elysia said to take."

He glanced at me, as he shook his left arm and massaged the forearm. "Elysia can be trusted."

"Can she? She sent us straight into the Forest of Echoes. She said it was a safer route than taking the road, which I wanted to do."

"So, it probably is safer. Travelling the road is no guarantee of anything. Not here."

"How well do you know her? Elysia?"

He watched his hand as he turned it over and back, working the forearm muscles. "Well enough," he said evenly.

"Then you really do cross over to Terranox a lot."

"Aethryn," he corrected me. "Get it right."

"Aethryn," I repeated. "How do you know Malachai?"

"Long story."

"And we're not in the forest anymore, plus it's dark and I don't fancy turning an ankle in the grass. So, talk, Kellan. I want to know exactly what we're going to find at the Heart of Aethryn."

"The Heart is probably the most unstable place in Aethryn," he replied, looking out over the grass. "It's a nexus point for tides of power, for all the chaos and magic that seeps through the portals."

"Which is why it is moving right now," I said, figuring it out. "Each time a portal closes, the junction point between those that are still open shifts. So why is Malachai there, if everyone else avoids it?"

"Because it's a nexus point," he said, with a tone that said this was obvious.

"Pretend I've never stepped through the portals before."

"Damn it, Riva, it *doesn't matter*. We have to focus on getting Chrissy back, and that's all." He turned so that the back of his shoulder was to me and looked out over the plain.

"The more you protest, the more sure I am that it really does matter," I told him. "Why did Malachai's avatar attack you in the woods?"

He didn't answer straight away, and I had begun to think he wouldn't answer at all, when he spoke in a low voice. "The portal that closed, that trapped Malachai here? That was me. My mistake."

I snapped up straight, the backpack moving over my back, brushing my coat. "You *can close portals*? You're a dynamo?"

He didn't look at me. "I don't know. I've never tested it."

"But you closed a portal…no one can do that."

"And it might have been a clash of thralls, or some joker on this side throwing too much magic around—they were trying to come through, and I was new and barely knew what I was doing. Malachai was at the museum that night. He went through to check on what was happening in Aethryn. To calm it down if he could, which would take the pressure off me. And the portal winked out."

I stared at him. Kellan must have felt my disbelief, for he looked at me, then away. "I looked for him. I tried to get him back. It took me two years, almost every day."

Understanding came to me. "That's why you spend so much time here. You were looking for him."

"Well, I found him. But by then, this place had infected him. He had no intention of going back to Terra. I told the Council that I'd found him here, and *they* assumed I had found his body—because no one ever survives here." His tone was infinitely bitter.

"You didn't correct them?"

"I figured it was best if everyone thought he was dead," Kellan said. "He was lost to the Wardens, and there was no one else on Terra who cared enough to want him back." He shrugged. "Malachai is a grown man."

"He went native," I concluded. "And now he's forgotten every scrap of training the Wardens put him through and believes that shutting down the portals is a good thing."

Kellan didn't look at me. "It's not the balance he cares about."

"Well, he *should*. He knows as thoroughly as we do what happens if the portals get out of balance. I mean, *look* at this place!" I waved my hand around. "Lakes floating, icicles pointing downward, upside-down trees, tropical heat next to Arctic coldness, farmers losing their land, which means food grows short...how can he think that this is a good idea?"

"And how fair is it that Aethryn has to bear the burden of Terra's chaos?" Kellan demanded, rounding on me. "Terra lives a stable life while Aethryn suffers."

"My god, *you've* gone native, too!"

"No!" Kellan slapped the back of his hand into the other. "*No!* But don't you see, Riva? It's monstrously unfair, the way the portals pull everything noxious from Terra and deliver it here."

It took effort to recover from my surprise and pull together an answer. "We didn't set this up, Kellan. We just make sure it stays in place. Maybe it is unfair. Or maybe we don't understand what Aethryn pushes through to Terra. No one has ever tried to measure that! All we know, after centuries of study, is that the portals must stay open, that the balance lets both worlds live."

"Live in chaos," Kellan said heavily.

"A little chaos, and a lot of magic, for Aethryn," I agreed. "No chaos and no magic for Terra. But it's sustainable. It's stable. If that balance is broken, then both worlds will destroy themselves."

After a long moment, Kellan let out a heavy gust of breath and nodded. "That's why we have to return Chrissy to Terra. And she must open the portals she has closed."

"Agreed." I looked across the plain, which was pale in the moonlight. "Now, where do we go from here?"

Kellan shifted his shoulders, as though he was shaking off the mood. "There's a shadowy shimmer way over there by the horizon, where the moonlight seems to ripple. Do you see it? I've been watching it for the last few minutes. I don't think I'm seeing things."

I peered in the direction he was pointing. "You're right. It is as though the dark is wavy, like the surface of a lake."

"That's the start of it," Kellan said. His tone was heavy. "That's the border of the Heart of Aethryn."

My heart thudded heavily. "Okay, then." I resettled the pack against my back.

Kellan settled the staff in his right hand, but didn't move. He studied the ground at his feet. "The last thing you feel guilty about really is something that happened when you were in grade school?"

"My mother popped up first, remember."

He shook his head, negating that. "You were still a kid. Your life really is so blameless, Riva? You genuinely have no regrets?"

"Regrets? I have thousands of them." I squeezed the straps of the backpack. Could I admit it aloud? I found myself saying it anyway. "They gave me a choice of portals, after training. Florence was one of them."

"And you picked *northern Alberta*?"

"Fort Chipewyan wasn't the other choice," I said. My heart was racing now. "Victoria was."

"You *asked* for the most remote portal in the world…" he breathed.

I nodded.

"Why?"

It was a simple enough question. I took a deep breath and was suddenly glad of the darkness, because my cheeks were hot. "When you're alone, when there's no one else around to mess things up, you can control things."

"You can follow all the rules," he added softly.

"Life is predictable, with no one in it," I said. "People don't...go away."

"Like your mother."

I nodded.

"There's been times in my life, Riva, when maybe I should've picked up and moved away from people, too. Maybe you had the right idea."

"I didn't," I assured him. "I keep thinking about the women you stood up—"

He groaned. "Really, Thorn?"

"You feel guilty about them. Lot of guys wouldn't even remember them, but you do."

He considered me a for a very long moment. "Come on," he said at last. "Let's finish this."

5: The Twisted Heart

WHEN THE FOREST WAS A blurred line on the horizon behind us, dawn was close enough that I could see where the sun would rise. It might not be east, not in Aethryn, but I labelled it so, just to stay oriented.

Ahead of us, the glistening wall of fractured images grew larger. "It's a circle?" I asked, tracing the way the line seemed to bend backward at either side.

"No one knows. It just is," Kellan replied. "Let's get inside before it decides to shift positions again."

We moved up close to the waving wall. "It isn't reflecting us," I pointed out.

"It isn't reflecting anything," Kellan pointed out. He gripped his staff and stepped forward, *through* what looked like a water surface covered in wavelets.

That left me out here alone. I drew in a deep breath and walked through the wall, too.

There was no sensation of passing through anything. And the land on the other side was exactly the same; a plain of grass, and low hills on the horizon. To my left, the sun was about to rise. I could see the glimmer of its leading edge.

Yet even though nothing looked different, it *felt* different. It took me a moment to grasp why.

"It's muffled, in here," I said.

"Everything is concentrated, in here."

"The nexus…" I breathed. "This is where all the

chaos and magic focuses. That's why Malachai is here."

"Watch yourself," Kellan said, moving forward. "Nothing works the way you're used to."

"Where are you going?"

"To the hills," he said over his shoulder. "Malachai isn't anywhere where we can see him, so I'm going to look behind things."

"Does the Heart go that far?"

"I don't know."

"Maybe Elysia lied about him being here, too."

"She didn't lie about where the Heart was," he pointed out.

Movement over the tips of the grass near Kellan's leg drew my gaze. His shadow was shortening, as if the shade was drawing into itself.

I looked around at the rising sun. "Kellan! The sun!"

The sun was well above the horizon, and as we looked, it climbed even higher.

"Time is speeding up," Kellan murmured.

In my chest, and spreading out to my limbs, I felt the warm bubbling sensation that rose whenever I dealt with the portals. Usually, it was a mild feeling of effervescence, that I had come to think of as an internal happiness at doing my job well.

But now the sensation was far more intense. The bubbling was closer to a rushing sensation. "There's something happening," I whispered.

"I can feel it, too," Kellan said. "Magic. All around us."

"Keep walking," I urged him.

We moved on, pushing through the grass. The sun passed over us and sank toward the land.

Now I could not feel the soil beneath my boots. And abruptly, a few steps on, the grass ended. It didn't stop, it *died*. The green faded to pale brown, then the stalks shriveled, crumpled and dropped to the ground.

The ground looked like soil, but it shifted under my feet in a way that reminded me of stepping on dirt or snow lying on top of ice — the heart-stopping sensation of having your feet skate unexpectedly, throwing your balance off.

I tapped the soil and dried grass stalks with the toe of my boot.

Kellan turned back to see what I was doing. "Ice?" he asked.

The sun went down, and darkness covered the land. Then, a heartbeat later, the large moon rose, and ghostly white light bathed us.

"It's not quite the same as ice," I murmured, swiping at the thin covering of soil. It revealed what *looked* like ice, especially in the inadequate moonlight.

"Glass," Kellan said. "But what is beneath it?"

I swallowed. "I don't think we want to find out."

He put his staff in his left hand and held out the other. "In case one of us slips."

I hesitated, then took his hand. I did feel a touch more confidence about carrying on, too, which bothered me.

As we walked, the moon sank, and the sun came up.

I blinked at the bright morning rays, as the sun climbed in the sky.

"It's getting faster," Kellan observed. His feet slipped, because he was watching the sun, and he barely caught himself. I held my arm rigid, as he yanked on my hand.

He pulled himself back upright. "That got the heart going," he muttered.

44

"Because nothing else here has?" I asked.

He gave me a look from under his brow and moved on.

Two steps later, he bounced off...something. He let go of my hand and rubbed his knee. "Far *out*," he breathed. "That hurt."

I moved forward, my hand up. My fingers rammed up against the same invisible barrier, which was warm to the touch, but inert. I pressed the flat of my hand against it and ran my hand over it. "Smooth and solid. A wall."

"We look behind everything," Kellan said. "Go around it."

I turned toward the east, kept my hand on the wall and let my fingertips slide along it as I walked. Kellan followed, swearing softly as his knee protested.

The wall ended, and I tested it with my fingers. "A corner," I said, as I detected the sharp angle. The plane of the wall continued perpendicular to the previous surface.

Kellan moved up next to me but was pushed back by something against his left shoulder. He tapped with his staff. "Another wall. Parallel to the new one. A passage."

"A maze," I corrected him.

The sun set. The moon came up.

"Day three," Kellan muttered. "We'll never find him at this rate."

"And the power of magic is increasing," I added, for the tingling rush through my nerves was increasing.

"We need to normalize things, if that's even possible."

"Let's try," I said.

Kellan looked at me, puzzled.

"We stabilize portals. Why not here?"

"Is that your solution for everything, Thorn?"

"Why not? You said you wanted normal."

Kellan blew out his breath. "Okay then."

"Together," I said, holding out my hand.

He took it without protest and his gaze shifted as he focused internally.

I pulled my own mental focus into the part of me where the warmth came from. Now the magic around us was pulling so fiercely upon it, it stirred the instant I touched it.

Stirred, and leapt.

I sent out the calming blanket. Threw it across the land and held it down until it settled and took. I could feel Kellan as a silent white light next to me. His power mingled with mine. They wove together, then fused into an even more powerful thrall, that fell softly upon the land, and sank, heavier and heavier....

I let go of his hand, breathing hard, and bent to put my hands on my knees. "...wow!" I whispered.

Kellan grinned. "You've never worked with another warden like that, have you?"

I shook my head. "Is it always so...?"

"Exciting?" He smiled. "Depends upon the warden."

My cheeks burned, but night had fallen again, which hid my reaction.

Kellan reached out with his hand up, feeling for the walls. "Not there," he said, taking a step forward. "I think we did it."

"We did," I confirmed. "You can't feel it? Inside you? All the magic is...sleeping."

Kellan considered that. "Which means it could wake up if we disturb it?"

"I think...yes."

"So, let's tiptoe past." He took a step forward, but his boot slid, and he held still, his hand out to maintain balance. Then he moved on, more carefully.

The land was still glass beneath our feet. We were still inside the Heart of Aethryn.

We walked in silence for a while. The moon wasn't racing toward the horizon now. The quietness wasn't as muffled. But I could feel something…. "Over there," I said, pointing to my right. "We need to go over there."

"What's over there?" Kellan asked. Then he added, "Besides trees that weren't there a few minutes ago."

"The land shifts," I reminded him.

"What is over there?"

"Magic."

He just looked at me.

"It's different from the wild magic here in the heart. It's…tougher."

"How come I don't feel it, then?" he demanded.

"I don't know. Perhaps it's women's' magic."

"There's no such thing!"

I lifted my chin. "How would you know?"

Kellan shook his head. "You're teasing. *You*."

"Perhaps," I replied. I pointed. "I do know we have to go there."

"Then we'd better go there," Kellan said.

6: That's Not Alberta

THERE WAS A RUIN AMONG the trees. A building that had once been tall and strong, with stone walls. Now only stumps of the walls remained, but they were still tall in places.

Firelight glowed and flickered over the jagged top of the walls.

"Behind the wall," I murmured to Kellan.

"Because the firelight didn't tip you off."

"I can feel her. Chrissy. She's there."

Kellan looked around, gauging what might be a threat, I presumed.

"There's nothing else here."

"It's warmer," he said. "Is the Heart waking again?"

"No." I knew that for certain. "There is time yet. It *will* wake again, but for now, it rests."

We moved forward cautiously. Kellan kept his staff up. We stepped through the lowest section of the wall, which came up to our knees. Our boots crunched on rubble strewn upon old tiles that covered a vast floor.

Not far away from us, a large fire burned merrily. A small black kettle sat upon a flat rock next to it, and a wooden spoon that looked identical to the spoon I had in my own kitchen drawer jutted from the top of it.

A divan covered in a dark green material, with scratched legs, had been pulled up to the fire. Next to it was a pallet of blankets. And over the pallet was a tent made of sheer fabric that might once have been curtains, looped up on one side to form a canopy. Like the divan, the curtains were dirty and showed great age.

A man lay on the divan, shivering under a thin blanket. He had red hair.

Malachai.

Beneath the canopy, curled up on the pallet, was a small child.

Chrissy. She looked as though she was asleep.

Around the divan and pallet were stacks of everything a person would need to survive. Food in baskets, and more blankets.

"What the hell?" Kellan whispered.

I hurried to the canopy. Chrissy was the priority. I knelt on the tiles and reached under the canopy to shake the little girl's shoulder.

She roused sluggishly and kept her eyes closed. "I don't feel good." Her hand crept to her belly.

"That's not a surprise," I told her. "Do you want to go home, Chrissy?"

She opened her eyes. They were a clear blue. "Malachai doesn't know how to get me home." And she shivered.

I picked her up. She was small and light. "We'll figure something out," I assured her.

I got up and went over to where Kellan was crouched by the divan, shaking Malachai.

The man woke as reluctantly as Chrissy had. He looked up at us, blinking. Then, "Delacroix!" He tried to sit up and fell back onto the divan with a soft curse.

"You're sick," Kellan said.

"I'm not sick," Malachai said. "I'm dying." He lifted a hand and waved it weakly. "It's been a year, almost. Once Chrissy shut down a couple of portals, we couldn't get out."

"The balance of the portals was broken, which disrupted the Heart," I murmured.

I meant for only Kellan to hear, but Malachai opened his eyes and looked at me. "A thing I didn't know until it was too late." He gave a great sigh. "Hoisted by my own petard, Delacroix. You always insisted the portals had to stay balanced, and you were right."

I stared at Kellan. "But you said…" I began.

"That Aethryn shouldn't be burdened with Terra's chaos? I did say that," Kellan agreed. "But shutting down the portals isn't the way."

"I know that now," Malachai whispered. "I figured we'd both die here. No one else could reach us and we couldn't get out. Even Chrissy—the imbalance affects her the most. She fell asleep last week, and nothing would wake her. I thought…" He looked at me. "But she's awake again?"

"Riva calmed the Heart," Kellan said.

"We both did," I pointed out.

"I just gave a bit of a boost,"

Kellan said, shaking his head. "It was all you, Riva."

"Riva…" Malachai breathed. "Riva *Thorn*?"

"Yes," Kellan said.

"Knew your grandmother," Malachai muttered. "A grand dame."

I let out a shaky breath. "We have to get them both out of here, Kellan."

"Now you're here, there's no way out," Malachai said. "Not while Chrissy is here. The Heart churns around her." He closed his eyes again. "I just wanted a place to hide while she shut down portals."

An idea came to me. "Or is the heart just reacting to the portals Chrissy closed?" I asked. "What if she opened them again?"

Kellan looked at me. In the last few minutes, the sun had risen again, and I could see his features clearly. He looked thoughtful.

"How many portals did she close, Malachai?" I asked.

Kellan shook the man.

Malachai didn't respond.

"He gets sleepy," Chrissy said. "And he snores for a long time."

I sat on the end of the divan and settled her on my knee so I could look at her. "Do you remember closing the portals, Chrissy? Did Malachai ask you to reach out with your mind and shut something down?"

"You mean scrunch it all up like a piece of paper?" Chrissy asked.

"I suppose, yes, that's a way to do it. Is that what you did?"

She nodded, her eyes wide.

"How many times did you do it?"

She held up her hand, two chubby fingers extended.

"You did it twice?"

Again, the nod.

"Am I in trouble?" Chrissy asked. "I did what Malachai said…"

"No, you're not in trouble…well, not with us. But what you did, Chrissy…it made the world sick. That's why you and Malachai both feel sick. And why you're stuck here in the Heart of Aethryn." I gave her a big smile. "Do you think you could open those portals once more? Maybe…smooth out the paper and put it back?"

Chrissy tilted her head, considering. Then she shook it.

Disappointment touched me. I hid my reaction, though. "It's alright," I told her. "We'll figure out another way to get you out of here."

"Couldn't I just make more doors?" Chrissy asked.

Kellan drew in a sharp breath. "Yes, Chrissy. New doors. Just like the old ones, but new and made by you."

"Why don't you try?" I asked her. "Put the doors where the old ones were."

Chrissy rubbed her eyes with a grubby fist. "I have to think inside," she said. "Malachai says I have to keep my eyes closed until I get better at it."

"You can do it however you need to," I told her.

"Okay." She shut her eyes, screwing them tightly closed, her nose wrinkling with the effort.

"Riva, look," Kellan said softly.

I looked up. The fire had lifted up from the ground. So had the divan we were sitting on. We drifted a foot above the tiles.

I reached out, smothering everything I could reach with a stabilizing thrall. I poured everything I had into it. My heart raced, throwing itself against my ribs, which hurt.

Slowly, we sank back onto the tiles. The divan grounded itself with a scraping sound.

Chrissy opened her eyes and yawned. "Two," she said, lifting her fingers once more.

"That's...not Alberta," Kellan declared.

I looked around.

A portal stood open, just by Chrissy's princess bed. It was raw and new and completely translucent. I saw a busy city street through it, and a dog peering at us, its head tilted.

I cast a curtain thrall over it, and the portal shaded itself, the interior a grey mist.

"So where did the other portal open up to?" Kellan asked softly.

I looked down at Chrissy. "Can you move the door somewhere else?"

"To Alberta?" Chrissy asked.

"Yes, where your mom and dad are."

"But they're not there anymore," Chrissy said sadly.

Kellan winced.

"Well, where they used to be, then?" I suggested. "The place where you came through to here. Do you remember that?"

"I don't like that place. The little men who came through the door there hurt my arms and legs."

Kobolds.

"If we can get you out of here, they won't be able to do that to you again," I promised her. "Try to move this portal to that place. It's important, Chrissy."

She screwed her eyes shut once more.

I could feel the divan trying to lift, and reinforced the stability thrall, smothering the area with calmness and balance.

Chrissy opened her eyes. "I found the place! A better place! It's all pretty!"

Well, Crowsnest Pass had spectacular scenery, including mountains and lakes, but I'd never heard anyone call it pretty.

I smiled at her and lifted the veil from the portal.

The portal neatly framed my house, the deep snow and the trees around it. The porch, and the woodpile just off it. It looked like morning, there, and the snow *was* bright and pretty. It sparkled.

So did the Christmas lights in my windows.

"Umm, that's not quite what I meant—" I began.

"Who cares! It will do." Kellan lurched to his feet. "Deal with it later," he told me. He bent and picked up Malachai, draping him over his shoulder. "We are *leaving*."

7: Boring is Good

Things happened quickly, once we returned to Terra.

Kellan's phone began to ring the moment we stepped through the new portal. While I got the stove going in my house, washed and fed Chrissy, and tended to Malachai, who appeared to be merely sleeping now, Kellan spoke to a lot of people, breaking the news, and making arrangements.

The helicopter arrived and took both Chrissy and Malachai away, but the pilot wouldn't take a third person. "I can come back and pick you up whenever you're ready," he told Kellan. "Let me get these two safely to their plane, first. That private jet of yours, right? What is that thing glinting in the front of the house, anyway?"

We tramped back to the house once the helicopter had clattered away.

"I'd better hide the portal," I said.

"I can do it, if you'll make breakfast," Kellan said. He angled toward the portal, which *did* shine in the sunlight.

I made breakfast. A *huge* breakfast. And I checked messages on my computer in between stirring the eggs.

Kellan settled in the other chair at the table with a long, hard groan. He hadn't asked which chair was mine. "I put all the usual guards on it, too," he said.

"Now there's two portals here."

"Lucky you."

I rolled my eyes at him. "Do you know what today is?"

Kellan pulled out his phone and put it on the table. He tapped it. "Christmas Day."

I put the loaded breakfast plate in front of him and settled into my chair. "It doesn't feel like we were there for four days."

"Clearly, we were."

"Time really got messed up over there."

Kellan picked up his knife and fork. "I have a feeling it's going to straighten itself out now."

"Balance restored?"

"Yeah."

He took a huge bite of toast loaded with eggs and chewed. While he ate, he looked around the room.

I could feel myself squirming, as he took in all the decorations. So I concentrated on eating my own breakfast.

When the coffee machine was done, I poured us both a mug each and pushed the cream and sugar toward him.

"It really *is* quiet here, isn't it?" he said.

I straightened my shoulders. "So?"

"So…after the last four days, it's nice. It's…" He grinned. "It's normal."

"It's boring, you mean?"

He shook his head. "Boring is good. Normal is good. Riva…"

I drew in a breath.

"The portals have to stay open," he said. "But we have to find a way to help Aethryn. You know that, right?"

"I do."

56

Kellan's lips parted. I'd surprised him. Then he smiled. His smile was nice. Warm. "There are two portals here now. The wardens won't demand you take care of both of them, even if you are the granddaughter of the great Vera Thorn. I thought that—"

"Yes," I said.

"I didn't ask yet."

"I'll help you help Aethryn," I said.

"Nope. Not what I was going to ask."

My heart battered at my chest. "What, then?"

He reached over and picked up my hand. His was warm and strong. "I've got a terrible record, when it comes to relationships."

"I picked that up, the last few days," I told him.

"Too many people around me, all the time. It's hard to focus on just one person, you know? But I think I want to try again. With you."

My heart squeezed. "And my excessively boring life?"

He shook his head. "It's quiet, Riva, but it's not boring. There's no way it will be boring with what we have to do now."

I let out a deep breath. "I think I'm done with being alone, anyway. For now, at least."

His eyes gleamed. "When we've done saving Aethryn, or when we need the break, we can come back here and be alone together."

"That sounds perfect," I breathed, as he drew me to him.

Taylen Carver is an Aurealis Award finalist, and is the pen name used by bestselling author Tracy Cooper-Posey. As Taylen Carver, she writes contemporary, epic, and urban fantasy stories and novels. TAYLENCARVER.COM

Winter Fruit
By Chelsea Mueller

I PUKED BEHIND A WALL of white asphodel flowers the day that Kiernan first took my hand. It wasn't his fault. Though I'm sure my mother would say otherwise.

I'd tilled the earth and beckoned blossoms and fruit day after day. I did it for so long that it must have looked easy. I passed bundles of grain to my patrons with cracked hands. They looked to my fresh stores and not to the new bruises marring my knees.

To call my garden fruitful would be an understatement. I had more than a green thumb; I had a touch. The Community Garden had become Chloe's Garden when I was merely a child. It had been my family's livelihood. Now everyone in the neighborhood came to me to feed their families, to adorn their homes with the fragrant flowers, and to be sated.

Everyone except him.

My dark admirer had never stepped atop my soil. He hadn't plucked an orange from the trees at the back or asked for a tomato to top a sandwich. He even ignored the poinsettias lining the front wall, a favorite this time of year, although harder to cultivate in our constant balmy weather.

He lounged across the street again today. Broad shoulders too wide for the chair, legs too long to wedge beneath the tiny two-person table. Like a dutiful uncle waiting for a child's tea party. He kicked his boots out to the side, crossed his ankles, and watched me. It was the third time he'd set up outside the coffeeshop. His laptop was a prop. His dark eyes ate every vegetable on the vines between us and still landed on mine hungry.

There was no hiding behind the trellis as my meager lunch launched up from my stomach and onto the rich soil. Vomit didn't count as fertilizer, but I'd done it enough times to know it wouldn't hurt the plants. My patrons didn't notice. Most had come in the morning or it was too early in the afternoon for those seeking arrangements to adorn their holiday dinner tables. He saw though.

He saw everything.

I swiped my mouth on the back of my wrist and a hand landed on my shoulder. A chill cut through my shift at the contact. I stepped over the sickness, getting room between me and my new guest.

"I didn't mean to startle you. I simply wanted to bring you this." My dark admirer extended a cup of water to me.

His dark hair fell past his ears in tousled waves. I'd assumed the petite table across the road merely made him appear large in comparison. Not so. He loomed several inches taller than me. Small whirls of dirt kicked up as he shifted his weight. Perhaps the looming was incidental.

His first step into my garden was to bring water? "Thank you, but why?"

His brow furrowed, brown eyes locked on my lips as if to will me to speak again. "You need to drink more, and…"

"My garden has water." I gestured to my flourishing beds.

"And yet your body does not. When did you last eat?"

Who said such things? He was right, but we didn't know each other.

"I assure you, everything is quite fine." I pointed toward the gate, the indication clear.

He caught my hand, gentle fingers skimming the chapped skin at my knuckles, the abrasions on my palms. "I'm Kiernan, and you, Chloe, deserve more."

"Excuse me?" His touch was kind, warmth simmering between us, but I still scanned my land for a patron.

"I said you deserve more." He let go of my hand, stepped away. "Can I tend to your hands? Let me see that you are well, and then I will go."

Agriculture, even with a touch like mine, was still hard work. It required connection and muscle. I'd grown accustomed to the aches in my palms and the rawness of the skin there, but now that Kiernan called it out, it's all I could think about. How tight my flesh pulled, the ache in my bones and in my heart. The fatigue I buried like compost in my belly.

I nodded once, and that was all it took for Kiernan to alight. His brilliant smile lasted a mere moment. Brooding pout back in place, he ran across to the bodega, returned with a lavender hand balm. He held out one hand, and I offered him one of mine. No one had noticed my pain before; no one had cared for my wounds. Kiernan massaged each muscle, revitalizing my hands, and cracking open the wall I'd built around my heart. Was I allowed to want this? To like it?

When my hands were buttery soft, he kissed the back of each of them. "I'll be back tomorrow."

It wasn't a question, but I wouldn't have been selfish enough to answer back then. "I'd like that."

Kiernan and I carried on like that for weeks. He never took from my garden, never asked for more. Patrons came with their children in tow, gathering garlands and mistletoe. But he brought me food crafted outside my walls and more water than was necessary. He soothed my aches and asked about what I loved most in my garden. It had always been the citrus fruits, but as the moon faded from full to new, I wanted to say he was the highlight of my garden.

●

MOTHER HAD NOTICED MY SOFTENED skin and my disregarded gloves. She'd asked time and again who was helping tend the Garden, as if she didn't titter about the town for praise from her daughter's bounty. If I weren't producing, she'd be the first to know.

My answers hadn't appeased her. Patron after patron tried to pry some secret from me. All at Mother's behest. As if they couldn't see the man who walked the softened paths with me while I worked in the late afternoon. Mother made no plans for a Solstice celebration; we never did. She was too happy to be invited to others' events, and I was too exhausted to do either.

Kiernan slipped into the Garden as the day faded. The sun had grown lazy in the sky, leaving him ringed in the echo of fire.

"You deserve more," was his greeting.

He'd said the same thing for weeks, but this day it came with action. He offered a night of freedom. Of escape. A night where no patron would find me, ask me to cultivate Solstice wreaths for them. One night to think only of myself.

And him.

I'd left the Garden before. I wasn't physically bound to it, but every time I left, I only found more beatific faces asking for *something*. And I wanted to help. I was meant to. Even going out for a meal, though, meant visiting those who cooked with the produce I grew. My efforts were everywhere and so I found solace nowhere.

And then there was the bucket of guilt I'd be dunked with. "Mother will know."

His laugh snatched my breath; its sinful heat licking up the sides of my neck. "I can promise you she will not."

"You don't understand her determination—"

"She hired me."

Every sweet flower budding in my heart dessicated with those words.

"Yesterday," he amended. "I took her money, and I won't apologize for that. But as long as she has a man determining who is 'doing all my daughter's work for her that she could afford weak hands' she will give us space."

"My hands aren't weak," I grumbled.

"Nothing about you is weak, Chloe." He took my hands in his. Smooth and warm. "I know an escape where you'll know no one, save me." Color warmed his cheeks but it was the smolder in his eyes that made me agree.

This neighborhood was cast in concrete and chrome. Was I kudzu come to reclaim this inorganic land? I hoped not, because for once I didn't have to think about the seeds beneath the ground or petals opening at the right time. There were no flowers here. I should have missed their bright colors. It was who I was....

And yet.

And yet.

And yet.

The building was tall and sleek and every bit as sharp as Kiernan. Inside the club, we breezed past security and hostess stands. He led me through a winding path of dark hallways to a plush sofa wrapped in black leather. Orange flames from a lone candle danced behind amber glass atop the low table, the fire multiplying against the slick, black surface.

The cushion dipped when he sat, sliding me toward him. I careened into his side and he caught me. Heat flooded my face, but Kiernan merely tucked a loose strand of hair behind my ear and then leaned back, those dark eyes heated again. "Do you have a favorite drink?"

No one had ever asked. "I don't think so."

"Not having one is better."

I'd missed out on so much. I grew the grapes for wine, the rye for whisky, the goddamned potatoes for vodka, but they were always for others. Everything for others. I cared for everyone else, but had no time left to do so for me. I continued to allow Kiernan massage lotion into my hands most evenings.

"I've experienced nothing. Not sure how that's supposed to be a good thing." I couldn't even look at him when I spoke. I wasn't a small woman, but this place made me feel tiny in the worst ways. I'd traipsed off with him, to this club, only to realize how little of the world I had enjoyed.

The couch dipped again. Kiernan's rasp was no more than a whisper. "Because then I get to help you experience it all."

His lips brushed the outer shell of my ear, and a shiver skated over my skin as if every drop of blood in my body had rushed to that point of connection.

"Oh." That tiny sound was enough for him.

He waved over a waitress — wrapped in the matching noir aesthetic of this club — and ordered for us both. The drink she brought me was the sunrise hue of near-harvest wheat. Small red pearls rested at the bottom of the martini glass.

His eyes blazed. "Sip."

The sweet drink overwhelmed me with silk and saffron and sex. Fire lit my cheeks, scorched my belly, and I flashed a feverish gaze at Kiernan.

Those dark eyes were on me. Always on me. Gloriously on me.

This wasn't like my patrons demanding quicker service, unhappy with current stock, expecting more and more and more from me. Kiernan watched me like I was precious, like he could absorb my joy and light by osmosis. I was the plant being watered. Was I simply being prepared for a reaping? I gulped my drink. Bright and bold, it warmed my body.

I stood too fast. I shouldn't be here. Mother would panic. The garden would need me to be ready in the morning. It needed my touch to grow.

Kiernan was on his feet too. This close, his height was imposing. "Don't leave me yet, Chloe."

He cradled my name like it was sacred.

"I'm not meant to be here." My cornflower blue dress somehow garish against the slick black of this place.

Kiernan leaned in, brows drawn. "Says who?"

"Everyone." I gestured widely. He caught my hand, cradled my palm to his chest.

"No, I say you belong here."

"My patrons will need wreaths, produce—"

"And what do you need, Chloe?" Why did he have to say my name like no one else mattered, like the shop was less important than me?

It had never been about what I needed. Even now, in this dark club with my heated skin and the slick surfaces and the intoxicating man in front of me, I couldn't allow myself to want this. To want this was to forsake my duty, my reputation. I'd been bending the rules in the Garden, but here I was shattering.

"I...I...I...." How to explain?

Kiernan stepped closer and my worries sputtered. Electricity snapped between our bodies, lighting my every pore with want. He lowered his mouth toward mine. Whisky and mint brushed my lips.

"Ask anything of me." The needy rasp of his tenor hooked my heart.

His lips parted. Soft and full and waiting.

"Kiss me," I said, passion and fear pressing the words into one.

Fire lit his gaze. His fingers gripped my chin, tilting me toward him, but the rest of his body stilled as though it'd entered the eye of a storm.

"Say it again." Flint met steel.

I pressed into his touch, the bite of his hold against my face. Muscles in his jaw tightened.

"Kiernan." It was my turn to turn his name into a match. Ignite it. "Kiss. Me. Now."

He didn't kiss me; Kiernan devoured me. His lips crashed into mine. His touch never gentling.

Hope and freedom bubbled beneath my breastbone. I speared my fingers into his hair, yanked him closer. Tongues, teeth, and grasping hands. We were all of them. In this dimly lit alcove miles away from my garden, I was no longer a harvest maiden. I became desire and temptation and pleasure. Kiernan's free hand found my waist, jerked me closer, and I could taste the darkness on his lips, feel the headiness of need swaddling us, pushing us closer, setting me free.

When we finally broke the kiss, I was out of breath and disheveled. He rolled up the sleeves of his shirt, and pulled me back to the sofa with him. I swiped my hair over one shoulder, let him eye my exposed neck like an invitation.

I drank the remainder of my martini in a swift move. "If we're going to do this again, we need to stay out of my neighborhood. I need neutral ground."

"There's no 'if.'" He signaled for another round of drinks. The wait staff pretended like they hadn't watched our collision. "I already know I will never get tired of your taste."

I lifted my empty glass. "Maybe it's the taste of the pomegranates."

The corner of his mouth ticked up. "Never had a taste for them until now."

●

I RETURNED TO THE GARDEN before the sun had risen the next morning. The bustle of town evaporated and the land took on a starkness, as if it were ready to reveal its secrets. Perfection. Leaves rustled in a low breeze; bunnies scurried near the small barriers I'd erected to keep them out. I padded around the pathways, readying for the day. To see if animals had nibbled their ways in, if fruit had ripened, to glimpse dew glistening on freshly turned petals.

I approached the back of the Garden when the sun crested the horizon in a riotous declaration of orange and yellow. Only the orchard corner where my favorite plum trees grew remained darkened. I hurried forward and started counting trees — seven were missing. How was that possible?

I broke into a full sprint, sputtering curses — at whom I didn't know — the ground suddenly gave way beneath my toes. I staggered at the edge of a chasm. My heart fluttered, my mother's groan of disappointment rumbling in the back of my mind. No point in fighting liquid legs now. I crumpled to my knees at the edge of the sinkhole swallowing part of my garden. I shifted forward. Clumps of dirt rained from the side. There were two dirt platforms below. The closer one bore the lost trees, but with fresh blades of grass jutting verdant beneath them.

It was what lay deeper that stole my breath. Steps. Clean and even and hewn from the earth itself, the steps led to the bottom of the space. Shadows obscured the details below, but the soft rushing of water was unmistakable. Had there always been a river beneath my garden? Was that why it'd been so bountiful? *Maybe it wasn't me at all.*

It had to be the shock that had me moving, because Typical Chloe would not be considering going down there. A girl does one night out with a smoke show like Kiernan and apparently gets bolder in everything else? There weren't stairs to that first level, but it wasn't *that* far down.

"I have to investigate," I told the nearby orange trees as though they cared. "Patrons will show soon, and I can't be ready if I don't know the status of this."

The fruit only had navels and therefore couldn't side-eye me. Small favors. I squeezed my eyes shut as tightly as I could and jumped. The ground caught me with an unexpected softness. The tree bark my forearm had slid against on the way down was less forgiving. I inspected the raspberry scrape. Not bleeding. It'd be okay.

Looking up, this was maybe a little farther down than I'd realized, but there wasn't an easy way to return to the surface. Someone would come to the Garden eventually and find a way to lower a ladder. Until then, I had a goal. I started down the stairs. The firmly packed dirt had no give as I walked down. What had looked like a handful of stairs before now continued on down and down and down. The air sharpened with a chill. Goosebumps marched across my skin. I moved faster, my shoes slapping against the steps.

A crispness of pine swirled around me and a cool light waited ahead. The river was close. Moments later, I reached the bottom of the sinkhole. Icy blue water rushed along in a slender river, evergreen trees lined the opposite bank. The ground crunched beneath my feet. Snow. I turned back, the opening to my garden now a small halo of yellow. A daytime moon hung low in the sky.

"You came." Honey slicked gravel tumbled behind me.

"Kiernan," I said without turning.

Warmth pressed against my back, and then over my shoulders as he laid a thick knitted sweater over my shoulders. When I finally turned, he remained close.

I had to tilt my head back to meet his gaze. "What is this place?"

A small plume of steam followed my words. Kiernan smiled as my breath collided with his chin. "It's your refuge, Chloe."

"I didn't ask—"

His lips parted in an amused smile. "No, and you never would."

I wasn't supposed to be taking right now. "I have customers who will need garlands and bouquets and fruits. It's almost the holiday. They'll need me."

"No." His huff blasted me with heat and mint, a tempting juxtaposition.

"No? What do you mean, no?" I jerked from his hold.

"They don't *need* you. They like your services and you're excellent at them, but they will survive if you aren't there."

"But the Garden needs to be tended."

"It'll be fine." He sounded so certain.

I opened my mouth, ready to argue he had no concept of what it took to keep my garden thriving and its impact in the community, and then I realized what he'd done. "You're changing the subject."

"I would never," he purred.

"Kiernan." I said his name like a plea and a reprimand.

His amusement dissipated, replaced by an earnest sincerity. He crouched to make our eyes level. "This is my home, and I want you here with me."

I gaped. What?

"Just take a day here with me. A day where you spend the holiday receiving for once. Let me take care of you."

"What does that even mean?"

Kiernan gnashed his teeth. "That you have to ask that is...frustrating."

"I'm sorry, I haven't had someone open a hole in the back of my garden before and then tell me it's a special place for me to *whatever*."

"To be taken care of."

"Okay. So you're going to feed me and give me cozy sweaters?"

"To start with." That devilish smile returned. Kiernan cradled my jaw in his palm and guided my mouth to his.

Heat suffused my skin. The frigid air forgotten, I leaned into his body, and his arms wrapped around me, bracing my lower back.

"Come with me, beautiful. Let's get inside and warm you up." His arm never left my back as he pivoted away from the stairs I'd descended.

It was unheard of to abandon the Garden, but my heart wanted me to stay connected to Kiernan. I followed him, hoping I'd understand this place — and him — before I let it go too far.

•

TRAVERSING THIS OTHERWORLDLY SPACE SHOULD have shaken me. Though I'd gone deep beneath the soil, gray clouds tumbled overhead. A hazy orb behind it could have equally been the sun or the moon. Either way, silver poured over the world around me. Snow crunched delightfully beneath my steps. Kiernan's pace at my side was silent. Firs and spruces rose on one side of the path, flanked by the crystalline waters of the narrowing river on the other. Galanthus flowers poked their heads above the powdery ground. I smiled to myself—I'd never seen Snowdrops in bloom. Living in a steady, warm climate didn't really necessitate the hearty flower.

"What is this place?" I hadn't meant to speak aloud, but there was magic in the air. This wasn't my home, and this shouldn't be possible.

"Does it matter?" Humor simmered beneath Kiernan's baritone.

I didn't know how I would get home. My mother would probably fear for me, and I was just going headlong into a snowy forest with a man who could easily fell one of these trees with an ax. And yet a contentedness I only ever felt when alone in the Garden surged beneath my breastbone. Kiernan stepped closer and my muscles instantly relaxed. He'd spent days merely watching me, bringing me lotion or water. And now my body expected it. Kiernan brought comfort. He meant safety. And when his hand skimmed my waist, he ignited a pulse lower and lower in my body until I wasn't sure if I should squirm away or lean closer to him.

Before I could decide, we rounded a corner. Icy air froze my throat as I gaped at the mansion. Red cedar had been hewn into a ski chalet and then magnified by castle proportions. Candles lit every window. Thick green and dark brown garlands swung from eave to eave, scarlet bows pinning them in place, as if the home had been built for the décor. While the rest of the world was silver and gray, this place emitted warmth. The honeyed glow of the candles, of the wood, of the crisp woodsy aroma around us drew me in.

"Let me show you my home," Kiernan said, taking my hand. He'd steered me through the woods with his hand around my waist, but apparently my gawking required literal handholding.

This house was magnificent. Warmth emanated from the cedar, as if the frozen landscape wasn't there. Even the railing on the steps to the front door was heated beneath my palms.

"It feels so alive," I marveled as we approached the door.

"I wanted a home that I could be myself in." Why did the words come with such longing? This was clearly his home. Everything about it mirrored him. Not merely the size, but the outward strength and inner warmth.

"That's how I feel about my garden." The giant room swallowed my admission.

But Kiernan heard me. Of course he did. "Your garden is work."

He led me into a cavernous room that carried a coziness. A mammoth fireplace on the far wall was taller than I, and the fire heated the space enough that I could have dropped the sweater around my shoulders. Two velvet wingback chairs sat together by the hearth. The fabric was a deep red, as though it'd been soaked in berries for weeks to capture every color from the fruit.

I dropped into one of the chairs. Both needing to feel if it was as soft as it looked — it was — and needing a breath of distance from Kiernan. "During the day, the Garden is work, sure."

"Your hands were ragged when I met you. Your knees are still bruised. Your beautiful lips were…" He stepped next to my chair and ran his finger over my bottom lip. My tongue darted out to follow the motion. A shiver snaked along my spine. Kiernan clocked the motion, his pupils flaring. "That place takes so much from you. Please don't tell me it's home."

I wet my lips again, letting him watch. "It is home, but mostly in the early morning hours. It's when it's quiet and dark that the Garden is calming. I love digging my hands into the soil and bringing forth something small and important."

Kiernan sat next to me. He dwarfed the chair. "Now *that* I understand."

"Good." I didn't need anyone to tell me my beliefs were correct, but Kiernan pushed against the Garden every time we spoke. This time, it was as though he had truly heard me.

"Who lit all these candles?" I changed the subject, lest he want to discuss injuries or, gods forbid, my mother.

His wistful smile had me reaching for his hand. "No secrets," I teased.

"I lit them, of course."

I raised a brow. There were hundreds of candles in this room alone. The chandelier in the center of the room had to have at least fifty. The room was bright with dancing flames. There was no way anyone managed a home this size without a staff.

"O-kay." My fake laugh didn't fool him.

His hand tightened on mine. "I would never lie to you, Chloe."

"So who are you, Kiernan? Really?"

"I am as I've always been to you."

I'd already descended into a sinkhole and walked through a forest. Now was not the time to be shy. "You say this is my refuge, but how does it exist? Who are you, Kiernan? What are you? Where am I?"

Maybe it was the trickle of fear that I let drip over my tumbling questions. Maybe it was the way I squeezed his hand back. Maybe Kiernan didn't want to keep secrets either. But he answered me.

"I made this house for you."

Too much. I shot to my feet. Kiernan did too.

He cupped his hands on my upper arms. "Please, Chloe, hear me."

Nocking my chin up was the best I could do, but I didn't leave.

"This is my home, this land. I couldn't make it open to you until you'd decided you wished to be with me, which I must admit took much longer than it did for me to be certain of you."

"What?" I blurted. "You're certain of me...how?"

"You're generous and kind and the most beautiful creature I've ever met. I knew the moment I met you I wanted you in my home and at my side."

"And that sinkhole opened because I feel the same?" Did I? Kiernan's presence was a balm to any dark thought. I sought his gaze, his touch. Okay, but still, a *sinkhole?*

"A gateway." He shrugged. "You needed to choose to enter of your own volition, but that I might spend Winter Solstice with you is more than I'd hoped for. For you to be surrounded with love and gifts. You deserve that joy."

The bounty of Winter Solstice was one that meant much work for me. I loved the colors and the smells and the smiles on others' faces. Of course, Kiernan knew I never had it for myself.

"We all deserve to be happy, but why does that need to happen here?"

He lifted a hand to my cheek, tracing my jaw with his thumb. I leaned into his touch.

75

His fingers slowed. "Besides the fact that you would never stop working if you were still in your Garden?"

I stuck my tongue out at him. Not above being petulant.

Kiernan groaned. "Don't tempt me, gorgeous."

I swallowed loud enough, he chuffed in response.

"In this place what I will happens." He held his hand out, palm up. "I need only call what I need, and it appears."

A ripe peach appeared in his open hand.

I narrowed my gaze at the peach. This was no trick. Even the light aroma of the fruit kissed my nose. "And what do you need of me if you can call forth food so simply?"

"You think I brought you here, made this place, because I wish you to provide for me?" He took a deep breath. Under his exhale, he muttered, "Damn your mother."

"What does this have to do with her?" Why did he speak like he knew her?

"Nothing to do with me." His implication poured another dram of tension into the room.

I stared at him. At the sharp jaw, at the full bottom lip, at his eyes of molten chocolate that I could fall into. Heat creeped up my throat. Kiernan speared his fingers through his hair, swiping it backward only to have it fall more perfectly tousled. My fingers itched to mimic his motion, to find out if the dark locks were as soft as they appeared.

"I wished to wait to tell you, but I should have understood you're far too smart to not question this."

I suppose that was meant as a compliment. I nodded for Kiernan to continue because I needed this man not to be a disappointment. I settled back into the plush cushion of my chair.

He didn't hesitate to lower himself to the seat next to me, but he leaned on his elbows like his head would ease to his hands in any moment. His swallow filled the room.

"This feeling is unfamiliar to me." His strangled laugh echoed around us.

"What feeling?"

"I'm nervous. I've waited for you to want to come here, to want to spend time with me, and...It matters not. You asked who I am and I must share. You are in the netherworld. I don't know if your family ever spoke of it, but this place exists beneath your own. Here is a place where existence can continue after life."

Merging into the velvet fabric wasn't an option, but I tried. "My mother spoke of such a place. A warning that there was no joy, celebration, or feasts in such a place. Maintaining the Garden is about making sure all experience life before fruits and flowers are gone." Her warnings rang in my mind, but my gaze bounced around this room. Holly berries adorned the mantle. Lush bouquets of rich reds and dark purples rested on tables at the edges of the room. "This can't be the same place."

"There is joy here. It's nearly the winter solstice and those thriving in the netherworld exchange gifts. I rule this place, Chloe, and I promise you my magic here is about gifting you what you need most. Never taking from you or demanding."

"You said this estate is the place where you can be yourself. Did you mean the conjuring of items?"

"I meant I can be vulnerable here with you. I use my gifts only to create for others. So this house, while it's solace for me, that's only because I made it for you."

"For me," I sputtered.

He leaned forward and kissed the back of my hand. "For us together, yes."

In the name of grand gestures, this was massive. It'd been so much for me to leave my garden to have a drink with him, and now he'd crafted an entire estate for me. Flowers and trees and a winter solstice celebration, but it was *so* much.

How much time and effort had gone into it? He'd conjured that peach quickly, but he'd had to think about what he wanted. This house was detailed. Flowers I favored, aromatic woods, the berries I loved most for the solstice, and who knew what other treasures lay in the rooms beyond?

"You made this place just for us to spend the holiday together?"

His chin rose, and somehow the move made his chest appear even broader. Like the buttons on the black button-down shirt he wore were going to spring forth. "You could say that."

"But would you?" We'd played these games enough that I spied a dodge for what it was.

He rose and took my hands in his, urging me to rise, but giving me no space to do so. "No, I wouldn't say I made this house simply for the holiday."

I stood slowly, letting the sweater he'd draped on my shoulders fall free. There was no chill in this room, and as my body slid up and up against his, a crackle of electricity ricocheted through my body; maybe through the room. His nostrils flared. It was my turn to smile. I pressed my palm against the center of his chest. His heart fluttered beneath my touch. The open collar of his shirt was its own invitation. I leaned in and let my breath heat the peek of skin. "What is this house for?"

His voice carried every bit of the danger and boldness of the river outside rushing over sandstones. "This is a home for my queen."

I went lightheaded and likely would have crashed to the ground if not for the sturdy man before me. Kiernan caught me, pulled me close. I nestled into the scent that was uniquely him — cold air, mint, and what I now realized was this careful blend of winter trees.

"I thought you'd like it, but I didn't think my strong woman would faint at my honesty."

"I didn't faint," I said, even though my body remained in such a languid state that he was the only thing keeping me upright.

"Let me know when you are ready to see more."

This was all so much. Was I ready to see more of this house? What did that mean for us? "If I say yes, am I agreeing to anything?"

"I'm not looking for an exchange, Chloe." He tucked my hair behind my ear, fingertips lingering on my neck.

I pressed my chest more firmly against his. For balance. Mostly. "You said this is for your queen."

"A gift. Only ever a gift." Kiernan tilted my head back and kissed me. Our lips barely touched, though there was nothing hesitant in the motion. Fire surged down my arms, making me hold him tighter. It licked up my neck, making me arch my back. It pooled in my belly, leaving me wanting in a way I doubted I could satiate alone.

He pulled back too soon, his features sharpened with predatory pride.

"While I love your presence, if you want me gone, I would leave you, though it would pain me." His tone left no room for disbelief.

"You...love my presence?" I shouldn't have pushed. I didn't even know if I wanted this. I was free when I was with him and happier than I could remember. But was this considered a proposal?

"Vigorously." He stepped away, not releasing my hand. "Come, let me care for you. Queen or not, you need to eat."

As much as I wanted his answer, I wanted to avoid giving my own more.

•

Kiernan led me down a long hallway. Warm wood surrounded us. He'd decorated both sides with artwork. Wheat-soft tapestries and watercolor paintings of sunrises — only sunrises — over fields of my favorite flowers. Each painting was more beautiful than the last.

We turned, finally, into a dining room. While the ceiling soared, this room had a coziness to it that sought to pull me in. A long table ladened with food awaited us.

"Has this been sitting in there the whole time?"

"Worried it'll be cold?" Kiernan teased.

"This is wasteful, Kiernan. I can't eat all this." Could he? The man was twice my size, but there had to be enough food to feed a dozen men.

"You forgot my skill already?" Kiernan swept his arm across the room and the food disappeared. He waved again and the full spread returned.

"A peach is one thing, but..."

"I made you a house," Kiernan muttered.

"It's one thing to hear it and another to see it. I need time to process." I didn't need to lie or hide my feelings here. That was the point, right?

"Indeed." Could he read minds? Would he tell me?

I squinted at him, waiting for him to reply to my thoughts. Instead, he pulled out a chair from the table. "Join me?"

We settled at the table and feasted. From roasted duck and beef loin to glazed carrots and potatoes dauphinoise to chocolate torte and lemon posset. The spread was decadent. We nibbled and we laughed and Kiernan poured red wine with a deep cherry note. And it was perfect.

Kiernan offered me a strawberry so large I was almost jealous I hadn't grown it. He pressed the red fruit to my lips. I opened my mouth to taste the berry, and his entire body stilled. Strawberry deliciousness had nothing on the perfection of Kiernan watching me with such intensity. It was as though not another being existed in this world. Juice dripped from my chin, but I couldn't risk breaking his gaze to find a napkin.

Kiernan tracked it, though. Lightning cracked, and then his tongue was on me, catching the juice. He pressed his index finger beneath my chin, and slowly licked away the juice. He moved toward my lip, nothing tentative in the motion. And then he was on me. This was not the soft connection of earlier. His tongue parted my lips. The berry had fallen from his hand at some point. Now both hands were on me. One found my hip, squeezing as if to ground himself. The other slipped around my nape and up into my hair.

I grabbed his shirt, twisting the fabric in my fist, yanking him closer. Was this what kissing was supposed to be like? It's not that I'd never touched another, but tiny bubbles rose beneath my skin. We were clothed, and this man was already turning me into an uncorked champagne bottle. I pressed my chest firmly against his, having to arch my back lewdly to get the contact I needed. The heat between us should have seared our shirts away. Kiernan twisted his hand in my hair, bringing the perfect bite of pain. He deepened the kiss, his tongue dancing with mine, but leaving no question about who was leading.

I tried to slip my hands between us, to grasp the hem of his shirt—or mine—to free us of this barrier, but Kiernan only held me tighter.

"Please," I eked.

He paused, releasing his grip on my hair and gazeddown at me witheyes flashing black flames. "Anything."

This man overwhelmed me. My breasts ached, nipples hard and begging for his attention. My hips writhed, seeking friction as if of their own volition. A chill skittered over my fevered body, as though I were a moth called back to his brilliant warmth.

Sweat dappled his temples and his nostrils flared. Could he tell how badly I needed this; needed him?

"I need to hear it, beautiful." His gruff tone was all want.

Gods, I was full of want, too. But he'd used words I understood. Asking for favors wasn't a thing I did. I took care of myself and everyone else. Only…Kiernan tended to my heart and my body and he could do this, too. Needed to?

I didn't know what I needed first or most or have the words to explain the bone-deep craving I had for him.

I started with a single word. "More."

He groaned and pressed his mouth to my clavicle. He kissed up and up and up my neck until his lips grazed the shell of my ear. "More what?"

My heart pounded and my breath was shaky, but more importantly I had a singular focus for once. "You."

He nipped my neck, and I moaned.

"Say it again, Chloe." Gods, the way he said my name. Reverent and filthy at the same time.

"I need more of you, Kiernan. All of you."

And then he was off me. The snow outside couldn't have chilled me more than the loss of his touch in that moment. He flicked two fingers at the table. The remnants of our feast were gone.

He turned back to me, the corner of his mouth quirked up in a way that almost made his hulking form appear boyish. "You didn't think I would deny you?"

"I don't want to think," I admitted. It was too late to be coy.

He lifted me from the chair and set me on the edge of the table. The mahogany was smooth beneath my palms. Kiernan unbuttoned his shirt. I snagged his waistband and pulled him close. He stood between my legs, looking down at me as if I was a treat. His dark hair fell forward. The firelight carving shadows beneath his cheekbones. Devilish delight played on his mouth. I pushed his hair back; it was every bit as soft as I'd imagined. I let my fingers wrap in it, and pulled him down. The kiss was light, but our connection was dizzying. When I planted my other palm on his bare chest, his groan vibrated down my arm. I pushed his shirt from his shoulders, marveling at the hard planes.

Kiernan slowed my actions. "No more thinking for you, beautiful."

Before I could question him, my clothes were gone. Did he even wave his hand that time? His pants remained in place.

"Are you going to join me?" I asked, inclining my head toward the trousers.

"I told you this place was about respite. I told you this holiday is about giving. I told you I needed nothing in return."

"Yeah, but—"

He continued like I hadn't said a word, rough hands coasting up my thighs. "And actions speak volumes."

Before I could question him, Kiernan was on his knees. I'd lost my clothes and I was spread out on a table—I should have been terrified or embarrassed or even cold. But only anticipation and the all-consuming need for Kiernan roared in my mind.

He lowered his mouth to my core and the first kiss blanked my mind. There was only my pulse and his tongue. Kiernan read every cant of my hips, catch of my breath, tightening of my thighs, adapting quickly as if he were an explorer mapping my desires.

"Ambrosia," he whispered reverently. Kiernan lifted his head and his focus alone should have left me in ashes. "I knew you'd be delicious, but your nectar is...I may grow addicted to you."

My throaty laugh echoed throughout the room. I hid none of my joy. "Thought this was about giving," I teased.

"Oh, I never said I wouldn't love every second of pleasing you. Getting to taste this perfect part of you? It's for me, too."

His words calmed a flutter of fret in my chest. He wanted me, but was holding back for now. I needed all of him on the table.

He narrowed his gaze at me, like he were parsing my feelings. He didn't call me out. Instead he grasped my calves, and spread me wider. "Don't hide from me now, beautiful."

By the time Kiernan finished with me, standing on my own was out of the question. I was sweat slicked and languid. And yet I still reached for him.

He practically purred as he pulled me into his lap. The high-back of the wooden dining chair feeling oddly throne-like in the moment. "We'll have time for that."

"I just need to hydrate, and then we can *make* time for that." Speaking desires aloud sent a rush of power through my veins. I pictured myself tracing my fingers over Kiernan's jaw.

He called me out. "What are you thinking so hard about?"

I lowered my gaze out of habit, but I wouldn't lie to him. "I would touch you like you're mine."

"I am." Authority shook the majestic walls.

I lifted my chin, and instead of merely touching his face, pulled him down to kiss me. Soft lips and warmth and need built between us, but it was the electricity and *power* cocooning us that made me break the connection.

"What was that?"

"I told you I would make you my queen…"

"I have no idea what that means, but I can't just disappear."

"They'd survive," he grumbled.

"Excuse me?" I scrambled out of his lap so quickly I fell to the floor. "I need to go."

"Chloe, please."

"You said my path here opened because I wanted to be with you. That means I should be able to choose to leave, right?" I gathered my discarded clothing.

Kiernan remained in his chair. His shoulders slumped, his brows drawn tight. "You're not a prisoner. This was a refuge and, I guess, a dream for us. But I wouldn't make you stay."

Scrubbing my hand over my face didn't provide any clarity. "I just need to think."

"Of course." He'd gone distant.

I shouldn't have continued this conversation, but perhaps I was addicted, too. "You truly want to be with me?"

He leaned forward like he was going to rush me, but squeezed the arms of his chair until his knuckles bled white. "It's the only thing I want."

A muscle ticked in his jaw. Each pulse like a white flag waving at me. But I wasn't used to being on this side of things. I was the one who cared for others. I was the one who had the job to help *others* enjoy the winter solstice. And here was this gorgeous man wanting to build an entire house so I could have one just for myself.

It was too good. Things this good don't happen, especially not to me.

●

THE HUMIDITY IN MY GARDEN was oppressive. Kiernan had deposited me near the asphodels, kissed my forehead, and left. He hadn't fought me on returning, but had simply given me a promise that I could return when I was ready.

How was I supposed to know when that was? Tears wet my face when he was gone. I walked to the back of the Garden. The sinkhole was still there. Whether because I still wanted to see him or because he'd chosen to leave it as a reminder of his invitation didn't matter; I wept at the edge all the same.

The sun was only considering cresting, so I rushed home to change into fresh clothes. I pulled a long sundress on and then headed to the kitchen to make coffee. My mother barreled into the house without so much as a knock.

"Just where have you been?" Despite her harried tone, Mother's hair was coifed to perfection and her golden gown neatly pressed.

"I do not need to explain my comings and goings to you." We both knew we were adults. But I'd never spoken to her bluntly. I'd trusted that she'd been the more knowledgeable, but now I trusted myself.

She flinched, but quickly recovered. "This community and this family depend on you. You left people without the foods and the decorations for their family gatherings. The winter solstice can't be celebrated properly without your centerpieces, without the oranges, without—"

"I wouldn't know," I cut her off.

Mother sputtered. "Excuse me?"

"Why have we never celebrated the winter solstice?"

She scoffed. "We celebrate."

I ignored my steeping coffee and planted my hands on my hips. "We don't feast, we don't decorate, we don't give gifts, none of it."

"We partake with our patrons." She held her hands up as though this line of conversation was too vexing. "I don't understand what's gotten into you, but you've put everyone at risk of missing joy. You want them to go to the netherworld without these memories?"

Nothing she said was new, but now I wondered how I'd so simply accepted them before. Perhaps because everyone else agreed with her. They wanted their ideal celebrations and I was the means. Kiernan alone thought I deserved to make winter solstice memories that were about belonging.

"I am not the only person who can deliver those items to them."

"They're all expecting you. The holiday is tomorrow." Mother pointed out the window, as if I didn't know where she expected me to be.

I shrugged. "Everything they need is in the Garden. Help them yourself if you're so worried."

"And what are you planning to do?" She choked on her incredulity.

Why had I bothered coming back here? I rapped my knuckles on the countertop. "Celebrate with a person who wants me there."

Mother trailed behind me to the Garden. Once she saw me walk in, though, she diverted herself to a local coffee shop. Patrons had already begun arriving at the Garden. I said hello, but didn't slow my steps.

Two white snowdrop buds had pierced the soil at the edge of the sinkhole. In the same place I'd cried earlier. Perhaps part of me was down there.

When I jumped this time, the fear was drowned in hope.

●

"YOU'RE BACK." DISBELIEF DREW KIERNAN'S words out. He rose from the rock slowly. "Not a phantom or a dream?"

"I shouldn't have left." Running to him was a foregone conclusion.

Snow clung to my hair. My dress provided no coverage from the cold, but the wind stopped the moment I leapt at him.

He staggered back with surprise, but his arm braced beneath my rear and bracketed my back. "I'm so sorry I pushed—"

I had no need for his apology. I kissed him hard and didn't let up. My arms wound around his shoulders, and our bodies fit in a way that made this embrace next to the icy river and surrounded by perfect solstice trees the most like home I'd ever experienced.

Kiernan took over the kiss and lit a blaze between us that should have melted the snowpack beneath us. Without breaking the kiss, he walked toward the home he'd built for me.

I arched up to nibble at his ear. "Can't you magic us to the house?"

"Do you really want me to?" He rolled his head to the side, giving me his neck. I didn't hesitate to press my mouth to the exposed skin.

"This is good," I said against his jaw.

His humor rumbled against my chest. "Whew, because I think I need to carry you inside."

He took me into the house. Every room we passed was probably more beautiful than the last, but as we littered our path with clothing discards, I had more perfect views before me. I lay on Kiernan's bed—our bed, he'd corrected—with his strong form hovering over me. Could anyone's winter solstice be as perfect?

Kiernan pressed his forehead to mine. "Let me make you my queen."

"Is that the same as your wife?" Because he hadn't been clear.

He dragged the back of his knuckle down my side. "It can be both. Should be. I will give you all of me."

"This place is remarkable, but I can't simply let the sunshine and the harvest go." Despite what I'd said to my mother, I loved cultivating my garden and I cared for the people in our neighborhood.

"This isn't the end of my realm, and I can conjure your desires." And how.

"You can't recreate my garden."

Neither of us moved or spoke for several breaths. Too much was on the line to get it wrong.

"Then we do both." Kiernan propped himself up on his arms. "Become my queen, my wife, and we spend half the year here and half there."

"Is that...possible?"

"For you, it is."

"You want winter?"

His answer was immediate. "I want you."

I kissed him, slow and full of promise.

Kiernan squeezed my hip hard. "That better be a yes."

"Yes," I whispered. A weight pressed on my head. I reached up and felt a spiked metal crown. I removed it, marveling at the black diamonds glittering on each of the seven points.

Kiernan steered it back onto my head.

"You look perfect in regalia." He meant it, already lowering his body to mine. "There's not a ceremony?"

"There will be for the wedding."

CHELSEA MUELLER (SHE/HER) WRITES FANTASY, romance, and thriller novels and short fiction for adults and teens. Her work includes the critically acclaimed Soul Charmer series and the YALSA Reluctant Reader Pick Prom House. She loves bad cover songs, good fight scenes, and every soapy YA drama Netflix can put in her queue. Chelsea lives in Texas and has been known to say y'all.

For the latest updates, join her email list at CHELSEAMUELLER.COM or follow her on Bluesky and Instagram.

Second Christmas Solstice
Meg Napier

Chapter One

"Merry Christmas to You
Merry Christmas to You
Merry Christmas, Happy Birthday
Happy Both of them to You!"

BARB'S SLIGHTLY OFF-KEY BUT heartwarmingly enthusiastic rendition of a combined Christmas/ birthday greeting brought a grin to Danica's face. Her mother never failed to call, even when Danny kept radio silence for weeks on end.

"Thank you. Merry Christmas to you, too," Danica said.

"What are you up to? Tell me there's something new and exciting in your life."

"Not really. Same old same old."

"Then come visit. It's been far too long, Danny. Todd and Jessie are growing up so fast, and they'd love to see you."

"Love to run me ragged, you mean." But she laughed. The last time she'd been home, the grandkids—her niece and nephew—had been two and four. That had been, what? Three years ago? Which would make them five and seven now.

"The pictures you sent are beautiful," Danica added. "I can't believe how big they've grown and how much Jessie looks exactly like you and Claire."

"They're beautiful and smart, just like you were and still are. Come see us, sweetheart. It's been such a long time."

Guilt crept up Danica's insides, but she gave it a hard mental swat and spoke with cheery reassurance. "I'm going to try hard to visit this summer, okay?"

"*Hrrumph.* If you got on a plane now, you could be here for Christmas dinner. And I could even make your favorite birthday cake."

"Mom, you know I'd love to see you. But I don't want to take time off work right now. We're going to be swamped for weeks."

Danny worked as a customer service supervisor at Genes4All, and countless subscriptions were gifted over the holiday season. Saliva samples would start pouring in, and the office director would send spluttering emails about preventing log jams before a single complaint arrived. Heaven forbid some princess in New Jersey had to wait an extra day to confirm that her ancestors had migrated from Italy.

"I'd bet my last dollar that lots of your colleagues have taken leave for the holidays," Danica's mother said.

"I don't think so, pretty lady. And don't throw away that last dollar. You taught me well the value of saving money. Now get off the phone and go start getting ready. What time are they all coming over?"

Barb recited the grandkids' Sunday School commitments and recounted the care she had taken to make sure Grandma's presents were wrapped in different paper than Santa's.

"Isn't it setting a bad precedent to have them believe that Santa leaves presents for them at Grandma's house as well as at their own?"

Her mother laughed. "You'd find presents here for you from Santa, too. Make my Christmas dreams come true and come home."

"You've already sent far too much as it is. And I love you for it. And for everything else."

"Happy Birthday, sweetheart. I love you, too. So very much. Merry Christmas."

Danny smiled as she disconnected. Barb and Jim had adopted her when she was left as a baby near the side door of the church they attended in Ireland. It had been Christmas Eve. They'd been posted there for Jim's work. Their daughter, Claire, who was fourteen at the time and bored with church socializing, had been the one to discover the basket. It had been so buried in blankets that it had taken the teenage girl's sharp hearing and curiosity to realize there was a baby inside.

The police were called and a massive investigation undertaken, but the family's willingness to take the baby home with them had been welcomed, given the lack of social services staffing during the holiday season.

First the fruitless searches and later the formalities surrounding a foreign family retaining custody of an Irish baby had been exhausting, or so she had been told. Danny remembered none of it, of course. Eventually Barb and Jim had been allowed to legally adopt Danica and take her to the U.S. Danny had grown up surrounded by love and secure in her place in their family. The McGlynnons never lied about her origins—always presenting the story as evidence of a Christmas miracle. But Barb, Jim, and Clare were fair-skinned, and as she got older, Danny became conscious of her own olive skin, dark eyes, and long, jet-black hair.

Her dad sometimes joked that she was descendent of the Spanish who had been shipwrecked in Ireland in the 1500s. Grandpa called her the family's sable-haired Leprechaun. The teasing was always given and received with love, but Danny wondered about her own birth family. What did they look like, and why had they abandoned her?

She learned early on not to voice her questions. Barb had admitted to Danny that she had longed for more children after Claire's birth. Finding Danica had been an answer to her prayers after their attempts at conceiving again had failed. The few times Danny expressed curiosity about her roots, her mom had grown quiet. She maintained that Danny coming into their life on Christmas Eve had been a true miracle, and she discouraged what she called pointless speculation. And since Danny adored her adopted family, she learned to keep her curiosity to herself.

She also remained silent about the odd sensation she sometimes had of watching life go by rather than participating. She got along with others at school but never had a best friend. She was fine playing on her own. She was content to wander the countryside in their Boston suburbs and study the deer, squirrels, and foxes that never feared her company.

When Claire married Brian, Danny determined that someday she'd track down her own roots. Brian came from a family numbering in the hundreds. Four brothers, two sisters, aunts, uncles, cousins, and grandparents, all of them looking alike with their fair, freckled complexions, blue eyes, and sandy-colored, curly hair. Danica didn't look like them or any of the other Irish Americans she had met.

Her curiosity spurred her interest in science and particularly in genetics. And once Claire gave Barb and Jim the grandchildren they so desperately desired, Danny felt less guilty about pursuing her own path in life. After graduating, when she received a job offer moving her not only out of state but also out of the country, Danica took the chance.

Working at the Vancouver offices of Genes4All was the answer to all her personal and professional aspirations, even if her actual work differed from her earlier expectations. Danny had applied for a highly competitive job in the lab, but personnel offered her a supervisory position in customer service. Complicated cases required an ability to explain genetic findings to customers who insisted their results were incorrect, so the department needed a scientist on board. Dealing day in and day out with people incensed over their genetic make-up had an oddly anesthetizing effect on Danny's own curiosity.

Instead of submitting her own sample for analysis, Danica focussed on settling into life in Vancouver and learning her new position. She liked her co-workers but hadn't yet made any close friends. Truly loving the field, she determined to keep her head down, work hard, and learn as much about the business as she could.

She liked the energy of the city and loved her quiet, simple life. She worked, did yoga, immersed herself in romance novels, and volunteered at the animal shelter. She loved spending time with the animals, especially the dogs, but the apartment she rented didn't allow pets. She wanted to keep her options open anyway. Who knew when the travel bug might hit?

Today was her twenty-third birthday. It was also Christmas Eve, and since she wasn't traveling and had no big plans, she had happily offered to go in and work. The shelter was closed to the public for the holidays, so no one would bother her as she changed water dishes, cleaned litter boxes, fed everyone, and walked the dogs.

Yet when she unlocked the door and went in, the first thing she saw was a figure — a decidedly male figure — straightening from the large tank in the corner of the lobby where a turtle, Lord Roberts, resided.

"This guy's pretty amazing," the stranger said.

Danny's head tilted as she struggled to make sense of the scene in front of her.

It was true. Lord Roberts *was* pretty amazing. He was at least forty years old

and was as much a part of the building as the walls and the ceilings. Danny felt a special tenderness toward Lord Roberts. She often stood by his tank and imagined he was communicating with her — sometimes fantasizing he was sharing images of his past.

"Yes, he is amazing," Danica told the stranger. "His name is Lord Roberts. But we're closed today. How did you get in?"

He was tall. Quite tall. Athletically built and with a cherrywood skin tone a few shades darker than her own. Her gaze was drawn compulsively to his.

The word *arresting* drifted through her consciousness as she waited for him to respond. And waited. Instead of answering her question, he stared as intently at her as she did at him.

She was almost certain she had never seen him before, but he felt familiar, like someone she had known and trusted long ago, or maybe always. But he was a stranger. Wasn't he?

His eyes were beautiful. Dark, large, perfectly spaced, and they seemed to gaze into her soul. When he finally spoke, his odd accent made her head tilt once more.

"I was hoping you'd come in today, Danica."

How did he know her name? How had he gotten in here? Had someone forgotten to lock one of the doors?

She dug her fingernails into her palms. She had to show some authority here.

"I'm sorry, but who are you? And what are you doing here? The shelter won't be open again until the 27th."

"I know. But today is your birthday. And this week is the most auspicious time for you to return to your home world."

Home world? Return? He was speaking English, but none of his words made sense.

Danica turned her head to check for other anomalies. She was in the right place, wasn't she? This didn't feel like a dream. And please, God, don't let this be some kind of weird surprise party. But no one else was in the lobby of the animal shelter she spent hours in every week. And no one in Vancouver, outside of human resources at Genes4All, knew it was her birthday.

"It's time to come back, Danica," the man said. "You were never meant to have been left here. But our people remain grateful to the McGlynnon family for taking you in and caring for you."

How did he know her family? Go back where? And what in the world did he mean by "our people?" He might know her name, but this man was most certainly both out of line and obviously unstable.

She shoved down the unreasonable notion that he was both known and trustworthy and loosened her fingers from the pendant she wore around her neck. She'd unconsciously reached for it and was compulsively rubbing it. *Show some backbone!*

Danny held up her hand. "Who are you, and what are you doing here?"

It was apparently his turn to assess because his head tilted much as her own had done just seconds earlier.

"I told you. It is time. We have a small window open to us at the solstice, and this land, this particular area, has respected and embraced the power of the solstice for thousands of years. The Granville Lantern Festival began when tribal elders here were allowed once more to celebrate their culture, but their understanding of the inherent connections between worlds goes back generations."

The Lantern Festival? The holiday bazaar that people in the office had talked about earlier in the week? And what in heaven's name did he mean about it being time for her to go?

"I think you have me confused with someone else." He obviously had serious mental issues. Half of her brain was warning her to back away while some irrational instinct was keeping her rooted only steps away from him. *His looks are not what's important here, idiot!*

"Is there someone I can contact for you? Then you can come back to the shelter after the holidays."

She should call the police. She touched the outside of her jeans pocket, making sure her phone was there. She didn't feel threatened, but the situation was definitely not normal.

"I'm not confused, Danica."

"How do you know my name?"

"It was the name your parents intended for you before you were born. You come from the stars, as your name indicates, but not the stars you think of when you look up at the night sky. But you were never meant to be born here. Your mother's unexpected weakness prior to your birth made passage through the portal impossible. Your father stayed with her, of course, invoking the ancient magic that allowed their souls to remain joined. And then he chose the only way he knew to keep you safe. He put your mother's stone around your neck and spoke the charm granting you protection in this world."

Yup. He had to be mad. But her hand instinctively closed around the pendant she always wore. Usually it was tucked inside her shirt, but she hadn't bothered today, knowing she'd be alone in the shelter. He must have seen it and was incorporating it into his psychotic ramblings. She touched her phone once more but didn't pull it out. He didn't seem dangerous, at least so far, but he was most certainly mad.

The police had assured her parents that whoever had left her at the church had wanted the best for her. Probably a young, unwed mother, they had said. There had been no trace of drugs in Danica's system and no evidence of neglect. She had been well-swaddled and protected from the cold with enough blankets to keep a Christmas dinner warm. The name "Danica" had been embroidered in beautiful script on the inner one.

Her parents had never hidden any of these facts from Danny but instead presented them as proof of her birth mother's love and of the miraculous gift she had been to Barb and Jim.

Danny still had the iridescent blanket that had enveloped her.

"Listen, Mr. — " She paused, but he didn't jump in with a name. "It was kind of you to stop by the shelter, but you need to leave. Come back again in the new year."

He stepped closer to her and took her hand.

She instinctively moved to pull away, but before she could, a tingling warmth spread from her hand up her arm and suffused her body. A frisson of energy passed between them. His eyes widened, and his breath, like hers, quickened as if in surprise.

She stared at him, her mouth dropping open. The sensation was not painful, but as the seconds ticked by, her disorientation increased. She was aware of an odd buzzing in her ears, and her vision narrowed.

No! She was not going to pass out. She focussed on the hand holding hers.

"Everything will be restored, Danica. Your greater family is waiting for you."

Why must every sentence he uttered be so incomprehensible? She had to get control of herself, had to take control of this situation. She lifted her head slowly. The dizziness abated, but something was different. She breathed cautiously in and out. She hadn't had a cold, but it felt as if her sinuses were clear in a way they'd never been before — as if she were taking in larger amounts of oxygen than normal. Could this be some kind of bizarre hallucination?

She narrowed her eyes and studied the man. His gaze upon her remained steady.

"Who are you?" Her words came out in a whisper, and his response was equally quiet.

"My name is Taariq." The sound he made when he said his name was unlike anything she had ever heard, and an image of ice cubes falling into a glass pitcher came to mind. A shiver of exquisite pleasure slid up her spine.

"I told you the shelter is closed."

"And I told you that is not why I am here. Although I am happy I had the opportunity to speak with Lord Roberts."

Oh God. She had to be dreaming. This couldn't be real. But he kept talking.

"We didn't know what you might remember, but it is apparent that you know little of your own story. Your parents were here as part of an aid mission attempting to imbed seeds to change the atmosphere and reduce temperatures. Everyone expected your parents would be home long before your mother was due to give birth."

Danny put up her hand once more, trying to stop the flow of nonsensical words.

"Are you saying my birth parents were aliens?"

"Alien is a harsh word, in any language. But modern vocabulary has lost the words to describe our differences. You and I cannot reach our home on a space ship as we are part of a world that coexists with this one in a different dimension. Your parents were here trying to help this world. The people here are puzzling. They are capable of almost indescribable achievements in art, music, and literature, and their science scholars have come to understand much of their universe. But the destruction exercised by small numbers of greedy individuals have put the entire planet in danger."

Yes, there was climate change, but he was still spouting nonsense. She wasn't alien born, no matter how he finessed the word. Her birth mother had likely been the victim of teenage hormones and inescapable poverty. She'd no doubt grown up in a poor section of an Irish city. She hadn't migrated between dimensions.

He continued to babble. The mission her parents had been part of had slipped through the portal in Newgrange, Ireland, during the winter solstice, the year before her birth. They were supposed to depart during the summer solstice. While the rest of their team was able to leave on schedule, her mother had contracted a virus that weakened her, making passage through the portal impossible. Her father manifested the power of the stone to join her in passing to the next realm, after ensuring that she, Danica, would live. Leaving her outside the church had been her father's last act.

The fingers of her free hand remained splayed in resistance, and he finally stopped speaking as they regarded each other.

His lips started to move again, but she cut him off.

"Hang on, Mr. Taariq. How do you know all this? Suppose for a minute you're telling the truth. Are you an alien as well? If my parent's team, as you call it, departed, how are you here?"

Taariq caressed her cold fingers in his warm, strong grasp as his eyes continued to bore into hers.

"We're not aliens, remember?" He smiled before continuing. "It's my job to know your story.

And it's my job to spend time in this dimension as part of the agreement our mutual ancestors made thousands of years ago. And it's just Taariq. No Mister."

Could any of what he was saying be real? She pulled her gaze away from his eyes to examine him more thoroughly. His clothing was dark—maybe black, maybe dark blue—and she couldn't tell where his shirt ended and his pants began. But they didn't resemble any clothing she was used to seeing. He wasn't wearing a coat. Everything about him looked at once normal and different. She had no doubt that if he passed her on the street, her gaze, and probably most women's, would follow him.

Whoever—whatever—he was, she was not in danger. The certainty of that conviction filled her, even as new concerns demanded attention.

She pulled her hand away from his and immediately missed the contact. She had to snap out of it. "I have to feed the animals. And walk the dogs." Odd that she hadn't heard barking from the dog room or the always persistent meows of the cats.

"No need. I took care of them before you arrived. I didn't want to miss you, so I got here early. And I was so happy to see animals again."

More inanities. How could he have known she was coming in? And what had he done with the animals? She moved quickly to the canine hall. Several of the dogs stood up and wagged their tales and Samson, the beagle mix she particularly adored, began his normal excited jumping. They all seemed content. No one lunged or strained at their crates the way they often did when they were anxious to get out or impatient for food.

"Hey guys, Merry Christmas." She greeted each one and spent extra time with Samson.

"Do you want to bring him with us? I think he can survive the shift," Taariq said.

She swung around to look at him. She hadn't heard him follow her in, and now he was suggesting she take Samson — *where, exactly?*

She exited the dog area and moved to the smaller room reserved for cats. There, too, all the animals seemed content. Their dishes were filled with kibble, and their litter boxes were clean.

"We need to prepare," Taariq said. "The portal will only remain open until midnight. You will not need any of your possessions, but if there is anything special you want to bring with you, we should get it now."

He had a beautiful voice. Too bad the words he spoke were ludicrous. Time to end this craziness.

"Nothing that you've said makes any sense. I don't know who you are or what you want from me."

He reached out and tipped up her chin. How had he approached so quickly without making a sound? Once again, from where his fingers touched, warmth spread throughout her body.

"I've been trying to tell you. I was sent to bring you home."

The space between them dissolved. She wasn't sure which one of them had moved. Maybe they both had. Right here, right now, in this most unlikely of spots, she felt a stronger pull toward this stranger than she could ever remember feeling toward another person. But she had to hang on to reason. Had to stop focussing on his lips which looked so very inviting.

"I am made of flesh and blood and live here. In this city, this province, this country, and this world. What you are saying is nonsense. You know it is. There are no portals to other worlds. I don't understand why you're doing this to me."

The skin on his brows lifted, and Danny gasped. He had no eyebrows. How had she not noticed that before?

Without thought, she touched the skin above his eyes. It was smooth, with a faint suggestion of darkening where his eyebrows should have been. She touched her own forehead, where every day she applied brow pencil to the merest hint of hair above her eyes.

Her mother had begun darkening Danny's brows in grammar school, when a cruel classmate had called her "naked face."

Was it possible he was telling the truth?

He gently touched her brows with both hands and then pushed her hair further back from her forehead. She shivered, but not from the cold.

"You are one of us, Danica. And you still wear the stone. That is how we found you."

Her hand went instinctively to the gem that glimmered brightly against the dark fabric of her sweater. It hung on a chain together with a gold shamrock her mother had given her when she went away to university. The stone pendant had been around her neck when she was found. The police had examined it, dusted it for fingerprints, and then shrugged their shoulders.

She had always known the stone was unique. It gave off a comforting warmth in the winter and was cooling in the heat. For as long as she could remember, she had always rubbed it between her fingers during times of stress.

Now she lifted it and bent her chin to study it. When she raised her eyes, she saw Taariq was holding a similar pendant, also on a chain around his neck.

Her knees gave out, and she sank to the floor.

He immediately crouched down next to her. He gently cupped her face in his warm hands.

"I'm not supposed to be here?" Her words came out in a soft croak.

"Your presence here has done no harm. In fact, your field of study has brought comfort and enlightenment to many. The more people understand their interconnectedness, the more likely they will be to support each other."

His touch sent tremors through her, but she wasn't chilled or frightened. Her breath caught as the orb-shaped pendant she was holding shimmered and pulsed, as if it were straining to make contact with his jewel.

Smart pendant. The unexpected thought made her smile, and she looked down.

She took several slow breaths. Maybe he was a market researcher sent out to see how people reacted to crazy stories for new movies or reality tv. Or maybe they were bringing *Candid Camera* back again. Or maybe, impossibly, he was exactly who he claimed to be.

He knew her name, seemed to know critical details about her life, and wore an ornament both similar to her own and equally unlike anything she had ever seen anywhere else. And while her brain continued to offer up reasonable objections, every other instinct felt pulled to him like a sunflower arcing towards sunlight.

Time seemed to freeze as she stared into his eyes. A kidnapper probably wouldn't ask her politely to come with him, would he? What else remained? Taariq, if that was his name, and if this wasn't all some sleep-induced hallucination, was either a villain, a madman, or he truly was from another world come to fetch her. She looked again at his naked brows, the stone hanging around his neck, and his eyes.

She remembered the terror that had passed through her at a birthday party she had attended long ago. All the kids had taken turns on a zip-line. She had desperately not wanted to jump. She had feared and hated being so high off the ground. But neither did she want to climb down and be humiliated for giving into her fear. She had let everyone else go ahead of her, but finally, she'd had to push off and jump.

Taariq's fingers were still interlaced with her own. She'd held a lot of hands in her life, but none had made her want to never let go.

Danny jumped.

Chapter Two

"I NEED TO CALL MY mother," Danny said as she started the car.

"Of course." Taariq buckled his seat belt as though he'd done it a million times before.

"How does this work, exactly?"

"There is an ancient portal. We need to get there before midnight, and the pulses from our pendants will synchronize and allow us passage."

"Passage? From here to where?"

Taariq hesitated. "We won't be going anywhere the way you understand the word." He chuckled. "Your parents and mine were fond of a television show here called *Dr. Who*. They said it was evidence that there was some lingering understanding of multiple dimensions, even if people insisted on calling it fiction."

"You're saying we're going to look for a no-longer-existent telephone booth and travel to another time period?"

"Not exactly. And I understand your confusion. This is all new to you, and I'm sorry we don't have more time. I came through on the 21st, the night of the solstice, but the plan was to wait for a moment when I could speak with you alone."

Danny drove the short distance to her apartment with Samson happily settled in the back seat while she marveled at the words coming from Taariq's mouth.

"And where exactly is this portal?" she asked.

Taariq laughed.

"In a most magical spot. It's in the back of the Granville Island Toy Shop."

"A toy shop?"

"Yes. It was full of shoppers when I came through three nights ago, which made it easier to pass unnoticed."

"Will they let Samson in?"

"It's late enough that the store will be closed, so there won't be a problem."

"If the store is closed, how will we get in?"

They were at a red light, and she turned to look at him. He gave her an impish grin. "It won't be a problem."

The light turned green, and she tried to focus on the road and not give in to nervous hysteria. Of course a lock wouldn't stop him. He hadn't used a key to get into the animal shelter, so why should he need one for a toy store?

In her apartment, she looked around, suddenly overwhelmed. Was she leaving for a visit or forever? Could she seriously walk away from her home, her family, her world? And what did one pack for transitioning to a different dimension?

"I have to call my mother."

"Yes, you said that before. Shall I walk outside with Samson and give you a few minutes?"

"Wait a sec. You said you were going to take me home, but *this* is my home. I can come back, right?"

"You can, of course. I think your family in our world hopes you'll stay."

She looked from him to the dog and then to the phone she had taken from her pocket and nodded. She had left a note at the shelter saying she'd been called out of town. Samson had taken it all in stride and was now happily following Taariq out the door.

She trusted Samson and Samson trusted Taariq. Was that logical proof, or was she under the spell of a master manipulator? Nothing Taariq had done or said had inspired fear or mistrust. On the contrary, watching him walk away with the dog left her feeling inexplicably bereft, even knowing he'd be right back.

Gripping the phone tightly with her left hand, she tapped her mother's name.

"Mom. Hi."

She was speaking to the only mother she had ever known, who had loved her unconditionally and shared everything she had. Barb had made Danny's twenty-three years in this world the best they could possibly have been. What in the world was she going to tell her?

"Hi, sweetheart. I love talking to you twice in one day. Happy Birthday and Merry Christmas! Shall I sing to you again? Have you changed your mind? Are you on your way?"

No, not on her way. At least not on her way to Boston.

"No. Thank you, Mom. No need to sing again. Mom—Mom, I have to tell you something strange. I'm going away. Maybe for a while. I really don't know."

There was silence on the other end. When Barb spoke, her voice was subdued. "Let me move upstairs where it's quiet." A moment later she spoke again. "I'm putting this on FaceTime."

When her face appeared on the screen, Barb looked both fearful and resigned. "Has someone come for you?"

Danny stared at her. "You know? How did you know? Why didn't you say something?"

"Because I never knew anything for sure. But I always understood something about you was different."

"Different? How? Why?"

"Oh, Danny. You were a gift from God, and you came to us on Christmas Eve. But at the same time I was thanking God for such a miracle, I knew there was more to the story."

"How did you know? And why didn't you tell me?"

"What could I tell you? I knew nothing for sure. But Danny, my precious girl, you know I've sewn and knitted my entire life. There's no fabric I've ever seen anywhere in this world that's anything like that blanket you were wrapped in. And who puts a fancy necklace on an abandoned newborn? I'm just grateful we had you for as long as we did."

"I love you, Mom. And I love Dad and Claire and the kids. I always have and I always will. You'll always be my mother."

"And I will always love you, my sweet Danica. And you will always have a home here with us."

Chapter Three

GOING THROUGH THE PORTAL WAS as easy as Taariq had predicted. One moment they were in the back of an eclectic toy shop Danny very much wished she had previously found time to visit, and the next, her pendant began vibrating.

She felt an odd swooshing sensation, then her entire body seemed to simultaneously compress and expand.

She wasn't aware of having closed her eyes, but when she opened them, she was in a wide, open field.

The air in Vancouver had been damp and cold, but as Danica breathed in, she was enveloped in a light spring breeze.

Samson gave an excited bark and pulled at the leash. It slipped from her hand, and Danny felt a flash of fear. But the group of people standing in a messy semi-circle a few meters away greeted him with delight, and he them.

"Hello, gorgeous boy," said one of the women, bending down to fondle the dog. Then she straightened and walked toward them. The smile that engulfed her face was at once welcoming and loving.

"Danica. I've waited so very long. My name is Alina, and I am your aunt. Your mother was my sister, and I am so very, very happy to finally meet you."

Once again, the sound of a name spoken aloud evoked curious but exhilarating sensations throughout Danny's being.

Alina came to stand directly in front of them, and Danny regarded her curiously. Her skin tone matched her own, her brows were similarly hairless, and her eyes were kind and welcoming.

Danny continued to gaze at Alina. Could this woman truly be her aunt? Warmth crept up her body as she recognized caring, curiosity, and longing in the older woman's gaze. The habitual sense of detachment that was as much a part of her as her limbs melted away. She smiled back tentatively at her aunt, and Alina pulled her into an embrace.

Her scent was unlike any Danny had experienced before, but it was delightful and invigorating, and she inhaled deeply.

After luxuriating for a moment or two in the novel sensation, Danny stepped away.

Alina was slow to release her. Danny saw tears glistening on her aunt's cheeks and realized that she, too, was crying. But she lifted her chin and worked to keep her voice steady.

"This is a little overwhelming. You've known about me my entire life, but I didn't know any of you, any of this" — she gestured with her arms to the wide open panorama that surrounded them — "even existed."

"I know. We all know. And while we mourned every day that kept you away, we knew you were cared for and loved. And we are so proud of the young woman you have become."

Laughter from some of the other adults nearby caught Danny's attention, and she looked over to see Samson sprawled on his back, legs in the air, head lolled to the side as a man and a woman vied for space to rub his belly.

"I guess Taariq was right, and it's okay that Samson came too?"

"Of course it is. We do not have dogs on our world, so he will be the focus of much attention, I am sure."

"But you know about dogs?"

"Oh, yes. We have windows that look onto your world. We knew what happened at your birth, and we've kept watch over you as you grew.

"Movement back and forth used to be common, but as time went on, fewer people in that world were interested in maintaining contact. Those who did were eventually labeled as witches or heretics, and the portals became invisible to the average person. Now they're accessed easily only on days surrounding each solstice and only by those who believe in what's come to be known as magic." She smiled at Danny.

"The stone is magic, of course," she continued. "But it's so much more."

Danny struggled to absorb all she was hearing. One idea leapt out and she zeroed in on it. "I'll be able to see my family?"

Alina studied her, as if trying to gauge how to respond. "Yes, of course you can view the family who raised you and loved you. We owe them an enormous debt. But I hope now that you're home, you'll be able to look forward."

There was that word again, sending a pang of uncertainty through her.

What did home mean?

"We've prepared your house for you, and you are welcome to stay there or anywhere else you'd like."

Alina moved as she spoke, her arm intertwining with Danny's.

Samson came running over, and Danny picked up his leash. She looked around but couldn't see Taariq. Where had he gone?

He had held her hand as they entered the portal, but in the shock of absorbing her new surroundings, she hadn't registered his departure. When had he let go of her hand? Would she see him again?

An odd ache niggled in her sternum at the thought that maybe their interaction was now finished.

Had he simply left her without saying goodbye?

"Where is Taariq? Will he be back?"

"He will, I'm sure, my dear. Though his work keeps him very busy."

Danny had marveled at the wonder of a newfound existence only seconds before. Now a small part of that light dimmed. She knew nothing about this world, these people, or how their society was organized. And the one person she had trusted, whose words she had heeded in deciding to put aside everything she had known, had disappeared.

Her aunt was moving them across the field and toward a cluster of small houses that resembled her imaginings of an English country village.

There were flowers she had never seen before and trees with fruit already hanging from their branches, even though the air felt more like spring than summer.

Everything was at once beautiful and orderly, familiar and foreign.

They walked a short distance, but Danny's head swiveled around so frequently that she began to tire. She had lost all sense of time. Where only minutes—or perhaps hours ago—she had feared Taariq might be mad, she now wondered if perhaps she was hallucinating.

Samson sniffed everywhere and was touched and cooed over by everyone they met. People moved about with purpose, all similarly dressed in shimmering garments whose style was hard to pin down. Lovely and comfortable seemed to be the only constant. Many nodded to Alina and smiled warmly at Danny.

What time of day was it? Were some of the people they passed farmers who tended the abundant fields? Or were people going to other types of work? Coming home? How did people spend their days, weeks, lives? What would *she* do here?

They stopped in front of a small cottage. Alina opened the door and stood aside for Danica to enter.

"This was your parents' home. They would have wanted you to have it. Your mother's stone—your stone now—serves to adjust the temperature and décor."

Danica stared at her aunt, perplexed. She'd worn the pendant all her life, had been aware of its coolness in summer and warmth in winter, but she'd certainly never witnessed anything resembling the magic Alina described.

"Wrap your fingers around it," her aunt prompted. "Close your eyes and envision what you need. Perhaps water boiling in the kettle for tea?" She smiled encouragingly at Danica, who, once again questioning her sanity, gave it a go.

A moment later, a soft whistling came from deeper inside the cottage. Danica shot a look of disbelieving delight at Alina and ran toward the sound.

She entered a kitchen outfitted with a perfectly-sized square wooden table. Four chairs surrounded it, and as Danny gazed around, she saw every appliance she might need. An old-fashioned tea kettle steamed on the range, emitting a gentle whistle.

Alina came to stand beside her and pointed at the cupboards. "It's all yours, my dear. Make a cup of tea and make yourself at home."

Danny made them both tea, and they sat together. Alina told her about her parents, their devotion to their work, and their happiness at Danica's impending birth.

Danica listened in amazement. The picture her aunt painted was of an all-encompassing community that sounded perfect. How, then, had she grown up with the McGlynnons?

"Why didn't someone come for me when I was a baby?"

Her aunt stared into her teacup, two of her fingers rhythmically circling its rim.

"Not everyone can pass easily through the portal. Forgive me if Taariq or I gave you that impression. Our stone's power is weaker in that world, and shifting is generally possible only on or near the solstice. And by the time you were six months old, it was clear to all of us that you were deeply loved.

"We watched Jim, Barbara, and Claire, and we recognized the gift you all were to each other."

As Alina finished speaking, the soft sound of gentle music filled the air. "You did that, my dear," she said, gesturing toward Danny's stone.

Startled, Danny looked down. Alina was right. Danny was unconsciously grasping and caressing the pendant as she had done throughout her life when tired or stressed. But doing so here brought forth soothing sounds that comforted her.

Alina smiled sadly at Danny, the first time any emotion besides confident happiness had shown on her face.

"You're tired. Today has no doubt been overwhelming. Get a good night's sleep, and we'll talk again tomorrow." She put her hands on Danny's shoulders and then pulled her into a hug as she had upon their first meeting. "Sleep well, my dear girl. And welcome home."

She left, and Danny looked at Samson. Her aunt was right; she was exhausted.

"This isn't what we expected when we woke this morning, is it?"

Samson licked her fingers.

"And since they apparently don't have dogs here, you're likely to end up a celebrity. But for now, you need a walk and dinner."

All the leashes at the shelter had doggie-bag holders clipped to them, so she could pick up Samson's droppings. She'd decide what to do with them in the morning, but for now, she'd leave the bag right outside the door.

Two bowls had been left in the kitchen — one on the floor filled with water, and another on the counter filled with something that looked like cereal, which Samson happily devoured.

Who had left the bowls for Samson and when? Had Taariq come here after disappearing from the field? Or had he communicated with someone in this dimension before they left home?

Home. Even as she thought the word, she wondered at its meaning. That very morning — both only hours ago and what felt like a million years ago — she had apologized to her mother for not going home for Christmas. Now she was somewhere else entirely that was also home. Everyone she'd met today had tried to persuade her to think of it as such.

But it was still Christmas, and she was once again alone and now so much farther from the family she so dearly loved.

Tears spilled from her eyes, and she brushed them away angrily. She had agreed to come here. Her aunt and everyone else she had met had been wonderful. But why had Taariq disappeared?

Samson claimed a spot for himself on the bed, and Danny sat next to him, stroking his back. He stretched out, greedily exposing more of himself to scratches.

"How is it that I didn't think it was possible to bring you home to my apartment in Vancouver, but you're here with me now?"

She chided herself for her pity party. She had nothing to complain about. On the contrary. She had lived through an experience that would leave storytellers open mouthed and adventure seekers green with envy. And though it hadn't been part of his mission, thanks to Taariq and his magic portal, she was not alone. Samson was here with her. Had she spent the night in Vancouver, as she had planned when she woke that morning, a loving, happy pup would not be sharing her bed.

She may have travelled to a different world, but the dog she had fallen in love with weeks ago still couldn't talk. He could push his head further into her hand for more extensive petting, though, and she obediently obliged.

There were so many things to think about, but her eyes were closing. She lay down next to Samson, and the last images that came to mind were Taariq's eyes as he had held her hands in the shelter.

Chapter Four

THE FOLLOWING DAYS AND WEEKS were unlike anything Danny could have imagined. The sun still rose in the morning and set at night, but all energy came from the stone mountain visible only faintly on the horizon. Everyone wore or carried a piece of that energy as they went about their daily lives.

The fruit trees she had noticed upon her arrival dotted the countryside, and more agriculture took place in greenhouse-like structures, with plants that astounded Danny in their variety. She saw birds and insects—some familiar and some more exotic than anything she could have imagined—but wildlife seemed not to exist. Samson remained a celebrity as he accompanied her wherever she went.

Everyone Danny met was friendly and welcoming, including cousins and other extended family, all of whom spoke warmly of her parents and said how happy they were that she was among them at last. She dined with many of them and enjoyed their company, but she never quite got over the sense that she was merely a visitor in a strange land.

Samson was universally adored, but she worried about him not having other dogs to play with.

Alina arranged for her to spend time in the medical research center and bio lab to see what work might best interest her. Each day brought introductions to new ideas and new people. Her previous understanding of genetics was blown away by the array of variations currently being studied through research that relied on both science and what Danny still thought of as magic. But to everyone around her, the stone and its power were as normal as the sun rising in the east.

When she asked questions, her new acquaintances seemed eager to help, but no one could satisfactorily explain why the stone's energy didn't extend into the world she had known as her own.

She longed to speak with her parents and relay everything she'd been learning, and she longed to see Taariq again. When she asked Alina about him, she was told that his work kept him extremely busy.

Finally, a few weeks after her arrival, she heard a knock just moments after climbing into bed. Samson barked excitedly, and she pulled a dressing gown over her underwear. She still didn't understand some of the garments that had been left for her.

When she opened the door and saw Taariq, the odd sensation of both not breathing and breathing more completely came over her once again.

He regarded her, and for a moment, neither one of them spoke. And then they spoke simultaneously.

"I wondered what happened to you."

"I'm sorry I've been gone. Have you been well?"

They laughed and then stood, silent again.

He gestured toward her and chuckled ruefully, keeping his gaze averted. "I see it's later than I thought. I should let you sleep."

Oh no. He wasn't going to disappear on her again.

"Taariq, wait. Don't go. Come in, please. I have so many questions." She pulled the wrap more tightly about herself and moved back to let him in.

He crossed the threshold and looked around the cottage, seeming to notice the small changes she had made as he smiled and nodded.

"Come into the kitchen, and I'll get us something to drink."

Once they were seated at the table, she took a deep breath and forced herself to speak calmly, not knowing if this was a courtesy call or something more personal.

"Why were you sent to get me and not someone else, like Alina? And why have you been gone so long? You said when we first met that it was your job to spend time in that dimension. Is that where you've been? How does this all work?"

"The how is simple. It's all through the stone. I can take you to the viewing center, and the stone will allow you to see and understand whatever you wish. Our two worlds have been linked since the dawn of time. There are elements of the stone imbedded in various locations around the planet, and those locations are where we successfully established portals, but it's possible to see almost anywhere."

"You're saying there are pieces of this same stone—" she pulled her own necklace out from under her wrap—"in Newgrange in Ireland and on Granville Island in Vancouver?"

"Yes. And in several other spots as well."

"Why don't people there know all this? How could I have spent my whole life not knowing anything about my birth parents, about this world?"

"We've learned over the centuries that societies and cultures embrace knowledge at different speeds and with varying levels of understanding. There have been civilizations that understood and appreciated the links between our worlds, but many others were happier putting up walls—both real and conceptual ones."

He hesitated and then looked at his hands while he spoke. "I wanted to give you time to settle in without influencing you. I understand how confusing it is to move from one dimension to another. I was born there, too. And you're right. I did say it's part of my work to spend time there."

He'd been born there, too? Why hadn't he told her that in the first place?

"What exactly is your work?" Danny asked.

"I'm an observer and an intermediary. There are still believers in that world who want to maintain contact and keep the portals open."

"You told me I'd be able to see my family. Can you help me see them?"

Before he could respond, a thought struck her, and she peered at him suspiciously. "Did you watch me before you came to the shelter that night?"

His hands were apparently fascinating because he continued to study them and didn't answer.

She leaned closer. His shoulders relaxed when she reached for his hand, and he finally met her gaze.

"I appreciate the time you gave me," she said. "And you were right. It is beautiful here, and Alina and the rest of my family are wonderful. But I miss my home."

As soon as she said the words aloud, an overwhelming longing to see her own world swept over her. And it felt like forever since she had heard her beloved mother's voice. Because no matter what she had learned here, Barb had been the only mother she had ever known. Her life here was vibrant and interesting, but at the end of the day, she was still alone. And her loved ones were infinitely more distant than they had been when she lived in Vancouver.

Tears rolled down her cheeks.

Taariq reached out and gently brushed them away. "Don't cry, sweetheart. We—I—hoped you'd come to see this world as your home."

"Part of me does," she reassured him. "But I think I understand better now why I always felt so different. But I'm different here, too."

They stared at each other in silence, but she drew strength from the warmth of his hands holding hers. "Please take me to see them."

"Are you sure you want to? I think Alina and the others thought you should spend longer acclimating here. They don't think you should be pulled in two directions at once."

"Yes, but the pull is there, whether I want it to be or not. Knowing both worlds was my parents' life, and it's obviously yours as well."

He hesitated, and she tilted her head, studying him more intently.

"You know everything about me, and I know almost nothing about you. Do you have family? Are you married? Do you have children?"

His eyes widened, and his response was instant. "Of course I'm not married. I wouldn't be here now if I were."

A shot of pure joy ran through her. "Parents?"

"Yes, of course. But they were observers, too. They knew your mother and father and worked with them for years. I grew up hearing my parents speak of them and of you. It's why I became an observer. I wanted to know for myself that you were cared for, and I began transiting between our worlds as soon as I was judged ready."

"You've been watching me all my life?"

"Watching is a strong word."

She looked at him and smiled. "You like that phrase. I remember you said something similar the night we met. What would you call it instead?"

He hesitated. "Admiring? Respecting?"

"Then why haven't you come by since I got here?"

"I was back there, working. I slipped back before the portal closed immediately after bringing you here. We've been attempting to adjust the oceanic currents to slow the polar melting."

"That sounds important."

"It is. But I'm still sorry I left you so abruptly."

She leaned closer. "Maybe there's a way you can make it up to me."

The smile that swept over his face took her breath away.

"I'd certainly like to try." He bent his head, and finally, finally, she got to taste the lips she had so yearned to know.

•

THE NEXT MORNING, HE TOOK her with him to the viewing center. The walk took them through parts of the community Danny had not seen before, and while she was curious and still awestruck by the beauty of her surroundings, her attention centered on the man holding her hand. The night they had spent together had been like nothing she had ever experienced. Her body had exalted in their union, but so had her soul.

Now as they walked together to the viewing center, the conflict within her increased. She yearned desperately to see the family she had always thought of as her own, but she was now joined to Taariq with a bond that felt equally eternal.

They entered a round building that stood alone in a clearing. People moved around quietly as though respectful of the nature of their work. Taariq led her into a large room that brought back memories of a planetarium she had visited long ago with Barbra and Jim. He brought her to the center of the room and gave her hand an encouraging squeeze.

"It's up to you," he said. "You are wearing your stone. Hold it in your hand and tell it what you want to see."

She looked at him, astonished.

"It's that easy?"

"It's that easy."

Danny closed her fingers tightly around the pendant and thought back to her passage through the portal.

Without warning, the toy store she had passed through in Vancouver was in focus before them, as clearly as if it were truly on the other side of a window.

Her breath caught. People were crowded in the shop, bundled up from the chilly weather with Christmas decorations everywhere.

"Why does it look like Christmas? It should be early spring."

"Time passes differently in different worlds. It's early December again there right now."

Danny gasped. An entire year had passed. Her family would be preparing for Christmas, and she would be absent for her birthday once more.

"Can I see more? Other places? Can you show me my family?"

"Of course you can. But it's not up to me. It's all within your power."

Danny closed her eyes and concentrated on thoughts of Barbra and Jim. She opened her eyes, and her family home came into focus. Jim was in his favorite chair, watching his beloved Patriots play football. A sharp pang went through her as she remembered the roars he emitted almost non-stop for the entirety of each game. Barb was sitting at the dining room table, boxes of Christmas cards spread out around her. She was writing a note on one, and tears were slipping down her cheeks.

"She's missed you very much," Taariq said quietly. "They all have."

"I need to go to her." Her words came out without forethought, accompanied by an overwhelming longing for the life she had left behind. This world had countless advantages, but Danny yearned for the sights, sounds, and smells of the world she had grown up in. She wanted to smell Christmas pine trees, taste her mother's cranberry pie, and hear Mariah Carey's annoying song playing everywhere she went.

The minor work she had engaged in at the various laboratories she had visited had been interesting, but not exciting or stimulating.

A memory came to her of a customer she had assisted at Genes4All not long before last Christmas. The woman's parents had acrimoniously divorced when she was young, and her mother had moved them out of the country.

The woman had recently returned and was desperate to find her father and his side of her family. Danny helped her make contact, and the woman's relief and gratitude had left her reassured that her job mattered.

Danica had been anxious to know who she was, where she came from. Now she knew. She knew, she respected her lineage, but most of all, she was grateful for the care her birth parents had taken to ensure her safety. Only her real family was in a simple house outside of Boston.

"Is the portal open now?"

"Yes. It will be open for another day by our standards. Four more days on the other side."

"I want to go back. I need to go back. But I need you, too."

He turned to face her and searched her eyes for several seconds. When he spoke, his voice was quiet.

"I thought you might want to return. That's another reason I stayed away. You deserved a chance to get to know this world, and your family wanted desperately to know you. But I didn't want to influence your decision."

Danny stared into his earnest, loving eyes and then swept her gaze up and down the whole of him. Could she say goodbye to all he had come to be for her? Her awareness of the mysteries of existence was now so much greater than it had had been before, but Taariq was the one person she'd spent her life waiting for. With him, that otherness she'd always felt had disappeared. Barb had once described having her eyeglass prescription fixed, saying she didn't realize how much she'd been missing until the instant she put the new glasses on. That's what being with Taariq was for her.

"Could you come with me?"

There was ambient noise in the hall, but the silence between them was absolute as he looked at her. When at last he spoke, his voice was quiet, but his words were clear.

"I fell in love with you on your eighteenth birthday. It was unreasonable and unrealistic, and perhaps even what you'd call voyeuristic. But it's what made me compete for the chance to go for you last year. And meeting you in person only cemented my feelings. If I go with you now, I'd very much want it to be forever."

It might not be Christmas here, but the wonder and magic seemed to have beamed across any barriers that separated their worlds.

"Is there a portal near Boston?"

He smiled. "There is, but you have to swear to secrecy. It's outside of Salem, but it is definitely not the commercial site called 'Mystery Hill.'"

"Can we make it in time?"

"We can, if we hurry. The magic of the solstice lasts through to Christmas Eve. You'll need to speak to Alina and collect Samson, and I'll need to tell my parents. They know my interest in your world has never waned. And I've mentioned you frequently enough that I doubt they'll be surprised. But we'll make it, and you'll be home for your Christmas birthday."

"My mother will love you." She knew it was true.

She had moved closer as they spoke, and now he closed the gap. As they looked into each other's eyes, their lips were only a fingertip apart.

"Are you sure?" They both whispered the same words, and then they both smiled, and their lips met again for the briefest, sweetest moment.

"Let's hurry," Taariq said.

This time the zip-line held no fear. Danica took Tariq's hand, and they jumped together into their future.

MEG NAPIER BEGAN DREAMING ABOUT romance sometime in second grade when she accepted her first proposal. It came with a tiny package of rock candy, and her addiction to love and sweets was cemented in one fell swoop. Sadly, she lost touch with her first beau, but the idea of life being better when hearts are entwined stuck with her.

Over the years, Meg allowed other commitments to take priority over writing, but she remained convinced that without love, nothing else has meaning. She has been blessed throughout her life to find love everywhere: in supportive parents and siblings, magnificent teachers, good friends, crazy pets, caring co-workers, cherished children, and a wonderful and supportive husband. The titles of Meg's books and stories all contain the word "second" because most things/people worth fighting for require more than we can possibly imagine during chapter one. And just as fine chocolate is often better savored on the second bite, love, too, always rightfully demands a second chance.

Meg's website: MEGNAPIER.COM
Sign up for her newsletter and receive a free short story at: MEGNAPIER.COM/MEGS-MAILING-LIST
Find all her novels here: BOOKS2READ.COM/MEGNAPIER

The Hanukkah Pretzel Prophecy

M. L. Buchman

First Night – Aaron

"You're an idiot, Aaron."

"Love you too, Miriam." I didn't. But being nice to your older sister on the first day of Hanukkah seemed like a good idea.

First Night of the eight days of Hanukkah, all Jews were mandated to celebrate. Actually, celebrate for all eight days, making it one of my favorite holidays. Miracles were handy that way. The Passover Pig Out, uh, Seder dinner, was another one where loads of good food was eaten to celebrate a miracle. In general, outside of the fast for Yom Kippur, The Day of Atonement, Jews were much more focused on feast. Probably because of all that famining we did in the times of the Torah.

Feasting was also good for the family; who'd have thought that Gloucester, Massachusetts—a decidedly Italian and Portuguese town on the

North Shore—would rock a Jewish deli and bakery for over a century.

Also, Miriam is dangerous in an evil-older-sister way, making cautious civility a functional strategy.

After I'd teased her about looking so different from the rest of us—saying maybe ten or twenty times too often that she looked like some demented denizen of Hell had pulled a fast one on Mom— she'd filled my pillowcase with whipped cream...liberally mixed with electric-pink dye.

When I'd plunged into bed that night, it had burst forth and splattered all over my room like a goopy shotgun blast. Everything it touched was stained hot pink: my clothes (which might have been all over the floor), my homework, my rug. My posters, the less said about my taste in under-clad female pop singers at that age...maybe it was high time they were ruined.

I've long since gotten my own apartment but Miriam had somehow arranged to have Mom guilt trip me into taking that rug with me. We're Jewish, guilt works. Jewish-mother-guilt is like an undeniable superpower even Superman could only wish for.

I still live with that rug; so sue me.

Over time, the bright pink polka-dots have faded from Madonna "Material Girl" hot-pink to *Barbie* pastel-pink. Since the movie, I'll admit that having cause to daydream about Margot Robbie knocking on the apartment door some day isn't an all-bad thing.

But I knew why Miriam—too tall and too much lush hair to be a proper Schwartzman—was calling me an idiot this time.

For this first night of Hanukkah, we gathered about the same table that we'd grown up around.

Mom and Dad, Uncle Max who's at least half as funny as he thinks he is, Aunt Max (short for Maxine), my two girl cousins (who at least *look* like they belong to the family, though I now keep my mouth shut on that point), and Grandma (on Dad's side).

She'd given me a Hanukkah gift on First Night. We aren't really a gift-during-Hanukkah kind of family. Dad may call our Christmas tree a Hanukkah bush, but he's not fooling anybody; he's into it as much as the rest of us.

No, for us Hanukkah is about fried potato latkes, cheese and blueberry blintzes drowned in sour cream, and smoked salmon on fresh-made sourdough bagels. It's about Mom putting Peter, Paul, and Mary's *A Holiday Celebration* album on because it had the "Light One Candle" song about Hanukkah in among all the Christmas carols. Mom isn't retro, it's Grandma's vinyl and she's never embraced CD never mind digital. We don't try to make the music ourselves as we *are* the Family Schwartzman-can't-carry-a-tune-for-crap non-singers and none of us, not even Miriam, look the least like Julie Andrews.

The most serious endeavor for us other than the lighting of the candles and a bit of feasting was playing the Dreidel game for gelt, gold-foil-wrapped chocolate coins. *Ganz, halb, nischt, schict,* the four sides of the spinning top, deciding who gets and who gives gelt. One year I'd spent hours trying to figure out how to load a Dreidel to always land showing *ganz* so that I could take all the gelt during my turn. But Miriam figured it out, switched our Dreidels when I wasn't watching, and cleaned me out. Worse, she shared her winnings with our cousins, but not me.

Anyway, our household? Not big on Hanukkah gifts.

But Grandma had given me a present—and only me. There are a few advantages to being the only male of my generation on either side of the house. First-born male has a certain gravitas in a Jewish household, especially to someone as traditional as Grandma, which I totally bought into because of how much it irritated Miriam.

It was one of Grandad's first recipes from when his grandad had first taken him to Schwartzman and Sons deli—back when Gloucester was more about fish and less about tourism. Except it was a recipe I'd never seen before, despite playing in the flour bins there since before I could walk.

The index card, faded to mud-brown and handled until it was as soft as fine leather, was covered with a child's scrawl. Half the ingredients were blurred past recovery. I could see there were a lot of steps, but the ones I could read made no sense. Of course, neither did the title.

Root Beer Rye Pretzels.

Grandma tapped the old card with a thwack of her knitting needle almost hard enough to scrape away a few more clues. "You make that. Make it good like your Grandpa. It will be very good for you."

My instinctual agreement to one of Grandma's mandates is what had earned me Miriam's, *You're an idiot* assessment once she'd managed to read the title. Which only made me twice as determined to resurrect Grandad's recipe.

It was just past sunset as I watched Mom set the central *shamash* candle on the Menorah and the First Night one to the far right of the nine-place holder.

Baruch atah Adonai, Eloheinu melech ha-olam...

As I echoed the blessing, watching Mom light the *shamash* then lift that to light the first candle, I could somehow see deeper.

Blessed are thou, Lord Our God, Defender of the Universe...

She replaced the *shamash* and headed for the kitchen. That's when things went kinda sideways. I half imagined that I could see something in the candlelight — Dad as a young man, kneading bread. I asked him if he'd ever seen Grandpa's recipe or eaten one of his root beer pretzels. He made a *Hell no* face not all that different from Miriam's.

That's when she kneecapped me with her chair as she rose to help Mom serve dinner.

Second Night – Tizzy

"No. No. No. And No!"

"You're being silly. Those soda flavors are all lovely." We'd just finished taste testing four different batches of root beer.

Mum the Encourager wasn't helping. Growing up, everything I did was a success, even when it wasn't. Mum Reality versus Real Reality wasn't often easy to reconcile as a kid. I thought I'd grown accustomed to it but on this one she was dead wrong. "You have Uncle Samuel's gift, Tizzy."

"Lizzy!" I don't know why I bothered. I'd been fighting that nickname since I'd been born. Since I was in Mum's womb. Since Moses first parted the Red Sea, followed closely by his wife Tzipora—the source of my nickname. Or at least that's what I decided. It couldn't be from Mum's favorite saying *Don't throw a tizzy, Tizzy*. I'm a redhead, I get upset. *Nyah! Nyah! Nyah!*

Okay. Maybe I should stop complaining, I don't want to be the *Pride and Prejudice* heroine Lizzy Bennet even more than I don't want to be the wife of Moses.

The fact that I was named for Great Aunt Elizabeth, for reasons no one could agree on, didn't enter into the matter. My vote was for our being the only two with flaming red hair. She'd been hot back in the day, I've seen pictures. Me? At least I got the thick red hair.

When GA Elizabeth had died last month, she'd left The Company to her namesake—me. Good thing or bad? The jury remained deadlocked on that one.

B-Dam—short for Beaver Dam of which we have a lot here on the Massachusetts North Shore but read it as Best Damn, please—was one of the last small independent soda pop bottlers in the US. It had folded three years ago when Great Uncle Sam had stroked out while lifting one of the last-ever cases of Birch Beer Tonic into his rattletrap delivery truck. Probably the way he wanted to go.

But *tonic?* It was a word that, like, one in a thousand people in this century still used for soda. Maybe. GU Sam had refused to change with the times. *Not soda, Tizzy, it was tonic in 1907 when my grandpa founded it, and it's tonic now.* When I tried to shorten his moniker to Gus, he'd shut me down on that too. *I was a newborn named for Uncle Sam during the war. Now that I'm your great uncle, that's good enough for me.* Stubborn old man. Three years gone and I still miss him every day.

Now the formulas and the ancient equipment in the front of the old house that had served B-Dam Bottlers for so many decades were mine. I fought the sniffles, again. GA Elizabeth hadn't let go of her throttlehold on his defunct business until the will had pried it from her dead fingers.

"You've always had the itch," Pop noted as he set the Second Night candles into the Menorah. "You got it from me."

"Maybe I got it from Tzipora," who had certainly patched up Moses enough times during *Exodus.* But he knew I was teasing. I'd inherited the need to fix broken things right down the paternal line.

Mum's eternal patience with the two of us escaped as a small sigh as she and I raised our shawls for the prayer before lighting the candles.

Baruch atah Adonai, Eloheinu melech ha-olam…

GU Sam's formulas were clear and legible. He'd made eight *soda* — because seriously, *tonic?* — flavors. I'd chosen to start with his all-natural root beer. I'd made the batch straight from his old recipe and three minor variations.

None of which were the flavor I remembered.

Thinking back, I'd never seen him use any recipes. I'd unearthed them on an archeological expedition, from which I'd barely survived, into what had laughingly been called his office. After all those decades, every nuance was in his brain, maybe even instinctively in his fingers as he hadn't exactly been all-there at the end — but his flavors had never varied. How he'd shifted the original recipes was gone, putting me most of the way back to square one.

I'd always loved to hang out with GU Sam while he was mixing syrup and I tried to see his motions as Pop lit the *shamash* and then the two candles, Second Night then First Night, as we intoned the prayers together. Tried to remember the taste. To savor each nuance in a lifetime of having it served on our dinner table. The business had slowly shrunk along with GU Sam's stature until our table and old-timer birthday parties became the only place B-Dam tonics were served. It had smelled of…cinnamon?

Mum set out the fried chicken seasoned with a touch of cinnamon, with a platter of fried leek *keftes*. I could feel my pores clogging simply from the smells. Yes, the oil in the original Menorah had lasted eight days when it should have lasted only one, so fried foods were big on the Hanukkah menu. But I was going to bloat and break out after all this.

Fresh vegetables. I'd get some...tomorrow.

I held out my plate for a taste of home.

Third Night – Aaron

DURING A BREAK AT THE bakery, I copied out every character I could read of Grandpa's recipe, but it left me little wiser about how to make Grandpa's *Root Beer Rye Pretzels*. Like a baker's version of the Dead Sea Scrolls, too many passages were missing to prove whether or not Jesus had married Mary Magdelene (my vote was yes because, hey, she'd been a babe).

I know how to make a good Jewish rye bread, what bakery boy doesn't—both yeast-risen and sourdough. Which is also yeast, but slower. And pretzels aren't exactly a big stretch from there. But—

"You think too much. I thought I should come by and tell you that," the small voice was high enough to make me wiggle a finger in my ear like a dog assaulted by a dog whistle.

"Like this is news." Then I startled. I'd thought I was alone in my apartment. The family managed to spend about half of the Hanukkah nights together at my folks'. This year, Third Night wasn't one of them, so I was on my own. Mom and Dad had a dinner invite. Grandma was off with her BWK group, pronounced Bwook—Books, Wine, and Knitting (heavy on the wine).

I looked around the place. It wasn't all that big. Bed, couch, coffee table, a good chair for slouching in, TV on the dresser, a small kitchen...I *was* alone.

And talking to myself in a high squeaky voice, apparently.

I glared at my own unlit Menorah. Grandma's actually. Mom and Dad had used the same one since they'd gotten married, so when Grandma had moved in, her Menorah came to me. Another bonus point to being the first-born male.

Miriam had some hot date. Guys never hung with her long, but she did better than I did. Miriams's dusky cream skin, that I'd never admit to envying, reeled them in like Gefilte fish into a poaching broth. A process that ground them up and spat them out in little patties that reeked of demoralization and week-old fish.

"If you looked like your sister," the voice again, "you wouldn't be the first-born male of your generation. You'd be the second-born female. I can tell you that isn't much fun. Try being tenth."

"Tenth?" I looked harder by the last of the evening light easing in through the front window. My room was neat enough — I don't leave things lying about since the fateful pink-pillow night. Of course, that meant the Margot Robbie-pink rug stains were on full display, virulent blotches glowing malevolently in the half light. Which, with my luck, meant I was more likely to get a visit from a pink Teletubby.

With the lack of clutter, it didn't take long to spot who was speaking.

Except it was hard to actually see her. She blurred in and out before coming into focus. Or maybe that was my perception as my mind tried to adjust. The foot-tall speaker sat opposite the Menorah, on the top of my TV, lightly kicking her bare heels against the glass with repeated little plonks. She wore a white smock, had a pleasant round face, and a mass of brunette curls. Half buried in the curls lay a skewed golden halo, like Saturn's rings at a weird angle.

"Aren't you going to light them?" She pointed a tiny finger toward my unlit Menorah. "You know, *He* doesn't care if you light them or not but your Mother does. She'll know if you burned the candles in your own Menorah or not."

"He?" The word stuck in my throat worse than a week-old peanut butter cookie.

"Adonai, Elohim, Yahweh, Joshua. You know, the One God?"

"Yes, I know the One God."

"Oh, you too?" The diminutive angel, I couldn't think what else to call her, clapped her hands together in excitement, making a little pitty-pitty-pat sound. "Isn't he the sweetest God? He can make me laugh until I think my wings are going to fall off. You still haven't lit your candles." She waved a tiny hand at the Menorah and the *shamash* burst alight. "There, that should help."

She said the lighting prayer with me, her hands clasped to her tiny chest and her eyes closed. A real believer. I go through all the motions, but faith comes hard. It—

"Well, if it came easier, then what would be the point?"

"Do you read minds?"

"No," she tapped what might have been a miniature smartwatch on her tiny wrist. "But the Software that Runs the Universe logs all your deeds and thoughts. Not that we really need that, those of us who've worked in Afterlife In-processing. Do you know how many humans come through every year? We've seen all the patterns. People love to *kvetch* even more in the afterlife than during their time here on Earth, so we hear it until our halos are drooping." She reached up to readjust hers but it simply ended up skewed at a different angle. "Of course, I suppose that it's no wonder with the Afterlife In-processing queues so far behind. We're only ten orders of angels—"

"Making you the lowest order. The tenth. I get it now."

Her sigh echoed inside my own chest like an aching void, and I only had the one sister.

To be tenth... "Sorry."

She wiped at a tear. Who knew angels could cry? Or could show up perched atop a guy's television?

"Uh, not to be rude, but who are you, what are you, and why are you here?"

"I'm Henrietta and I thought the angel part was pretty obvious." She plinked a finger against her halo. It set up a tuning-fork vibration that filled the room until the plates and glasses in the cupboard were rattling together. She yelped in dismay and grabbed her halo, holding tight until the last vibration stopped and the glassware finally settled.

My ears were the last thing ringing in the room.

After carefully releasing her halo and no new sounds emanated, she relaxed. "Don't forget when and how," abruptly so bright and cheery it was like she glowed far whiter than justified by the light of four little candles. "They're very important, too. They'd get lonely if you left one of them out."

"Well, the when *is* kind of obvious, as in now." But I couldn't go any further.

It all sort of caught up with me at once.

What would be...Henrietta the angel? I was talking to a tenth-order angel who claimed to know God and be conversant with the Software that Runs the Universe — *that explained a lot* — which would make sense if she was what she said she was. Which made no sense at all.

"Being the smallest angel, of the lowest order of angels, can be very trying. I was telling Michelle just the other day about —"

"Who's Michelle?" I managed to slip into her stream of consciousness. It was a fast-flowing stream, so I was pretty pleased with my success.

"The Devil Incarnate. I was helping her weed her garden, which she is *most* inconsistent about. Would you believe that she simply throws seeds wherever they land in her garden and lets them grow? It's so a-jumble, the bees hardly know which way to turn next. I drew them little maps and set up signs for them — in bee, of course." She stood up on top of the TV and did a little dance, not quite falling onto my pink-polka-dot rug or tumbling back to get snarled in the tangle of wires behind. "It's like those word-jumble things, I can never do those; they're even more confusing than Michelle's garden. What was I talking about?" She sat back on the narrow top.

I opened my mouth, but as I had no idea, I closed it again. The angel didn't slow down for even that long.

"I'm here *now* because you called out in some pain."

"Pain?" I looked down at myself. I hadn't nicked myself at the bakery in ages. Nothing broken. No —

She pointed a tiny finger toward the index card I'd set by the Menorah and my insufficient attempts to transcribe it.

"Oh."

She fluttered down to stand on the coffee table that was also my dining table and my footrest.

Fluttered, as in flapping a pair of white feathered wings as tiny as she was. I don't remember a lot of dreams, so that didn't seem likely. I was male, so no holy angel was about to pull an immaculate conception number on me—I hoped. Besides, that was New Testament, not something the Jews were big believers in.

I had the *who* (kinda), the *what* (though I still wasn't fully bought-in on that), and the *when*. The *how* and *why* still remained elusive.

Walking over to the index card, Henrietta bent forward to study it by the light of the four candles. She picked it up, as big as a poster in her grasp, and twisted and turned it in the light. "Nope."

"Nope, what?"

"No secret script visible only by Third Night candlelight."

"Is there such a thing?"

She put the card back down with a sad sigh. "Well, it worked during Bilbo's quest to the Lonely Mountain. I thought that maybe if it worked for a hobbit, it might work for me." Her voice faded to a whisper. "You know, one of the little people." She placed a hand on top of her own head as if measuring herself, again tears glistened in her eyes.

I blinked...and was alone.

Me, the stupid recipe, and the glowing Menorah that absolutely I hadn't lit because I didn't have any matches or a lighter in the apartment.

I carried the Menorah over to look at the TV. There was a little dust-free stretch on the top, about the width of a cloaked angel's butt, and two little clean spots on the screen that might have been heel marks. Hey, I said I pick up my clothes, I didn't say I was on top of my dusting except before a Mom visit.

Back to the coffee table with the card.

I tried studying it in the Menorah's light. I tried looking through it with the candles behind. All it did was show quite how primitive the writing was. Grandad must have copied it down when he still counted his years in single digits. But what if he hadn't copied it down? What if he'd been as much a bakery boy as I'd become—and invented it himself?

I stared into the light and thought about Root Beer Rye Pretzels. Definitely a kid's recipe.

Pretend you're a kid, Aaron.

What I saw in the flickering light was the back of a girl's head with a long red ponytail. She wore a poodle skirt as bright pink as the original splotches on my rug (and clothes and homework). Sitting at a strange machine, she appeared to be...filling soda bottles.

Fourth Night – Tizzy

I SKIPPED THIRD NIGHT. AND Fourth. Not dinner, just the family gatherings. I'd been weak and swung by the Clam Box in Ipswich for fried haddock and double onion rings. I like their fried clams better, but I'm Jewish, it's Hannukah, and shellfish are *treyf*, forbidden by Jewish dietary rules. So I skipped the clams — this time. If they didn't want Jews to eat shellfish, GU Sam shouldn't have put his bottling operation so close to the best fish-and-chips shop in the state. Okay, maybe it wasn't all that close, on the opposite side of Ipswich, but Ipswich isn't all that big a town.

I wasn't used to this being my home yet. The back of the building was a lovely little apartment but without my GU and GA there, it felt too strange. Instead of easing into my new home, I'd slept for the last several weeks in the old second-floor syrup room.

This setup dated back to before pumps ran the world. Despite its awkwardness, the mixing room still resided on the second floor so that once the syrup was ready, it could be piped down to the bottler in the room below by gravity. But that meant carrying lots of extracts and sugar, especially those heavy, heavy bags of sugar, up the ancient narrow stairs that creaked like they were tempted to drop me into the basement out of spite. I guess I was lucky there wasn't a basement.

Toward the end of GU Sam's life, I'd get off the high school bus each day after school at B-Dam Bottlers to carry the sugar upstairs for him. A hundred pounds of sugar to nine gallons of water, made one batch of simple syrup. Add the extract...and that was the magic I was missing.

I began with cataloging the one- and five-gallon carboys of extracts GU Sam had lined up along the back wall. There had to be some reason he'd left those behind. Most had been there as long as I could remember. Some missing only a few batches' worth. Others must have been more promising but still they'd been sidelined with extract remaining in them, there since even before I got dumped on him for babysitting after Kindergarten let out.

No empties to give me a clue as a syrup-making room had to be kept meticulously clean. The layer of dust over everything when I'd inherited the place hadn't been there the day he died. After a purge worthy of Hercules cleaning the Augean Stables, I'd set it to rights again. It would have been easier if I could have diverted the Ipswich River to flush it clean, but not being the half-god child of Zeus, I'd been stuck with more prosaic methods like a vacuum and mop.

Now, I sat on the cot he'd had installed for toddler Tizzy to nap on that would later support his own after-lunch siestas while the syrup was mixing. As I finished the last onion rings, I poked through the few keepsakes I'd gathered from the apartment but that had been kept here during GU Sam's day. Their Passover Seder goblet, simply beveled with a translucent rim of red-purple glass. I'd always loved its elegance and someday it would sit upon my own Seder table.

Their Menorah and an unopened packet of forty-four candles, the number needed for eight nights of Hanukkah. I placed the candles for Fourth Night, halfway through Hannukah. What would I pray for other than God's blessing?

The patience to relaunch B-Dam Sodas.

But I had a double handicap there. I was about as patient as you'd expect from a *Daddy's-girl* Jewish redhead and Pop's genes telling me to just fix the thing, no matter what it took.

I scrounged some matches and lit the *shamash,* then lit the other candles in turn.

Baruch atah Adonai, Eloheinu melech ha-olam…

I almost dropped the *shamash,* when a small face stared back at me through the lit candles.

Like *Alice Through the Looking Glass'* Cheshire cat. Just the little face, almost overwhelmed by the anime-huge brown eyes. Those eyes studied me intently through the flames for a long moment.

"What? Who?" At least that's what it looked like she said. Then a perky and mischievous smile shone through the light.

I may have screamed. I didn't mean to, and I kept it short, but I was the only critter of any genus or species bigger than housefly in the building, at least that I knew about. There hadn't even been field mouse tracks in the old dust before I'd done my girl-version of being Hercules. And I certainly wasn't built like Xena—I had Mum's lack of big curves despite wishing I'd inherited GA Elizabeth's instead—so that didn't fit any better.

When I dared look into the flames again, I saw a man with an Elvis pompadour, dressed in a dark apron spattered with flour. He was pouring a bottle of something into a mixing bowl. I'd know that label anywhere.

I tapped the side of the Menorah like, I dunno, slapping the side of a malfunctioning computer. The candles were all knocked askew. And the image was gone.

But I knew what I'd seen.

A baker pouring a bottle of B-Dam Root Beer Tonic into his dough.

Fifth Night – Aaron

HANUKKAH CANDLES ARE MEANT TO burn at least half the night, and I had stayed up far longer than that hoping for another glimpse of the redhead at the bottling machine. After the first two minutes, she'd left the machine, gathered one of the wooden cases of glass bottles she'd been filling, and disappeared.

Instead of being voyeuristic about someone's back and ponytail, I was left to stare at the machine she'd been running for hour after hour.

With nothing better to do, I'd tried looking it up online. That's how I figured out it was a Dixie bottling machine…an old one, circa 1950. Back when poodle skirts first became a thing. And I'd had to look those up to see what they were called. Googling *redhead in poodle skirt* didn't help at all except to prove that they did have poodles on them and that they were now worn like costumes.

Yet the girl I'd seen, or maybe imagined, hadn't looked out of her time.

Twice I went and checked. The angel-butt clean spot was still there atop my TV. I thought up an excuse to text a buddy just so I could check the time and date stamp on his reply. It was the day I thought it was, indicating I hadn't fallen into some *Star Trek* time warp.

The more I'd stared at the machine, the more detail I'd picked out. Until I noticed the stack of empty cases beside the machine. Staring harder into a Menorah mostly made my eyes dazzled and watery. I'd finally tried taking a picture with my phone.

Yep, the image was definitely there. And by zooming in, I could almost read the print on the cases but none of them were turned quite right, not even after I thought to rotate the image so that the cases were right side up. But...something about them was familiar.

Getting up for baker's hours wasn't worth it. I'd stayed up so late that it was morning. I'd headed into the bakery early and started working on my root beer rye pretzel recipe. Being part of a Jewish deli meant that we stocked several varieties of root beer.

Over the last two days I'd prepped and baked a batch of rye bread dough for each variety.

Which put me behind on the morning's baking, and the deli was chaos straight through lunch as I scrambled to make bagels and bread fast enough to meet demand.

By the time I returned to my rye dough, it had overproved. I baked it anyway to test for flavor but I was so befuddled with lack of sleep that I'd forgotten the caraway seeds and salt. It didn't matter, none of them had the root beer taste I was after.

The second day, after no more angel visits or visions of redheads, and getting a bit of sleep, I tried again. This time I simmered the root beers until reduced by half to concentrate the flavor. I dropped the barley malt and molasses as being too strong a flavor that would be combative with the root beer.

Closer, but not magical.

Fifth Night I once again sat in my own apartment,

staring at my Menorah and the recipe card. No foot-tall angel, so maybe that vision had been an overdose of cheese knishes.

Just as I tried to give up staring into the candlelight for the third time, the image returned. This time a man with graying hair and the first hint of a bald spot was operating the machine. Not nearly as scenic as the redhead. My gaze drifted from his bottler to my card.

With the light passing through the card, there was a word that was clear but made no sense. I checked my transcription notes: *Splotch-Dam Root Beer-Smudge.* I'd never seen *Dam* as an ingredient or instruction in any recipe I'd ever made. Yet there it was, staring at me.

It was also staring at me from the Menorah.

Right there.

On the bottles sliding along the track.

Dam.

In fact, B-Dam Tonic.

I compared it to the size of the splotch patterns on my card. That would fit. I did a quick search on my phone for the word *tonic,* archaic term for soda. So, that fit too.

Then I put in the full search string.

Permanently Closed.

Three years ago. It had gone out of business after a hundred and fifteen years.

No way this could be happening. There was something special in the Best Dam Root Beer Tonic that I wasn't going to find anywhere else.

I set the card down and looked at the image in the Menorah. An image seventy years out of date. As old as…my grandparents' Menorah.

If I was going to believe in foot-tall angel visitations, I might as well go for broke.

Sixth Night – Tizzy

No MATTER HOW MANY THINGS I tried, none of them felt right. Had GU Sam used sassafras extract, with the FDA-banned safrole removed? Or had he gone to the sarsaparilla root instead? Had he added licorice root, vanilla, nutmeg, acacia…

The more I guessed, the worse it all muddled up in my head.

But I couldn't move on to the ginger beer or the lemon tonic — *soda!* — until I'd solved the root beer. It had been B-Dam's most popular flavor and I was going to find it! Hopefully before I died of old age and frustration.

In addition to causing liver damage and various cancers, safrole had provided much of the root-beer flavor.

GU Sam's recipe must have pre-dated that discovery and the banning of it in the 1960s. Which meant he'd had to adapt, but hadn't written down the changes.

I tried to picture him combining his extracts and spices but —

A knock sounded on the door downstairs. The building had been abandoned for three years, no one except me cared about the place.

"Go away!" I shouted toward the window closed against the December chill. I'd been close to seeing —

It became a pounding.

Any useful image gone, I stormed down the stairs and threw open the door. "What part of Go Away don't you understand?"

The man standing at the door looked at me wide-eyed. "Red hair," he whispered.

"Yeah. So what?"

"Do you have a bright pink poodle skirt?"

Okay, red hair gets a girl some strange pick-up lines, but that was a new one on me. I shook my head.

"Weird," he squinted at me. "Can I show you something?"

Perfect, a total creep on my doorstep. I was halfway to slamming the door in his face, when he reached into a bag and pulled out a Menorah.

The door slammed loudly enough to make me jump in surprise.

I took a deep breath and eased it open to peek out. "You're still here."

He nodded.

I glanced down toward the Menorah clenched in his fist. Old brass, as old as mine. "Not quite what I was expecting."

After a brief puzzled look, he nodded. "Oh, right. Yeah, I'm not exactly brilliant about thinking through what I say before I say it."

"Are you licensed to be out in Ipswich after dark wielding a Menorah?"

"If this is the building where the Best Damn Root Beer Tonic is made, yes."

"*Was* made." And then I thought about the man with the Elvis hairdo in the Menorah's light. The same strong hands like the man on the doorstep, I like good hands. And, if I ignored the hair—good jaw, nice face—maybe even related? "Are you a...baker by any chance?"

159

He offered me a lopsided grin.

"This *is* seriously weird."

"You don't know the half of it." He reached into his bag again and pulled out an empty quart bottle printed with the B-Dam name and logo. The flavor would have been printed on the cap.

I glanced once more at the Menorah still clenched in the other of his big hands. Actually, I'd bet that I knew *precisely* half of it. "I'm not giving you back the five-cent deposit."

"Not asking for it."

"I guess I've got something to show you too."

He teased me with raised eyebrows and we both laughed. Mine sounded maybe a little hysterical. His wasn't all that different.

Still Sixth Night – Aaron

ENTERING TEMPLE HAD NEVER QUITE felt like this, not even on the High Holidays of Yom Kippur and Rosh Hashanah.

Crossing the threshold left a shiver up my spine like I'd just entered somewhere holy. Either that or how I'd arrived here had been so surreal that I was going to be freaked out for the rest of my life.

This morning at the deli, I'd asked Mom and Dad about B-Dam Root Beer Tonic and got a whole load of reminiscences dumped on my head. Stories about dates walking along the Ipswich River, splitting a bottle of B-Dam Orangeade. Then, at Grandma's suggestion, I'd prowled the back of one of the deli's basement storerooms we no longer used and come up with the empty I'd shown at her door.

From the outside it had looked like a house. Halfway up the drive there was a big picture window that I couldn't help peeking in before I'd knocked. The shadowy view, lit solely by a vague wash of light coming from a narrow stairway, had revealed what simply had to be the same machine I'd seen in the Menorah.

Even thinking a sentence like that rated as a serious indicator alarm for a mental breakdown. Yeah, maybe less with the holy and more with the freaked out.

But the machine stood there in the shadows.

"Does it still work?"

The redhead, who was as fine looking as the machine beside her, patted it like a good puppy dog. "My girl works wonderfully." Then she glanced up at the ceiling and the briefly radiant smile evaporated faster than wine out of a Passover goblet.

"Then why did you go out of business?"

At that she looked sadder than the teary angel Henrietta had in the moments before she'd departed.

"I just inherited it a few weeks ago. Great Uncle Sam operated it. We didn't have a lot of customers by the end. The Ipswich Riverfest. Long-term customers might order a case or two for a birthday party or wedding celebration. By the bottle if you came to the door." She waved a hand vaguely toward the door I'd entered.

Just inherited. "I'm sorry." For more than one thing. I wanted some of whatever they'd put in those bottles.

She wiped her eyes. "Sorry, my mess, not yours. What did you want to show me?"

"Aaron."

That earned me half a smile. "Please tell me you don't have a younger brother named Moses who I'm supposed to marry?"

Aaron was Moses' older brother in *Exodus*. "Why, is your name Tziporah or something? No younger brother, just an older sister named Miriam." Who had been named for Moses and Aaron's older sister.

She groaned in pain. "I'm Tizzy. No, Lizzy. Wait. Maybe call me Elizabeth."

"Tizzy? Seriously? As in Tziporah the wife of Moses?"

"No, yes, well, mostly no. Just…don't call me that." She covered her eyes and groaned in exasperation. "Everything's a mess, including my name. Run. Now! I highly recommend it."

"I still have something to show you." I turned back to the machine. "Could you sit on the operator's stool for a moment?"

Lizzy, no, I liked her as Elizabeth all proud and with a dancer's erect posture. Elizabeth watched me carefully as she moved to do so. She sat with her back to the machine, facing me.

I shuffled until the alignment was right then turned to look behind me. An empty shelf ran above the big picture window. "That's where your great uncle kept his Menorah."

"Elijah's Passover Goblet as well. He was very sentimental that way. He—" She jolted to her feet. "Wait! How did you know that?"

I held up my Menorah as if that explained anything. "Redhead in a bright-pink poodle skirt with a long ponytail almost as pretty as yours."

"Great Aunt Elizabeth had red hair and—" she glanced down toward her body then blushed brightly enough that I could see it in the soft light from the stairwell. "*But*…she never wore it long."

"She used to."

"Huh. And the Elvis imitator?"

I knew who she meant; I'd seen Grandma's wedding photo. "Dad's father."

Tizzy-Lizzy-Elizabeth-Tziporah glanced at my hair.

"No, never. Not even as a Halloween costume."

I didn't know what to make of her thoughtful hum.

"Do you have any of the root beer?" Seemed like a safer topic.

And that brought back the über-sad face. She shook her head. "GU Sam died with the recipes in his head. I can almost see it—" Her fine fingers traced pouring motions through the air, then fell lifelessly into her lap. " —but not."

I was too close to give up now. There was the shelf behind me, the machine in front of me. And pipes going up through the ceiling... "What's upstairs?"

"The syrup room. That's where the trouble is. The bottler maybe be older than our parents, maybe our grandparents, but it works fine."

I tipped my head toward the stairs.

"It's not very exciting. Yeah. Sure. Whatever. I'm lost at this point."

The syrup room could have been a surgical laboratory for how clean it shone. Maybe in need of a fresh coat of paint but sparkling from a fresh scrubbing. What was also strange was how simple and empty it was. The single workbench filled with historic equipment might have been more appropriate in a museum.

"That's from when they were making their own extracts for flavorings. For years GU Sam was using commercial extracts, but mixing and matching." She tapped a neat pile of crinkly old invoices. "I've ordered the extracts he used, but I can't get the mix right. Maybe he added other stuff. I can't remember. I'm missing something, I just don't know what."

"I've got no idea how the Menorah-flame-vision thing works, or what Henrietta did to make it happen..."

"Henrietta?" she asked then continued before I could answer. "Little round face and big brown eyes?"

I nodded.

"I saw her face in the Menorah's light. She looked like she was up to something."

"Like lighting a burning bush in my apartment." Okay, the Lord of the Universe had not commanded me to go free the children of Israel from Pharoah, but it gave me some idea of how Moses must have felt. Up until then he'd escaped Egypt then become a shepherd for his father-in-law and had a couple kids with Tziporah. Renowned as a great beauty, I could only hope for the old man's sake she was as pretty as Elizabeth.

"That must have been fun."

"Not even close." I looked at the rest of the room and I saw that Elizabeth had spoken the truth about not much here. There was a stainless-steel tank two feet wide and four deep with a motor at the bottom. I peeked inside and saw a big stirring paddle. Beside it, stood a series of three smaller tanks.

She touched the big tank. "Simple syrup of nine gallons of water and a hundred pounds of sugar. GU Sam only used saccharine once and didn't like it. Pure cane sugar only." She pointed at the next smaller one but didn't touch it as if it might burn her. "This is where small batches of syrup are flavored with extract to create a particular flavor. Then it goes through those filter tanks and is piped down into the bottling room. There the bottler adds a splash of the syrup, a blast of carbonated water, and a bottle cap. We mix it by hand."

I made the motion I'd seen Elizabeth's forebears make as they took each bottle off the line. They grabbed either end, gave it three fast, end-over-end twists.

"That's it."

I resisted having a panic attack mostly because I didn't want Elizabeth to think I was that lame.

The rest of the room included shelves of labeled extracts, a cot, and a table on which sat a Menorah as old as the one I still clutched as one might a talisman against evil. "What did *you* see?"

Elizabeth shook her head in a swirl of red hair down past her shoulders. She wore a black turtleneck and had jammed her fists into the pockets of an unzipped forest-green fleece vest. She practically vibrated with nerves.

I stepped over to the table and managed to unclench my grasp to set my Menorah beside hers. My fingers throbbed from holding it so hard. "I saw someone, who must be your great aunt, bottle a wooden case worth of some flavor. She was all dressed up with a pink poodle skirt, a yellow sweater, and black-and-white shoes, like for a party, and took it with her."

"Saddle oxfords," Elizabeth mumbled. "That's the shoes."

"Later I saw a balding man making up a lot of bottles."

"I never met Great-Grandpop, but it had to be him if my GA was in her teens."

"What if…" I waved a hand toward the two Menorahs.

"…we light them both?"

"It is sixth night." I dug into my bag and pulled out a box of candles and a lighter that I'd stopped off to purchase on my way here.

Sitting side-by-side on the cot, we each lit a *shamash* then began the prayer.

Baruch atah Adonai, Eloheinu melech ha-olam…

Seventh Night – Tizzy

"This is crazy."

"No argument from this boy." Aaron hovered without quite...hovering.

At this point I figured anything was possible, but his feet remained firmly on the floor.

Putting our two Menorahs together last night was like cutting their age in half. At least that was our best guess.

Through my Sixth Night-candled Menorah, I'd seen his father—without an Elvis pompadour— making pretzels. No sign of B-Dam soda, or tonic, anywhere in the process.

"We stopped making them back when I was a kid because they just weren't selling."

Through Aaron's Menorah, we'd seen GU Sam and GA Elizabeth making batches of syrup. It went by too fast but Aaron held up his phone; he'd been recording it.

The images were blurry, the blinding light of the seven lit candles of Sixth Night washed out half the image, but—

Well, tonight we'd see if it was enough. We'd sat shoulder-to-shoulder on the cot for hours afterward, playing and replaying the video. What was blurred out in one batch, showed clearly in another.

I felt like I was eavesdropping, but I never so wanted anything more than to watch those endless batches of syrup being made. My notes were a mess and got worse with each repeat. But, by the time the candles burned out, we had them in a reasonable order.

I'm not an idiot.

I might have only been interested in the recipe but I couldn't miss Aaron's growing interest in something else.

Finally, I was holding what simply had to be GU Sam's recipe. It had many unexpected twists and turns, I definitely had to go shopping, but each step felt right in my memory. The excitement of being so close coursed through my body like a shot of syrup through my bottling machine. I turned to look at Aaron while thinking about what might be fun to do with all that energy.

I'd missed when he'd collapsed sideways onto the cot and passed out.

By the time his alarm roused him—I checked my watch, baker's hours were harsh—I was too deep planning my batch testing to do more than wave.

"I'll bring some by later if this works," I'd called after him as he creaked down the stairs.

"Okay," drifted back up the stairs accompanied by a big yawn.

Next time I looked up, he was gone and the sun was coming in through the window.

I raced downstairs and fired up the bottle washer and the bottling machine to start the first test batch.

Eighth Night – Aaron

Baruch atah Adonai, Eloheinu melech ha-olam…

Blessed are thou, Lord our God, Defender of the Universe…

The table was jammed. Mom, Dad at the far end. Grandma, Miriam, and two cousins down one side. Elizabeth's mom and dad with my Aunt and Uncle Max on the other. Elizabeth herself squeezed in close beside me at the foot of the table. I wasn't complaining.

Four Menorahs, each with nine candles alight, blazed over the Eighth Night feast. My parents, her parents, and Elizabeth and I had each brought our own Menorahs.

Every place setting included an unopened bottle of B-Dam Root Beer Tonic — as there hadn't been time to make new labels. Each person also had a Root Beer Rye Pretzel waiting on their plate. Maybe not the most brilliant of meal openers, but no one was complaining.

Grandma patted my knee and whispered, "Such a good boy," before kissing me on the cheek.

"We haven't even tasted them yet." I hadn't dared.

Her smile only grew bigger. I didn't need her glance toward Elizabeth to hope that her prophecy of this recipe being good for me just might come true.

This afternoon, foggy from so little sleep, I had snapped awake when Elizabeth strode into our deli as if she'd never been anywhere else, and thudded down a case of fresh bottled root beer.

Did you taste it?

She'd shaken her head. Nervous energy, that I was coming to see was an Elizabeth trademark, wasn't enough to sustain her after the long mostly sleepless nights. She collapsed on the small couch in the deli's tiny office and passed out. Lacking blankets, I'd spread my jacket over her.

Then I had turned to do my part. I mixed and rose dough. I wanted to take a sip of the soda to test the flavor profile, but it wouldn't be right if I was the first to taste something Elizabeth cared so much about. So, I'd baked it blind, and managed to track down her family to invite them to dinner while she slept.

Now we were packed around the table, everyone staring at the twist of pretzel on their plate. Caraway rye, Kosher salt sprinkled onto the boiled dough while still wet before baking. Yet no one reached for theirs.

"Well, somebody try it!" Elizabeth finally called out, not reaching for hers.

I took up my pretzel and broke off a bite. I inspected the crumb, many tiny airholes just as a relatively dense pretzel should have. When I squeezed it, it sprang right back showing it was cooked through. I sniffed it carefully. Rye, wheat, salt—I'd decided to leave out the molasses or barley malt that I'd have put in without the soda—and...root beer. The smell was there. As to the taste...

"Elizabeth?"

"What?"

The moment she opened her mouth, I tucked the bite in, giving her no choice but to take it. She rolled those lovely blue eyes at me.

But her focus slowly shifted to the flavors going on in her mouth, and a final whispered, "Oh my God."

I took a bite myself and savored the hard hit of the salt, the chewy texture of the rye bread with the slight crunch of caraway, and then the long after-note of the root beer. Schwartzman and Sons were definitely going to be bringing back these pretzels.

"You know what would go really well with this?" I asked her.

She smiled and we both reached for our bottles of root beer.

It was as good as I imagined.

The kiss that followed was even better.

Somewhere in the background of the buzzing in my ears and the applause around the table, I swore I could hear a small high voice cheering herself hoarse.

USA TODAY AND AMAZON NO. 1 bestseller M. L. "Matt" Buchman is the author of 75-plus action-adventure thriller and military romance novels, 200 short stories, and lots of audiobooks. PW says: "Tom Clancy fans open to a strong female lead will clamor for more." Booklist declared: "3X Top 10 of the Year." A project manager with a geophysics degree, he's designed and built houses, flown and jumped out of planes, solo-sailed a 50-foot sailboat, and bicycled solo around the world…and he quilts. For more tales of the Deities Anonymous World, visit: MLBUCHMAN.COM/DEITIES-ANON.
For the author's Root Beer Rye Pretzel recipe, visit: MLBUCHMAN.SHOPIFY.COM/BLOGS/NERDGUY-COOKS/ROOT-BEER-RYE-PRETZELS

Crowning the Snow Queen
Michelle Moras

Chapter 1

THE LAST NOTES OF TCHAIKOVSKY'S *WALTZ of the Snowflakes* echo through the theater, as the velvet curtain closes at the end of Act 1. As soon as we are out of view, my partner brings me down gently out of our lift. My muscles ache from the weeks of performances, but the exhilaration of performing pulses through my veins. It's always bittersweet to end another season of *The Nutcracker*, but it being my seventh year with my company, I'm ready for a break.

"Freya, you were magnificent!" My fellow dancers swarm around me as we exchange congratulatory hugs. I smile, accepting their compliments and offering my own, but my mind is already drifting away from the stage, back to the emptiness that waits for me beyond the theater doors. Unlike most of my fellow company members, I don't have family waiting for me outside, nor a significant other.

My parents have both passed away in the last five years—my father to a heart attack and my mother to cancer. As an only child, I've never felt lonelier. In my grief, I tried to find comfort in the arms of men I dated, but nothing lasted. After a year of botched relationships, I decided I just wasn't in the right headspace to be with someone. So, for the last couple of years I've focused on therapy, my career, and as much self care a girl can buy. I'm in a much better place now, but still haven't met anyone worth the effort of committing to and sometimes the loneliness is too much to bear.

As I get back to my dressing room, I take a moment and stare at my reflection in the mirror-like floor. My costume sparkles under the lights—a white tutu adorned with silver snowflakes, my black hair pulled into an elegant bun, and a crown of ice crystals perched on my head. I've danced every lead principal role in *The Nutcracker*, but the Snow Queen will always be my favorite. Winter's always been my favorite season, and this role feels the most magical.

I take my time wiping off all the stage makeup, noticing how tired my blue eyes look. Once finished, I look at who sent the various bouquets on my vanity. Among the flowers, I notice a small, intricately wrapped package, which seems out of place. Curiously, I pick it up, noticing the fancy handwriting on the attached note:

To my dearest goddaughter, Freya. Every wish deserves to be made. Love, Drossamier.

I smile softly, thinking of my godfather. He was my father's best friend, and although I rarely see him, he always knows how to surprise me. I do not know how he got the gift here, as I don't believe he's even in the country at the moment. He's always sending me letters telling me about whatever far-away adventure he's on, but I'm thankful for his support even from afar. I unwrap the package carefully, revealing a delicate snow globe nestled inside.

It's beautiful — inside the glass, tiny snowflakes swirl around a miniature version of a winter wonderland. An elegant castle made of ice stands tall in the center, surrounded by evergreen trees dusted with snow. Feeling a little silly, I shake the globe gently, watching the snowflakes dance around the castle. The note's words echo in my mind: "Every wish deserves to be made." With a wistful sigh, I close my eyes and make a wish, whispering it into the silence of the room.

"I wish...I wish I wasn't lonely this Christmas."

As I open my eyes, a strange sensation washes over me. The air in the room grows colder and the snow globe glows with a soft, white light. I stare at it, wide-eyed, as the light intensifies and a swirl of sparkling white dust bursts out of the globe, enveloping me.

"What the — ?" I say, but the words are stolen from my lips as the world around me spins. The dressing room fades away, replaced by a whirlwind of snowflakes and icy winds. I'm caught in the middle of it, weightless, suspended in a storm of light and snow.

And then, as suddenly as it began, the whirlwind stops. I land softly on something cold and solid, the light fading to reveal a breathtaking scene before me. I'm no longer in my dressing room. I'm standing in the middle of a snow-covered landscape, with towering evergreens and snow-capped mountains in the distance. The sky above is a deep, twilight blue, dotted with twinkling stars and a full moon that bathes everything in a silvery glow.

I gasp, my breath visible in the crisp, frigid air. Everything around me sparkles as if the snow itself is made of diamonds. It's beautiful—like stepping into one of those old-fashioned Christmas cards that capture the magic of winter.

"This...this can't be real," I whisper to myself, but the cold seeping through my thin ballet costume tells me otherwise. I wrap my arms around myself, shivering slightly as I take in my surroundings. "I must be dreaming."

In the distance, I spot a figure approaching through the snow. As the figure draws closer, I see that it's a young woman; her features sharp and ethereal, with pointed ears peeking out from beneath a hood lined with white fur. Her eyes are the color of ice, and her gaze locks onto mine with a mixture of curiosity and something that feels like recognition.

"Welcome to the Winter Realm," she says with a smile. "You must be Freya."

Chapter 2

WHAT ON EARTH IS HAPPENING right now?

One moment, I was in my dressing room and now I'm standing in a place that shouldn't exist — a place straight out of a fairytale.

I stare at the elf woman, my mind reeling with a thousand questions, but all I can say is, "How do you know who I am?"

"I'm Lumi," she says, her voice pulling me from my thoughts. "I'm one of the attendants at the royal palace. The King and Queen have been expecting you."

"Expecting me?" I repeat, the confusion clear in my voice. "How is that possible? I think there's been some mistake. I'm pretty sure I'm dreaming, actually."

Lumi's smile is kind but knowing, as if she's heard this before. "Your godfather informed the royal family that you would visit our realm. They've prepared to host you and are eager to meet you."

I glance around at the snowy landscape, still struggling to accept the reality of it all. The snow beneath my feet is soft, crunching lightly as I shift my weight.

The air is crisp, filled with the scent of pine and something sweet, like freshly baked cookies. It's enchanting, but also completely bizarre.

"Come," Lumi says, extending her hand to me. "We should get you to the palace. You must be cold in that outfit."

Glancing down at my tutu, I can't help but laugh at how strange I look in it compared to the warm clothing Lumi is wearing. She's dressed in a long-sleeved gown made of purple velvet with a green wool hooded cape over her shoulders, and brown lace-up, pointy-toed boots. Clearly a tutu, pointe shoes, and tights are not adequate here.

Figuring that this is all a figment of my imagination, I might as well go along with it. I shrug and take Lumi's hand.

Lumi leads me through the snow, into a grove of pine trees where a large brown reindeer awaits.

"Hop on," Lumi says. "Hansel won't bite."

As I approach him, I swear he winks at me. This is all so strange, but I'm just going with it. I put my foot into the stirrup, my pointe shoes making it slippery. But when I hike my leg over and settle onto the blankets, it's surprisingly comfortable.

Lumi grabs the reins and guides us as we walk out of the forest and onto a well-worn path. In the distance, I glimpse something shimmering in the moonlight. As we draw closer, the source of the light becomes clear. It's a castle, made entirely of ice. The structure is both delicate and grand, with towering spires that seem to reach up to the stars. The walls of the castle reflect the moonlight, casting a soft glow over everything, and the windows sparkle like pastel diamonds.

"This is the royal palace of the Snow King and Queen," Lumi says, her voice tinged with pride. "The heart of Winter Realm."

"Wow," I say, gazing up at it. "It's beautiful." My eyes widen in awe as we approach the gates, which are carved with intricate patterns of snowflakes and icicles. The gates swing open silently at our approach, and I'm led into a courtyard filled with more elves, all dressed in elegant winter attire. They bow slightly as we pass, their eyes filled with curiosity. I feel completely out of place. I'm guessing they've never seen a ballerina sitting on a reindeer before. I smile and nod at everyone we pass, and I can't help but let a baffled laugh escape.

Lumi leads me through the courtyard and to the stables where we leave Hansel before going into the castle. The interior is just as breathtaking as the exterior, with walls of ice that are as clear as glass, revealing the soft glow of lights embedded within. The floor is polished to a mirror-like sheen, reflecting the chandeliers made of antlers that hang from the ceiling.

The palace is filled with the sound of soft, melodic music, and the air carries the faint scent of pine and cinnamon. It's as if the entire place has been enchanted to embody the very essence of winter and Christmas.

"I'll take you to see the King and Queen now," Lumi says, guiding me down a long hallway. The walls are lined with tapestries depicting scenes of winter celebrations and occasional statues of elves frozen in graceful poses, as if captured mid-dance.

My heart pounds as we approach a set of massive double doors at the end of the hallway. Lumi nods to the guards stationed there, and they open the doors with a flourish. Inside is a grand throne room, the walls adorned with garlands of holly and evergreen, twinkling with tiny lights that appear to be floating candles. At the far end of the room sit the King and Queen, their thrones made of ice and adorned with shimmering snowflakes. My jaw is on the floor with how magical this place is.

The King is tall and regal, with a crown of silver on his head and a short white beard. His eyes are a piercing blue, as cold and clear as the ice that surrounds us, but there's warmth in his gaze that eases the butterflies in my stomach.

The Queen is equally striking, her shimmering silver hair cascading over her shoulders, her gown sparkling like the night sky. She smiles at me, her eyes twinkling with kindness.

"Welcome, Freya," the King says, his voice deep and resonant. "We have been expecting you."

I step forward, my nerves on edge, but there's something about their presence that calms me. "I...I don't understand how I got here."

The Queen chuckles softly, her laughter like the tinkling of bells. "Your godfather told us you'd be visiting, and we're honored to have you here. He's always been full of surprises, hasn't he?"

I nod slowly as I try to make sense of what they are saying. "He is. But I didn't know he had connections to...a place like this."

The King's smile broadens. "Yes, well, only those with Elven blood can pass through the portals. Most from your realm do not get the chance. Your godfather has always been one to not stay in one place for very long, but he convinced us that now was the right time for you to join us here, especially with the Yuletide Ball coming up."

I can't even begin to process that the the King is implying I may have some Elven blood. Besides, I'm still convinced this is all a figment of my imagination, so asking might throw off my dream, and I'm quite enjoying it so far.

"Yuletide Ball?" I ask, my curiosity piqued.

"Yes," the Queen explains. "It's an annual tradition here, a celebration of our favorite season. This year's ball is especially important because our son, Prince Eirwen, will select two maidens to vie for his heart. Only one can be his future Queen to reign alongside him when we step down."

"Oh, wow, that's lovely. Congratulations."

The Queen nods gently. "Thank you, dear. Just so we're clear, that means you, along with the other maidens of the realm, will dance with the Prince to see if you form a connection."

The words take a moment to sink in. "You mean...I'm supposed to...?"

"Yes, it is a requirement of our realm that all eligible maidens must attend and you, being twenty-three, are of the correct age-range to take part in the selection," the King explains.

I stare at them, my heart pounding. This can't be happening.

But the longer I stand here, the more real it feels. The cold, the smells, the sounds—it's all too vivid to be a dream.

"I...I don't know what to say."

"There is no need to say anything now," the Queen replies gently. "You have time to prepare. The ball is tomorrow night. For now, rest and make yourself at home. We have tasked Lumi with preparing you for tomorrow."

Lumi steps forward and gently takes my arm. "I'll show you to your quarters, Freya."

I nod, still in a daze, and allow her to lead me out of the throne room. As the doors close behind us, I can't help but glance back, catching one last look at the King and Queen. There's something comforting about them, something that makes me feel like I'm exactly where I'm supposed to be.

But as Lumi leads me down another hallway, my thoughts race. Elven blood? A Yuletide Ball? Prince Eirwen? A magical Winter Realm? It's all too much to take in, and it feels oddly similar to the Snow Scene that I just danced in *The Nutcracker*. It's as if that part of the tale has come to life. Yet, deep down, a small part of me—a part that's tired of loneliness—wants to believe this is real. I want to hope that maybe, just maybe, this magical place can give me what I've been searching for.

As we reach a beautifully decorated room filled with soft, warm light from floating orbs, Lumi turns to me with a smile. "This will be your room, Freya. Get some rest. I'll be here first thing in the morning to start preparations and teach you about our realm. Tomorrow is a big day."

I step inside, the warmth of the room wrapping around me like a comforting blanket. The bed is covered in a thick, white fur blanket that looks as soft as a cloud, and a fire crackles in the hearth, filling the room with a cozy glow. On the nightstand, there's a tray with a cup of hot cocoa, topped with whipped cream and dusted with cinnamon. There's also a plate full of an assortment of baked goods. It's not quite dinner, but more like dessert. My stomach grumbles and I realize I'm so hungry that I'll eat anything, even if it's pure sugar.

I walk over to the window, pulling back the heavy, red velvet curtains to reveal a view of the snow-covered landscape outside. The moonlight reflects off the snow, casting everything in a silvery glow. It's breathtaking, magical, and completely unbelievable. I spot a white owl in a large pine tree outside the palace gates, and I get the odd sensation that it's looking right back at me. I close the curtains and turn back towards the bed.

I sit on the edge of the bed, wrapping my hands around the warm cup of cocoa. As I take a sip, the rich taste filling my mouth, a sense of peace settles over me. This room, this palace, this land — it's all so wonderful. It's hard to imagine living in such an ideal place.

After eating, I crawl into bed, the soft furs enveloping me in warmth. I close my eyes and let the sounds of the crackling fire lull me to sleep. Tomorrow, I'll face whatever this realm has in store for me, while hoping this dream lasts long enough for me to attend the ball.

Chapter 3

THE MORNING SUN FILTERS AROUND the drapes, casting a soft glow over my room. I stretch and yawn, the warmth of the bed contrasting with the crisp air. I'd had the strangest dream, last night, of wandering around the woods and being trailed by a wolf until a handsome man rescued me.

Rubbing my eyes, I can't believe I'm waking up to this reality. I thought for sure I'd wake in my little apartment in New York. I wished my godfather was here so I could ask him why he kept this from me for so long. He's always been mysterious, popping in from his travels to check on me, but never in a million years did I think his travels were to other realms. I laugh out loud at the thought, because it's just all so unbelievable. And yet, deep down, I think this might be real.

"Knock, knock," a voice calls out while tapping on my door. "It's Lumi and I've got breakfast for you."

"Come in," I call out.

Lumi enters, carrying a basket and a pot of what smells like coffee. She sets it down on the tray table next to my bed and pulls a teacup and food out of the basket. "Here you are, Freya. Warm pastries and fresh fruit."

"Thank you so much. It all smells lovely."

"Of course. I'll go run you a bath while you enjoy the food. Then we'll get you ready for the day."

I nod, as I pour myself a cup of steaming hot coffee that smells as if it's already been laced with cacao and cinnamon.

The delicious aroma fills the air and I can't help but moan as I take the first sip. I've never had coffee so good. I could get used to this.

After eating and soaking in the massive claw-foot bath, I meet Lumi back in my room and find her sitting on one of two big velvet chairs in the corner surrounded by stacks of books.

"What's all that?"

"Your history lesson for today."

"Oh, alright. Which book do I start with?"

"Well, I'll need to talk you through them, as many of these are in our ancient Elven language. The King and Queen felt it was important for you to learn not just about our Kingdom, but the entire Realm of Noxtania."

"Noxtania?"

"Yes, that is our world, made up of four Elven kingdoms: Winter, Autumn, Summer and Spring."

"I see. And do they all get along? Can you visit them all?"

Lumi giggles. "Of course, you can visit them all, and for a millennium there has been peace between the kingdoms."

That's reassuring and excitement fills me with the idea of someday seeing all of Noxtania, but for now I need to focus on Winter.

Hours go by as Lumi teaches me everything she thinks I need to know, as well as important customs so I don't make a fool of myself tonight.

I am thankful that it is a peaceful place where all people are treated fairly and provided for by their King and Queen.

I'm still quite curious about how I may have

some Elven blood, but Lumi didn't know about my ancestry. As our studying continues, I yawn.

Lumi smiles softly at me. "I think that's plenty for today. How about you take a nap and I'll come and wake you when it's time to get ready for the ball."

"Okay," I say quietly, barely able to keep my eyes open. As soon as my head hits the pillow, I fall into a deep slumber filled with dreams of the prince I'll meet tonight.

Chapter 4

A COUPLE HOURS LATER, I'M woken by Lumi, who holds up a pale blue gown. It's a magnificent creation, made of delicate silk fabric that shimmers. When it catches the light, it has a sparkling effect reminiscent of fresh snow. The bodice is adorned with intricate patterns of frost and stars in silver thread.

I quickly get up and with Lumi's help, pull on the gown. It fits like a glove and the color compliments my dark hair and pale blue eyes. When I look in the full-length mirror in my room, my breath hitches at how beautiful I look.

"It's so gorgeous. Who made this?"

"The Queen's seamstress, I believe. You're quite lucky to wear her handiwork."

"Please send my sincerest gratitude."

"Of course, Miss Freya. Are you ready?"

I swallow thickly, my nerves kicking in. I've never met a prince before and even though, as an outsider, there's zero chance he would pick me to be in the running for his queen, I still feel like I could throw up.

As I follow Lumi into the main hall, the palace is alive with activity. People bustle about, putting the finishing touches on decorations. The walls are adorned with garlands of holly and the scent of pine fills the air.

Lumi guides me through the hallways to the grand ballroom. We pass through a large archway made of antlers. It's not too crowded yet, but the excitement is palpable, and my heart races with anticipation of what's coming. Not to mention, it feels like all eyes are on me, probably wondering what an outsider is doing here.

I can't help but fidget with the sleeves of my gown as I scan the room. I'm not sure anyone can tell if I'm Elven or not, for I've purposefully left my hair down to cover my non-pointy ears.

The ballroom is breathtaking with a domed ceiling made of ice, and chandeliers that look as if they're made of ice, in the shape of large snowflakes. The floor is polished to a mirror-like sheen, reflecting the light from above. I watch as elves dressed in their finest dance and mingle, their laughter and chatter echoing through the space.

In the center of the ballroom stands a grand staircase, leading up to a platform where the Prince will enter. I swallow thickly, feeling very out of place. I'm so thankful to have Lumi by my side.

"Remember, Freya," Lumi says as she leads me to a group of maidens. "You will have your chance to dance with Prince Eirwen tonight. Just be yourself and enjoy the evening."

I nod, trying to calm the fluttering in my stomach as I anxiously await the arrival of the prince. I can't help but wonder what he's like. So far, the Winter Elves seem like kind people and Lumi has assured me that I'd be lucky to marry the prince. But the thought of me staying in this realm and becoming a queen is laughable. Although, I must say, I am not missing life back home either.

The music starts, a beautiful, ethereal melody that seems to echo through the ice of the palace.

Couples dance to a lively waltz. Despite being a professional ballerina, I've never danced a real waltz before, and I can't help but feel like I'm going to royally mess this up.

It's not long before the Prince enters. And holy hell, he's gorgeous. Eirwen walks down the staircase and into the room with an air of confidence, his silver hair slightly tousled and his eyes a deep, mesmerizing blue. He's dressed in a navy blue velvet suit, the jacket adorned with silver buttons that glisten like frost. I can see the resemblance to his parents.

As he takes his place at the center of the ballroom, next to his parents' thrones, the crowd falls silent. The King stands and booms, "Welcome, our loyal subjects, to our annual Yuletide Ball. We hope this evening is one to remember. It is a special night for our family as our son begins his journey to find a mate to reign alongside him."

The crowd claps and cheers loudly as the king sits back down.

Eirwen steps forward to address the crowd, and my heart skips a beat when I hear his deep voice. "I want to thank all the maidens who have come tonight. It is an honor I do not take lightly. Please be patient with me this evening as I give everyone a fair chance to dance with me. If you could please come forward and stand along the north wall, to await your turn."

Lumi pushes me forward and I stumble as I follow a dozen other maidens across the floor to line up. This has got to be the oddest way to meet your future wife, but who am I to judge their traditions?

The music shifts to a new, more romantic melody, and Prince Eirwen greets the first maiden and brings her out to the middle of the dance floor. They dance for only a few eight counts before he walks her back to the line and greets the next woman.

Each maiden takes her turn, and I watch in awe as he moves gracefully from one to the next. He doesn't dance with any of them for very long, but all of them return to the line blushing and wearing bright smiles. I can only imagine that they've all had crushes on him for years. I wonder what he's looking for in a future wife and queen?

When it's finally my turn, my face flushes as our eyes meet for the first time. As I step forward, the rest of the world seems to fade away as I am lost in his midnight eyes. He extends his hand to me, and I place my own in his, feeling a spark of warmth at the touch.

"Freya, isn't it?" he asks, his voice warm and inviting.

I nod, trying to steady my nerves. "Yes, Your Highness."

He smiles brightly, his eyes crinkling, and my heart flutters. "Shall we?"

We dance, and I lose myself in the music's rhythm. The way he moves is graceful and fluid, and as we dance, he strikes up conversation.

"So, you are the mystery maiden who my parents said is visiting our realm. I'll be honest, I didn't expect to meet someone new tonight, especially someone as beautiful as you. I didn't know it was possible to travel outside our realm, but my parents explained your godfather has something to do with it."

"Yes, I'm still quite in shock. It's hard to wrap my head around the fact that I'm in an entirely different world right now, especially one as magical as this. I keep wondering if this is all a dream."

"That would be overwhelming. I have so many questions for you about your world. Does it not have any magic?" He continues to twirl us around the dance floor. His hand feels so perfect wrapped around my waist.

"Well, not really, no. There are people who do magic tricks, I guess, but those are all a hoax. The only thing that might be like magic is love, I think."

"Ah, yes. Love is the greatest source of magic, even here."

I can't help the smile that spreads across my face.

As we talk, I find myself captivated by him and how easy it is to converse. There's a natural ease between us, and I feel as if I've known him for much longer than just this evening. I'm not sure how long we twirl and glide across the floor before I notice that the other maidens are watching us with a mix of envy and admiration. Prince Eirwen seems to be completely absorbed in our time together—his focus solely on me—and I feel a pang of guilt for hogging his attention.

The music ends and he leads me to a quieter corner of the ballroom where we can speak without the noise of the crowd.

"I really enjoyed dancing with you, Freya," he says, his eyes reflecting the warmth of his words. "I'd like to spend more time getting to know you. I've known all the other maidens since I was a young boy, so I think it only fair if I spend extra time with you."

I blush, feeling a rush of pleasure at his compliment. "Thank you, Prince Eirwen. But I'm not sure the other maidens would agree." I glance back at everyone, feeling their gazes on me.

He chuckles softly, a sound that makes me tingle all over. "It'll be fine, I promise."

"Okay."

He ushers me over to sit on a settee with him. We share stories about our childhoods and lives. I tell him about my parents being gone and becoming a ballerina.

He isn't familiar with the term, but I explain I dance and perform for a living. Eirwen listens with genuine interest, and when he looks at me, it's as though he can see into my soul.

He surprises me with how he talks about his connection to the animals in his kingdom, and my jaw drops when he says he can understand them.

"Do the animals talk to you?"

"Sometimes, but always with my familiar."

"Familiar?"

"It is an animal who is a companion with a special kinship. Familiars are meant to protect you," he explains, as if what he's telling me is no big deal.

My eyes widen in amazement. "That's incredible. And what is your familiar?"

"A white fox, named Valko. I'll have to introduce you."

"I'd like that," I say, grinning. I can't get over how surreal this realm is. "Well, I think we'd better head back. I'm sure there's another maiden you want to spend time with. I can't imagine the pressure you must feel to pick someone so quickly."

Eirwen's eyebrows furrow for the briefest moment, before he clears his throat. "Well, like I said, I know everyone else well and went into tonight sure of who I would select to move forward, but now...now I'm quite perplexed."

"Why?"

"Because of you. I've met no one like you and I've also never connected so quickly with someone. Something about being near you feels so right. Like there's this tug towards you that's even making it hard for me to walk away right now."

He's right—there's a connection between us that feels both magical and meant to be.

"I feel it too," I whisper as we gaze into each other's eyes. Iit's as if fireworks go off inside. Our faces inch closer, but just when I think he's about to kiss me, someone clears their throat from behind.

I turn my head and see another handsome man, probably the same age as Eirwen, standing behind us.

"Alvar, my friend, you have impeccable timing, as always," Eirwen says with a slight groan.

"Forgive me, but your parents asked me to bring you back. It's getting late and everyone is eager for your announcement," he says with a smirk. Alvar has bright red hair and freckles along his nose and cheeks, with dimples that give him boyish charm. "And you must be Feya. I'm Alvar, this bloke's best friend." He holds out his hand and when I place mine in it, he lifts it up and kisses my knuckles.

Eirwen stands quickly, bringing his body between me and Alvar. "Watch it," he says through his teeth. His jaw is tight as he puffs his chest out.

Alvar lifts his hands up in surrender. "Calm down, I'm only being polite. Are you alright?" he asks Eirwen with a quirked eyebrow and concern creased across his forehead.

Eirwen shakes his head, as if coming out of a haze. "I'm sorry, I just…"

Alvar tosess his head back and laughs. "No need to explain. I get it." He turns, walking off, chuckling.

"I'm sorry, Freya. I don't know what came over me. Alvar is the best of friends."

I stare up at him from my seat, unsure of what to say. Eirwen doesn't seem like the possessive type, but his reaction has me feeling flushed.

"It's okay. We should head back though," I tell him as I stand.

He takes my hand in his as he leads us back into the ballroom.

Everyone is still enjoying the celebration. The other maidens are no longer waiting.

Eirwen brings me over to where Lumi is sitting with some friends, and when she smiles at me with a knowing look, I feel my cheeks heat.

"Thank you for a wonderful evening, Freya," Eirwen says, his voice soft and sincere. "I look forward to spending more time with you."

I smile, completely smitten with this man. "I look forward to it as well, Eirwen."

"I have much to discuss with my parents before I make an announcement, so I'm afraid I must leave you now."

"I'll be perfectly fine here with Lumi. Don't worry about me."

"Alright," he says and then he kisses my cheek, lingering a bit as if inhaling my scent before he walks away.

I can't believe I just spent the whole evening with an Elf prince.

"Well, you and the prince seemed to really hit it off," Lumi says.

I'm not sure what to say, because I don't know how their people would feel about a stranger being in the running for Eirwen's heart. So, instead, I just nod and distract myself by perusing the food table.

The royal family is noticeably absent for several minutes, and I wonder if I have something to do with it. When this day began, I would have never in my wildest dreams envisioned the night going the way it has. But now that I've met Eirwen and got to know him, I will be sad if he selects other maidens and I don't continue getting to know him beyond this perfect evening.

I'm terrified that this will all be over and I'll be swept back to my world. I don't want this to end, especially now that I've met him.

I have no clue when my time here will be up or if I can return to New York. But right now, the idea of returning to my lonely little life is much worse than staying here where everything and everyone is so joyful.

The King and Queen re-enter without Eirwen. They stand at the top of the staircase and the King holds up his hand to silence the room.

"The Prince has asked that he have the night to sleep and consider the important decision of which maidens he would like to invite to live at the palace while he gets to know them better. We have granted his request and will announce his selection tomorrow. Please enjoy the rest of the evening, eating, drinking and being merry together. We bid you a goodnight."

They turn and leave through two large doors, as everyone else continues to enjoy the festivities. As I glance around the room, I can't help but see some maidens fretting, and others glaring at me. I find Lumi and tell her I'm going to head back to my room. When she offers to escort me, I'm very thankful.

Once I'm in bed, my thoughts linger on each moment spent with Eirwen. Before sleep takes me, I send up a wish to be one of his chosen maidens.

Tomorrow we will see what fate has in store for me in the Winter Realm.

Chapter 5

I COULD HARDLY SLEEP, THE events of the evening still fresh. I can't believe the prince and I have such a strong connection. It's easy to still feel as though this is all a dream, but as I wake in the realm again, it's getting harder to believe it's not real.

Lumi arrives with a warm breakfast, and I notice the smile she's trying to hide as she greets me.

"What is that look for?" I ask her with a quirked brow.

"Oh, just that I have just come from the King's office where I received the names of the maidens the prince has chosen," Lumi says, her eyes sparkling.

"And?" I ask, my heart beating wildly in my chest. I'm both nervous that it won't be me and desperate to find out.

"It seems Prince Eirwen seemed particularly taken with you."

I smile, feeling a flush of warmth and fighting the urge to jump up and squeeze Lumi. "Oh...my...god! He picked me?"

Lumi's expression turns thoughtful. "Yes, my dear. You've certainly made an impact. Apparently, the Prince has been talking about you non-stop and supposedly, he didn't want to pick anyone else along with you but his parents forced him to keep to tradition."

"Wow," I say, letting out a relieved breath. "Do the other maidens hate me? And who did he choose along with me?"

"I don't think anyone hates you. After last night, it was quite clear you'd be chosen. But, Layla, who he also picked, is twisting the truth and telling people she knew he'd select her and that choosing you was just so his choice of her to be queen was easier."

"Oh," I say, my heart sinking. I don't want to cause trouble here. "Do they have a history?"

"They've been seen in the village pubs together, but more so in larger groups of friends. She's actually an outsider, too."

"She's from Earth?"

"Earth? No, she's from the Spring Kingdom. Her parents sent her here to study," she explains.

"Is that common?" I ask.

Lumi shrugs. "Not really, no. But she has an affinity with weather magic and her parents wanted her to gain experience in all seasons."

I keep forgetting that everyone here has some sort of magical ability, and I wonder about my supposed Elven ancestry.

As we finish breakfast, Lumi informs me I'll have the day to relax and prepare for my date with Eirwen tonight. He chose me for the first date and will go on a date with Layla tomorrow night.

After I get ready for the day, I decide to explore the palace and the surrounding village. The fresh air is invigorating, and I enjoy the peaceful beauty of the snow-covered landscape.

The palace gardens are enchanting, with their frosted trees and glittering pathways. I wander through the grounds, marveling at the winter wonderland.

I come across a small, secluded clearing surrounded by tall, snow-laden trees and flower beds full of snow-drops and daffodils. There's a bench in the center, and I sit to take in the tranquility of the setting. Snowflakes drift lazily, reminding me of the snow globe my Godfather gave me.

I wish he was here so I could ask him about this place and why he waited all these years to tell me about it. And why did my parents say nothing? They had to have known.

I'm lost in thought when something nudges my knee.

Looking down, I find a white fox snuggling up to me. When I let out a surprised gasp, it lifts its head and looks at me with its piercing blue eyes. I've never seen such a majestic creature.

"Why, hello, there. You are so lovely. May I pet you?" I ask, even though there's no way for it to understand me.

It quirks its head, as if assessing my words, then stands on its hind legs, puts its paws in my lap and lowers its chin on top.

"Well, I guess that's a yes." I can't help the giggle that escapes me. I slowly and gently place my hand on its head and pet it. "What's your name, I wonder?" I ask as I smooth its soft fur.

"That would be Valko."

I turn to see Eirwen approaching, and my breath hitches at his beauty.

"I was hoping to find you," Eirwen says, "but it looks like he beat me to it."

"This is your familiar?" I ask, glances at both of them.

"Yep, and he looks as smitten with you as I am," Eirwen says, with the sexiest wink I've ever seen.

I smile, feeling a flutter of excitement. "I thought I wouldn't see you until tonight."

He sits beside me, his gaze thoughtful, a hint of a pink in his cheeks that quickly fades. Do I make him as nervous as he makes me? "I admit I couldn't wait to see you again."

Gosh, he's so sweet. "Thank you," I say, dipping my chin. "I'm happy to see you. And thank you for selecting me. I'm sure it was a hard decision."

He lifts my chin with his fingers, bringing my eyes up to meet his. I could easily get lost in his gaze and feel like I'm melting.

"It wasn't difficult at all. I wanted you to know that despite the rumors swirling, I didn't want to choose anyone else."

"I understand," I tell him, laying my hand on top of his and squeezing gently. "I am worried that your kingdom will not be happy about you being with someone who isn't from here and isn't full Elven."

"You belong here, Freya. More than you know."

My heart pounds as I wonder how he knows that.

We sit in silence for a moment, our hands entwined, the snow gently falling around us. The quiet of the clearing is almost magical, as if time itself has paused for us. The world outside feels distant, and all I can focus on is the warmth of Eirwen's hand in mine.

His gaze softens and he leans in slowly, giving me time to pull away if I choose. But I don't want to. I want to be close to him, to fully feel the connection we have.

When our lips meet, it's as though a spark ignites between us. The kiss is gentle and tentative at first, but it deepens as we both give in to the emotions that have been building. The cold air seems to vanish, replaced by the heat of our kiss.

When we finally pull apart, Eirwen's eyes are filled with need. "I've been wanting to do that since I laid eyes on you," he whispers, his breath mingling with mine in the frosty air.

I smile, feeling a deep sense of contentment. "Me, too." I've never felt this close to someone so quickly, and it's crazy, but it feels so right.

As we stand up and walk back to the palace hand in hand, with Valko trotting alongside us, I feel a sense of hope that I haven't felt in years. I wonder if maybe dreams can come true?

Chapter 6

AFTER PARTING WAYS FROM EIRWEN, the day passes with excruciating slowness as I await our date.

Once evening comes, Lumi helps me get ready. She brings a dark amethyst velvet dress and matching winter cloak trimmed in fur. She gives me strict instructions on how to get to the village entrance where Eirwen will meet me.

As I make my way to the palace gate, Valko trots up and nuzzles me. I tickle his chin and he wags his tail.

"Are you my escort, tonight?" I ask him. He walks through the gate ahead of me. "I guess that's a yes."

We walk toward the village, the snow crunching under my boots. My heart rate increases with each step. The village comes into view. It's picturesque, with charming cottages adorned with twinkling lights and festive garlands.

I spy Eirwen waiting for me by the entrance, his face lighting up with a smile as he sees me and Valko approach. He's dressed warmly, a cloak wrapped around his shoulders.

"Freya," he says, extending his hand to me. "Are you ready for some fun?"

I take his hand, feeling the warmth of his touch despite the cold. "Absolutely."

"Alright, Valko. You've done your duty, you can go now."

I watch them stare at each other for a bit too long, and then I realize they must be having a silent conversation in their minds. Valko lets out a little bark and sits down by the gate.

Eirwen rolls his eyes. "Fine. Stay here if you must."

We leave Valko as we enter the village.

"What was that about?"

"Oh, just Valko being overly protective."

"Does he not want you with me?"

"No, never. He just thinks there's danger lurking, but he's been saying that for weeks now and nothing has happened."

"Oh. You don't think we should be concerned? Is it not safe in the village?"

"You have nothing to fear. I'm the most lethal weapon in the Kingdom, and besides, I have no enemies. Everyone is a friend here and it's perfectly safe."

"Lethal weapon?" I ask, my lips twisting into a smirk, as we keep walking.

"Part of my training to be king someday is to become the best warrior in the realm."

"Well, that makes me feel better. And, I'm sure everyone loves you, but I fear I've made myself enemy number one of all the maidens in the realm by being on this date with you," I jest, although I partly believe it.

Eirwen stops and turns to face me. He cups my face in his hands and looks deeply into my eyes. "I swear that no one in my kingdom would dare harm what's mine."

"Oh," I say, not able to say more because I think he just glitched my brain. He thinks I'm his, but not in a possessive way—just utterly romantically—and I think I might faint.

202

"Yeah... oh," he says, winking at me again, as if that doesn't make me swoon harder.

We continue our stroll through the village, taking in the sights and sounds of the festive atmosphere. The streets are bustling with activity, as villagers shop and dine. The air is filled with the delightful aroma of roasted chestnuts, spiced cider, and burning wood.

Our first stop is a small, quaint café nestled back into a quiet corner of the village. The café is cozy and inviting, with a roaring fire crackling in the hearth and soft, golden light casting a warm glow over the room. Everyone we pass by says hello and asks Eirwen how he's doing. I get the sense that the kingdom is like one big happy family.

We settle into a small wood table, and Eirwen orders us both mugs of hot mead. I smile, feeling a sense of contentment. "This is perfect, Eirwen. I'm glad we have this time together."

"This is just the first stop. I thought I'd take you to all my favorite places."

"I love that idea. It's so lovely here and everyone is so friendly."

"I'm glad you like it. What is it like where you live?"

"Quite different from this, unless it's Christmas time, then I guess it's kind of similar, just add in a million more people and noisy cars."

"A million people?" Eirwen asks with eyes wide.

"Or more," I say, and then I try to explain what New York city is like, but I'm not sure he can fathom it.

"I would think that would be quite overwhelming," he says.

"At first, but you get used to it. It's lonely, more than anything."

"Why's that?" he asks with furrowed brows.

"Well, when you have no family and live in a place with so many people, it's easy to feel insignificant."

"I'm sorry, about your parents."

"Me, too." My eyes get misty, thinking about how I wish I had more time with them and all the questions I'd ask them but can't. "Have your parents mentioned anything about my Elven ancestry?"

"Nothing concrete, only that your grandparents were from here."

"Really?" I ask, my heart pounding in my chest. "Who were they?"

"I don't know, but I know just the place that might help you find the answers."

"Really?" I ask, my heart lodged in my throat.

"Really. Let's go."

After finishing our drinks, Eirwen leads me through the village until we come to a large three-story stone building. As soon as we walk in, and I see all the walls lined with bookshelves and smell the familiar musky scent, I know this is a library.

"Prince Eirwen," a little old man with a long gray beard says as he walks towards us. "To what do we owe this pleasure?"

"Aatos, this is Freya and she is seeking information on her ancestors whom my parents believe are from here. Can you help us with the archives?"

"Hello, Freya. It's lovely to meet you. And yes, I'd be happy to help you with such a task. Follow me." Aatos leads us through to the back of the library and into a room off to the side. There are large tomes laid open on pedestals. "This is the archive room, and this book here is the ancestry book going back to the original families of Winter Realm. Now, what is your surname, my dear?"

"Mustanen," I tell him.

"Ah, fitting," Aatos says as he flips through the pages.

"Why's that?"

"It means the color black, like your hair. Your ancestors must have had the same onyx locks as you."

My heart swells with that knowledge. Eirwen reaches out and squeezes my hand in his. He's truly the sweetest man I've ever met.

"Here we are—Otso and Ilti Mustanen. It says Otso was a hunter and bear shifter, and Ilti was a forest witch."

"I'm sorry... but, what? How are those things possible?" I ask, my mouth gaping open.

Eiwen chuckles next to me. "It's quite normal in our realm. Quite an impressive match though. Does it say anything about them leaving the realm?" he asks Aatos.

"No, I'm sorry Miss Freya, that's all it says."

I let out a deep breath, wishing there was more, but so thankful to have one piece of the puzzle solved. "Thank you so much," I tell him, wrapping Aatos in a hug.

"You're quite welcome."

"Ready to go?" Eirwen asks.

"Yes, but I'm definitely coming back here to check out some books."

As soon as we are back outside, I grab Eirwen's arm before he leads us somewhere else. When I pull him back toward me, I wrap my arms around his chiseled neck and kiss him. Our lips meet and tongues dance together, both of us moaning into each other's mouths. Minutes go by as we get lost in each other's arms, but when we finally come up for air, both of our chests are heaving.

"What was that for?" he asks.

"For bringing me here, and being so thoughtful."

"I'm quickly finding that I would do anything to make you smile."

After we kiss some more, we decide to take a stroll through the village park. We walk hand in hand as the moon and stars above illuminate our path.

As we approach a secluded spot near a charming, snow-covered bridge, Eirwen suddenly stops, his expression growing serious.

"Freya, get behind me."

Before I can respond, I hear a faint rustling sound from the nearby trees. Eirwen and I exchange a worried glance, our senses on high alert. I spot a figure moving stealthily among the shadows—a figure I recognize as Layla.

Layla emerges from the trees, her face contorted with anger. "How dare you flaunt this outsider throughout the village?" she yells at Eirwen.

"Layla, please calm down. We can talk about this like adults."

"I will be queen," she yells back. "And I'll be damned if anyone gets in my way." All too late, I notice she holds a sleek, silver bow, and in a blink of an eye I see her nocking an arrow, ready to strike.

"Eirwen!" I shout, pushing him aside as Layla releases the arrow. It flies with deadly accuracy, except it's not Eirwen who gets hit, but me.

I collapse to the snow, feeling a sharp, searing pain. Eirwen rushes to my side, his face pale with fear. "Freya! No!"

I struggle to stay conscious, my vision blurring. I can hear snarling and Lyla screaming in the distance. Eirwen lifts me gently, his expression a mix of anguish and determination. "Hang on, Freya. Try to stay awake."

With great urgency, Eirwen carries me through the village, his stride quick and purposeful. The snow-covered streets blur around us as he rushes towards the palace. Villagers and guards look on with concern, and I can hear Eirwen shouting for help.

When we arrive at the palace, the royal healer is waiting. The healer takes one look at me, her face grave. "We need to hasten. The poison is powerful, but we can save her."

Poison? Maybe this dream just turned into a nightmare.

Chapter 7

I WAKE WITH A START, my eyes flinging open and confusion fogging my brain. I'm in a small dark room with a warm fire in the corner. The air is filled with the faint scent of medicinal herbs and the comforting aroma of fresh lavender.

I try to sit up but as soon as I prop up on my elbows, pain radiates down my left arm. As I lie back down, closing my eyes, teeth gritting through the searing pain, the events of last night flash through my mind.

Layla shot me with an arrow.

I thought for sure it had been my beautiful dream turning into a nightmare and that I'd wake up back home in my tiny apartment in New York. But now, I truly believe that this is all real. I'm in another realm and this is all really happening.

Relief floods through me, and another realization dawns on me, that I would be devastated if this had all been a dream. For the first time in years, I feel like I belong somewhere. And that somewhere is here in the Winter Realm with Eirwen.

I turn my body to lie on my right side and come face to face with my reflection in a large standing mirror.

My once-dark hair now cascades in sparkling white waves around me. I gasp out loud. What happened to me?

Across the room, a large wooden door opens slowly, causing light to flood in. I squint my eyes as I try to see who's entering.

"Freya, you're awake?" Eirwen asks as he rushes to my side, running his knuckles down my cheek. I lean into his touch, my heartbeat slowing, feeling better now that he's here with me.

"What happened to me?" I whisper.

"Layla struck you with a poisoned arrow, strong enough to kill a full-blooded elf. We believe she meant it for me, but you—my brave, foolish Freya—pushed me aside and got hit with it instead. Valko attacked her and ripped her throat out to protect us. You don't have to worry about her any longer. Apparently, letters were found between her and her parents regarding their plan to become queen and overthrow my family. Her parents have been arrested and locked up in their kingdom for treason."

"Wow, that's horrible." I may not like that Layla tried to harm us, but I feel awful that she's dead because of it. "How did I not die as well?"

"Our healer believes that it's your human blood that saved you from its effects. Had you been full Elven, you might not have survived. You've been in an induced coma for a week so that your body could heal."

"And what about my hair?" I ask, as I twist a lock between my fingers.

"We aren't sure, but the healer senses a shift in your aura. And there's something else..." he says, biting his bottom lip. My heart sinks into the pit of my stomach.

"What? Just tell me... please."

Eirwen lets out a high pitch whistle through his lips, and I hear a rustle of feathers behind me before a white snowy owl flies over my head and perches at the foot of my bed. My eyes go wide and I wonder what it's doing here.

I'll be by your side forever now.

My breath hitches as I think I just heard it speak into my mind. Is this for real?

Yes, I'm your familiar. I've been waiting for years to meet you. I'm Brita.

Hello Brita. I'm so happy to meet you, I tell her through our mind connection. My eyes well up with tears.

"Is this really happening? I can speak to animals, like you can?" I ask Eirwen.

"I believe so," he whispers as he wipes a fallen tear from my cheek. "Something about being hit with the arrow awoke your magic. I told you, you belonged here." He lifts my hand and kisses my knuckles as joy radiates through me.

Eirwen has been by my side throughout my recovery, his presence a soothing balm to my restlessness. I'm very ready to leave the infirmary room, but the healer insists on me staying until I am stronger.

Each morning, Eirwen arrives with a new gesture of affection—fresh flowers, hand-knit blankets, and books to read. He brings a small pot of tea each day, the aroma of cinnamon and cloves filling the room as we talk or play a card game, or just sit together and read. We talk about everything and nothing, sharing dreams and hopes for the future. His presence is a steady anchor, helping me through the slow process of healing.

Today, he's brought a delicate tray of pastries, and I salivate at their sweet, sugary smell when he enters. "Good morning, Freya," Eirwen says, his voice a warm melody. He sets the tray down on a small table beside the bed and takes a seat in the chair next to me. "How are you feeling today?"

I sit up slowly, taking in the sight of his kind eyes and the care he's taken to brighten my day. "Better, thanks. And these pastries look delicious."

Eirwen smiles and hands me a pastry, his touch tender. "I thought you might enjoy something sweeter than all the soup the healer makes you eat. It's important to have a little indulgence while you're recovering," he says with a wink.

As I nibble on the pastry, I look around the room, feeling a mix of gratitude and introspection. The white hair that now frames my face is a visible sign of the magic that has rooted inside of me, and it makes me excited for a future in this world. I don't think I could ever go back to New York, and hope I never have to make that choice. I'm quite attached to Brita, who keeps me company when Eirwen has royal duties to attend to, and I'm obviously quite taken with the prince at my side.

Eirwen takes my hand, his fingers warm against mine. Even the slightest touch from him creates a flutter of emotion in my chest.

"I hope you know how grateful I am for you keeping my company every day, Eirwen."

He nods, his gaze softening. "It's easy to care for someone as wonderful as you. I want to be here for you, no matter what," he says as he tips my chin up with his fingers.

"Thank you," I say, my voice husky, as he leans in closer. Our lips meet in a gentle, lingering kiss. It feels like a promise of the future, a symbol of the love that has grown between us despite the short time we've known each other.

As we pull away, I look into his eyes, feeling a profound sense of connection.

He clears his throat as he tucks a loose strand of white hair behind my ear. "Freya, I know it's fast, but these last couple of weeks with you have been the best of my entire life. And I can't hold it in any longer. I love you."

"Oh Eirwen, I love you, too. So much. Once I get out of here, I can't wait to be together, like a proper couple."

The night deepens, and we continue to sit together, enveloped in the warmth of our shared love. The journey ahead is filled with uncertainty, but with Eirwen by my side, I feel ready to face whatever comes next.

Chapter 8

WEEKS PASS QUICKLY, AND THE day of Eirwen's Birthday Ball arrives. I've been out of the infirmary for over a week now, and it's been pure bliss, falling more and more in love with him.

The palace is adorned with sparkling icicles and shimmering garlands, transforming it into a dazzling wonderland of festive cheer. The atmosphere is electric with excitement, and the entire kingdom buzzes with anticipation for the evening's grand event — Eirwen selecting his future queen.

I'm dressed in a gown of deep emerald green, its fabric flowing gracefully around me. The dress has been chosen to complement Eirwen's black velvet suit with green embroidery. Our outfits remind me of the kingdom's pine forest.

As I stand before the mirror, I can't help but feel a mix of awe and nervousness. Tonight is the culmination of everything we've experienced — the magic, the danger, and the love.

Eirwen appears in the doorway, his eyes widening as he takes in my appearance. "Freya, you look absolutely stunning," he says, his voice filled with admiration.

I turn to him with a smile. "Thank you, Eirwen. I'm excited but also anxious. This is a big night for you and for the realm."

He steps closer and takes my hand. "It's a big night for us, but you have nothing to worry about. Just be yourself, and everything will be perfect."

His reassurance soothes my nerves, and I nod. "I'm glad you're by my side."

"I'll be by your side forever, my love," he says before kissing me softly. Oh, how I love him. He knows all the right things to say to calm my nerves.

As we enter the hall, the guests turn to admire us as we enter down the staircase, following his parents who I've grown close with over the last couple of weeks. I feel like I have a family again.

The murmurs of awe and admiration follow us as we make our way through the room. Eirwen's presence beside me is a comforting anchor amidst the whirlwind of activity.

He introduces me to the other guests, his pride clear as he speaks of my bravery and how I saved his life.

I smile and engage in polite conversation, but my thoughts keep drifting back to Eirwen and the promise of our future together.

As the night progresses, the atmosphere in the hall becomes even more festive. The guests gather for a grand feast, and the sound of laughter and celebration fills the air. Eirwen and I join the festivities, enjoying the delicious food and the cheerful company. I love seeing how much his kingdom adores him and his parents, and how happy they all are here.

With the ball in full swing, Eirwen leaves me to stand by his parents who sit upon their thrones as he makes his way back up to the top of the staircase to address the crowd. The room falls silent as Eirwen taps his crystal goblet with a spoon to get everyone's attention. His face is filled with a mixture of excitement and emotion. He clears his throat and looks out at the gathered guests.

"Tonight has been a magical evening, thank you all for celebrating my birthday with me. As you all know, it's customary for our kingdom's prince on their twenty-fifth birthday to select a maiden to be his future queen. I think it's quite clear that there is one maiden who has captured my heart in a way that I never expected. Freya, will you come forward?"

My heart skips a beat as I make my way up the stairs on shaky legs while the room erupts into applause. As I step forward, I place my hand in Eirwen's, and that familiar rush of magic stirs between us. He takes a deep breath and looks at me with a mixture of love and hope.

"Freya, you've brought a new magic into my life, one that I never knew I needed," he says softly. "I want you to stay here with me, to build a life together in this realm as my mate." My heart stops at his words as something deep within me clicks into place. His mate. The words feel so right. That must be what we are, why we feel this way together, as if all is perfect in the world when we are near each other. "Freya, will you be my Snow Queen?"

Tears of joy well up in my eyes as I look at him, my heart overflowing with love and gratitude. "Yes, my mate. I would be honored to be yours."

The room erupts in cheers and applause as Eirwen pulls me into a tender embrace. We share a kiss, sealing our promise to each other and to the future we will build together.

This truly is a wish come true. I found my soulmate, my prince, my Eirwen.

Michelle Moras is a romantic at heart and a lover of all things that make her swoon. She finally put her degree in History to use when she decided to write her first novel. When Michelle is not reading and writing, she loves to travel, drink wine, take naps and dream up her next book. Follow Michelle on her Instagram and TikTok @michellemorasauthor

Ornaments of Ice
Erin M. Hartshorn

AS BRAN WORKED TO WEDGE his car into the half-a-parking space left in the lot, he reminded himself that he loved his family, he loved his younger sister, and he loved that said sister had asked to name her firstborn child to honor him — Bronwyn if it was a girl and Brand if it was a boy. He especially loved that she had agreed not to, instead opting for their favorite uncle, Liam, as a name source. As he told Sherry, the name "Lee" worked for anyone.

Hard not to see his nibling's early arrival as annoyance at the name change, but he resolved to find even that cute.

The reminders helped him calm down so he could climb out the passenger door and shimmy between the car and the building. He really hoped the jerk who'd parked diagonally, blocking three spots, was gone when he got back. First, though, he had to brave the overcrowded gift and souvenir shop on its last day open until mid-January.

If he'd known Sherry was going to have the kid early, he would have picked up a gift when he'd done the rest of his shopping. Instead, here he was at the last minute, trying to find something baby appropriate along with half the travelers on the road.

Inside, Bran ignored the obvious kitsch right next to the door, walked past the section of old-timey toys like the yo-yo that was a surefire choking hazard, and squeezed through the narrow gap leading to the consignment items. A child-sized quilt would be ideal, but quilts vanished quickly here. Everyone knew their value.

"Hey, Bran. Don't usually see you here this time of year. Thought you'd have your holiday shopping done months ago."

He didn't remember her name, if he ever knew it, some older acquaintance of his mother whom he hadn't seen in years. If she hadn't heard about Sherry, he wasn't going to tell her.

"Got roped into a Yankee gift swap. You know how it is." He gestured at the ornaments displayed on the wall behind her. "One of these should be perfect. I just have to decide which one."

"Oh, you play nice. I should have guessed." She stepped to one side. "I'll get out of your way then. Tell your mother I said hello."

"I'll do that."

An ornament probably wasn't the best gift. The kid wouldn't know about it for years and wouldn't care for at least a decade or two. On the other hand, it could be the kid's first heirloom, something to grow into. And then Bran could get a stuffed bear or moose or something that the kid would love to death before they were school age. He was surprised to discover he was looking forward to being an uncle and staying more in touch with his family.

But which ornament? Not one of the wooden plaques — that would look too cheap. The quilled ones looked pretty but wouldn't last long outside a scrapbook. The blown glass with swirls of color were beautiful and delicate. He tipped one of them side to side, eyeing the patterns of purple and green. It could work....

A glint of light caught his eye, and Bran turned to see a pale blue frosted globe with a scene painted on it, a small ice-covered pond nestled in a copse of birch trees. The only bright spot of color was a pair of cardinals, the male vivid red, the female soft brown, both with yellow-orange conical beaks. So much detail in such a small space, so much, as if he could reach out and touch it.

His hand moved.

The cardinals took wing, singing their alarm, and Bran realized he was standing in the scene.

•

EIRLYS SKIPPED A STONE ACROSS the pond in front of her. It bounced twice, then skidded across the last bit of ice. Winter wasn't as much fun as fall. Then, a rock from her hand would send out spirals of frost as it hit, crafting grace. She wrought change.

But after she set things in motion, others took over. "It's past the time for frost. Now is for real cold and snow."

She flicked some of the snow she sat on and huffed a sigh. Was it truly better for being deeper and thicker? When she breathed chill into the wind, it was artistry. If she touched a leaf, she left bright spots of yellow, orange, or red. The snow elves left brown husks that rattled in the wind or fell to lie on the ground. Everything she touched was a thing of beauty.

No one cared. Her work was done. Now there was nothing for Eirlys to do but rest in her favorite

219

places and wish for some way to create her art the rest of the year.

"You're easy to find." Karre's voice came from behind her. "Are you going to the winter ball this year?"

She didn't turn around. "You say I'm predictable, then ask if I'm going to do something different?"

"That's not—You know you're missed every year."

Karre meant well, she knew. Would even have an answer if Eirlys asked just who missed her. Not that she needed to ask—her parents wanted her to attend just as much as Karre did. That didn't change Eirlys' mind.

"They don't believe I belong. I'm not a snow elf, I don't belong to winter."

"Even the sun elves come."

Now she did turn, furious. "You don't believe I belong to winter either!"

Karre flinched, their mouth open in shock. They quickly recovered, standing straight and shaking their head at her. "I was trying to tell you it doesn't matter what anyone thinks. But fine. Stay alone and lonely."

Without another word, they melted into the rock they were standing on, vanishing from sight. A pang of guilt stung Eirlys, and she rubbed her breastbone as if that could make the ache go away. She hadn't meant to chase away her best friend; she merely wanted others to value the same things that she did.

Her head drooped. Did people truly care about her if they didn't care what she found important?

Her back warmed as though an out-of-season sun rested on her. Confused, she turned back toward the pond. On the far side, brightness grew along with warm wind. A moment later, both vanished as if they'd never been, and in their place stood a man at least a head taller than her, with dark brown wavy hair, a sturdy build, and one hand raised in the air as though he were trying to touch something. She'd never seen clothes like his, thick cloth that covered him from toe to neck in discrete pieces. They looked warm enough for the snow, but she wondered briefly how he would look clothed in the lighter garments she was familiar with.

His eyes focused on her. "Where in the world am I?"

•

THAT WOULDN'T NORMALLY BE THE first thing Bran said to a beautiful woman, but this was decidedly not normal. He'd thought about how real the scene looked, and as he reached out to take the ornament, he had found himself there, in the depiction. No, not just "not normal" — decidedly weird. He'd stopped believing in Narnia before he was a teenager. Not that this was Narnia — Mr. Tumnus had never been depicted as a woman with a sheer gown sitting on the snow.

The woman tilted her head to one side, causing her long black hair to spill over her shoulder and pool on top of the snow where she was sitting. "You're on the edge of the forest, of course. The meadow's not far behind you. You should be able to just turn around and go back." Before he could say anything, she added, "If you walked here, that is. If not, you should probably reverse your magic."

"My magic?" If he was here, he would stipulate for the moment that magic was involved, but — "I can't do magic. Someone or something else brought me here."

"Why would someone bring you here? Are you to be a guest for the winter ball?"

Winter ball? Dressed in his jeans and flannel? Not likely.

"I don't know. I was admiring ornaments, and there was this one with a scene on it. It looked so peaceful, and I remember thinking it seemed so real I could almost touch it—and then here I was, inside the scene."

"Ornaments?"

"Christmas ornaments. We hang them on trees in our homes to celebrate the season." Mostly true, and a simple enough explanation.

She stood up and stretched out her hand. "This ornament, may I see it?"

He glanced down at his hand, confused. He hadn't realized he was even holding it, yet there it lay, a globe barely darker than the icy pond in front of him. The image on it remained the same, complete with the cardinals that had already flown away. He stepped forward, glanced at the ice, which didn't look nearly thick enough to hold his weight, then walked around the pond.

She crossed the pond to meet him, her toes brushing across the ice and raising puffs of frost in curlicues around each step. Not a single crack formed beneath her, but he wasn't about to meet her halfway.

When she stepped onto the snow, he realized she wasn't leaving footprints. Maybe the ice didn't have to be that thick if you floated above it. He couldn't do that.

Bran handed her the ornament and she took it, eyeing the metal hanger curiously before examining the scene in detail. Her eyes glanced toward the bush and said, "The birds were there, last I looked. A very recent image captured, then." She stared off into the distance. "Whose magic could have done this? Not Karre, they have not this power. Portals are things of transition, and Karre is all about settling into what *is*."

"Who's Karre?"

She startled as if she had forgotten he was there. "A friend I spoke with just before you arrived." She tapped one fingernail against the globe, making it chime. The note carried, and faint echoes came back from beyond the copse—not the trees, but something nestled more deeply inside. Judging from the faintness, the source was in walking distance, but not *close* walking distance. "The ornament came from here."

That seemed obvious. Either that, or someone on Earth could see this world *and* create magical portals, and that just didn't seem likely. "But why?"

"We will have to find the source to find out why, and to enable you to return home."

"We?" He didn't mind the help, since he didn't know the area, but—"This isn't your problem."

Her laugh had a sour note to it that he didn't understand. "I'm not doing anything else at the moment, and this is the most interesting bit of magic I've seen in years. I would like to know more about it. Unless you would rather be alone?"

"I'm happy for the help. I just wanted to make sure I'm not interrupting anything important."

"You're not." She slid the ornament into her skirt. That must be a well-made pocket to not show at all from the outside, even with an ornament in it. Sherry would be envious when he told her, since she was forever complaining about the dearth of good pockets in women's clothing. This pocket, though, would have been unusual even in men's clothing. More magic at work, no doubt.

She strode off in the direction the echoes had come from, and he did his best to follow her, tracking through the snow. It was a good thing he'd treated the boots recently, or the leather would be soaked through. As it was, a small bit of snow worked around the tongue on his left boot. Not enough to cause any real problem, but enough to be annoying.

"Sorry for slowing you down," he said. "Must be awful convenient to walk on top of the snow like that. My name's Bran, by the way."

She paused and glanced back at him, eyeing his boots stuck more than ankle-deep in the snow. Shaking her head, she met his eyes. "Eirlys. I'm a frost fey."

"Is that why you're not sinking, why you could walk across the ice?"

"I've never thought about it, but yes, probably. Ice can neither slow nor halt me." She frowned down at his feet again. "I might be able to do something about it grabbing you."

He hesitated. She meant well and it would be nice, but he wasn't sure he trusted magic. So far, his only experience of it was something yanking him from Earth to wherever this was with no obvious way back, while his family was expecting him. What if she tried to keep the snow from touching him and he wound up bounding into the sky?

"Maybe not. I'm used to snow."

She nodded and kept walking. After a while, she said, "You said you are used to snow. Is it winter in your world as well?"

"A fairly mild one so far. They're predicting a blizzard for next week, and we're overdue for a good one."

"Predicting? Do you not know? Surely those whose job it is must tell people!"

"The meteorologists' job is predicting the weather!"

She gave him a confused look before going around a fallen tree. "Who makes the weather, though?"

"No one *makes* it. It just happens!"

"What types of magic does your world have, then?"

"I told you there isn't any!"

Now she stopped and stared at him. "You said that you didn't have magic. That's not unheard of here, although it's rare. But no magic at all? Then how did you come?"

Bran was getting tired of talking in circles. "I don't know how I got here, remember? I don't have magic, my world doesn't have magic, and I just want to go home." His voice had risen, and he felt bad. He didn't mean to yell. He just had no idea how any of this was possible.

"Fine," she said stiffly. She pulled out the ornament and flicked it again. The echoes didn't sound any closer. "I'm sorry it's taking so long." Eirlys stalked away silently.

Bran followed.

As they walked, Eirlys paused at bushes and plucked berries that hung, dark red and purple, unnaturally bright in the winter landscape, and offered some to him. He knew they weren't holly or yew, though he wasn't sure what they were. He accepted the offerings, eating them one at a time and trying to decide what their flavor reminded him of.

Occasionally, they paused to rest by a large rock or another fallen tree.

At one point, Bran remembered that he'd put a granola bar in his pocket because they were easy to eat on the road. He pulled it out and unwrapped it, then broke it in half and offered half to Eirlys. She looked at it doubtfully but nibbled at it. It was obvious when she hit the chocolate chunk—her eyes opened wide, and she stared at the bar.

"Is all the food from your world like this?"

He laughed. "No, and not everyone likes these, but sometimes they're convenient."

"And delicious! Do you have more?"

"Unfortunately not. I wasn't expecting to be gone for hours when I walked into the shop."

"Oh." She looked at the uneaten portion in her hand. "I'll save the rest for later, then."

It vanished into her pocket. She straightened up and nodded in the way they'd been going. "There's a traveler's shelter ahead that I use sometimes. We should probably stop when we reach it."

Stop, as in stay overnight. He knew the echoes hadn't been close, but he hadn't expected to be here this long. He wondered what the shop owners were going to think when they closed for the night and his car was still in their lot. Maybe that he'd broken down and gotten a ride from someone else? Worrying about it wouldn't change anything, though. He kept walking.

A while later, Eirlys led the way over yet another ridge. When he followed her, the crust on the snow broke and he slid down the other side of the slope on his ass, getting completely soaked. After he came to a stop alongside a small rill he could hear tinkling underneath the ice, he sat up and looked at her. "Is that offer still open?"

226

To her credit, she didn't laugh out loud, although a slight smile crossed her face. "Certainly."

The disturbed snow was no more difficult for her to navigate than the smooth surfaces she'd been using. She seemed to simply step forward, trusting her foot to stop atop the snow as she went. She halted next to him and reached down to grasp his hand.

How could he express his skepticism without being rude? Even if she could do fancy things with frost and snow, that didn't mean she had the leverage or the strength to help him up out of the snow.

Before he could say anything, frost swirled from where she touched him, coating him in a layer of rime that felt cold for only an instant before both the appearance and the feeling vanished, and with them the feeling of cold sodden clothes clinging to his backside. Bran turned awkwardly to eye his back. His clothes were still wet, but he couldn't feel them. None of the snow, wet or dry, was touching him as far as he could tell. He'd take it. "Thank you."

He leaned forward and twisted his legs under him to push himself upright. Without the friction of the ground, standing was much harder than he'd expected—not slippery as though it were coated in ice, but more as if he were pushing against the air itself, with as much success in changing his position.

This time, he heard a slight chuckle. "You really aren't from around here." She put one hand beneath each elbow and hauled him upright. "Stay close until you figure out how to walk. I'll keep you as steady as I can." An apologetic smile came with the next words. "At least you'll be able to dry out when we reach the shelter."

•

THE SHELTER WASN'T MUCH — A cabin with cots and blankets, a couple of chairs and a table, some root vegetables and dried herbs and a place to cook them. Eirlys breathed on the light globes to activate them. Afterward, while she busied herself with making a simple meal, Bran hid under a blanket and removed his wet clothes, then wrapped the blanket around himself so that it passed over one shoulder and around his body. "I thought my days of toga parties were over."

"Toga parties?" She glanced up from the vegetables she was cutting. His arms and exposed shoulder looked every bit as good as she had imagined. "This is not much of a party."

Laughing, he shook his head. "Sorry. No, where I'm from, when people are young and foolish, they sometimes dress like this and drink too much. I'm surprised I still remembered how to fasten it."

"If you place your clothes on the backs of the chairs, they will dry by morning."

The damp clothes made sitting at the table for dinner slightly awkward, but they managed, balanced on the forward edges of the seats, knees brushing against each other whenever either of them moved. She knew she blushed often, but she tried to focus on the conversation, answering questions about the herbs she'd used and where they grew.

After dinner, he insisted on cleaning up before settling onto one of the cots with another blanket. She walked through the shelter, tapping the globes so they would gradually dim, leaving only the faint glow of coals from her cooking fire.

"Stars watch over you, Bran."

"Sweet dreams, Eirlys."

Dreams she would most certainly have, but she was certain she would not tell him what they were.

In the morning, after Bran retrieved his clothes and put them on, they refolded the blankets and left the shelter ready for other travelers. On the point of stepping out the door, she reached out a hand to touch him again, renewing the frost protection that she had given him the day before. Some charms faded with the sun, and she had never done this for another person. Better to be safe.

And if she got to hold his hand again for a moment, that was simple happenstance.

Today as they walked, she listened to the birdsong. As she'd noticed the day before, the birds would flutter away as they approached, and occasional motion in the bushes indicated a hare or squirrel darting away from their presence. Still, with Bran here, she was less lonely than she usually would be on this walk.

"Tell me more about your friend Karre," he said.

What was there to say about them? "I've known Karre my entire life. I wasn't surprised that they are a rock fey. They've always been the steadiest person I know."

"Sounds like they mean a lot to you." There was something odd in his tone, but she didn't pursue it.

"They're my closest friend, but sometimes, they are stone stubborn. When we were talking yesterday, they were trying to convince me to go to the winter gala. I've only been once, and they've been trying to get me to go back ever since."

"Why don't you want to go? Dress up fancy, dance, laugh—"

"You make it sound so simple, but I don't fit in. I'd rather be alone at home than feel alone in a crowd."

"Karre would be there."

"And Karre will be dancing with half the fey in attendance, whether I'm there or not. They don't need me."

"It sounds like they want to see you, though. Can't blame them for that."

That was sweet. A brief smile crossed her face, but she only responded to the first sentiment. "They know where to find me if they want to."

His comment was muttered almost too low for her to hear. "They're a fool if they don't."

Their travel was similar to the previous day, with her trying to pick a route that he could easily follow. They made frequent stops and she plucked berries along the way. A couple of weeks back, she might have added nuts or seeds, like those that had been in the bar he'd shared with her, but any that remained now needed to be left for the animals.

She enjoyed his presence, sometimes quiet, sometimes talking about little things, like which of the berries she enjoyed most, and what type of fabric her clothes were made of. In turn, he told her about the summer berries he knew, and how his own clothes were made far away from where he lived.

Sometimes, though, he lagged behind, and Eirlys paused to let him catch up with her. Even without sinking into the snow, he wasn't used to walking in the forest. This time, she spoke words of encouragement. "We are almost there."

He peered around eagerly. "Where?"

"Where the echoes of the magic lead." She pulled out the ornament again and flicked it with her fingernail. Answering chimes came louder this time. They arose from the pond in front of her own home. She had recognized where they were headed the day before, but she had hesitated to tell Bran. Would he think she had brought him here to this world? But she couldn't have, could she? That wasn't what her magic did.

Now he looked past her as if assessing the walk yet to be made and squared his shoulders, ready to get to the task. She remembered the shoulder displayed with his toga and thought again about what those shoulders would look like under the sheer fabrics her people favored, displaying his muscles; what they would feel like under her fingers — and where had that thought come from? He was attractive, yes, and very different from those she was used to. Perhaps it was simply the allure of novelty and change.

Whatever. She would not let the attraction distract her from learning more of this magic and returning him to his home. A new form of magic would give her something interesting to do, a way to fill her time once her autumn-to-winter tasks were done and the snow fey chased her away from their work. That was why she was doing this.

Still, it was a slight pity that he had fallen behind so she couldn't watch him as they went.

The tall bushes on the approach to the pond were bare at this time of year, leaves fallen and fruit long since eaten, but the branches were thick enough to slow Bran's progress as he attempted to walk forward in a straight line. Eirlys backtracked and motioned him to one side to follow the animal trail. He muttered a gruff "Thank you" and plunged ahead, not waiting for her.

She slipped onto the trail behind him, grateful for the opportunity she had hoped for. He would be gone soon, but she would enjoy his presence while she could.

This time, she started the conversation. "These ornaments for trees, do you buy them every year?"

His chuckle was soft. "No, no. We reuse ornaments each year, but sometimes we buy new ones for a special occasion. When I moved into my own place, I took some ornaments with me, but I bought new ones, whole sets of matched ornaments that made my tree look more like an adult lived there rather than some underage hooligans."

The thought of a younger Bran as one of the sprites that reveled in mischief amused her.

"So you were admiring someone else's ornaments? Could they have a tie to the magic that brought you here, then?"

His steps slowed. "I don't think so. The ornaments were on display in a store. Leaving the magic there to catch any who might pass by seems dangerous."

"Yet it caught you." She didn't mean the words to be anything more than an observation—the magic *had* been there, and he *had* been affected by it—but he took the words personally, nonetheless.

"Do you still think I did this?" Hurt suffused his voice.

"No. If you had brought yourself here, you would not need any help to return, and you seem to gain nothing by trekking through the forest with me."

"Thanks for that at least."

He didn't seem mollified, but she hadn't finished her thought yet. "Whether the magic originated there or here, it became active when you touched the ornament. I don't know if it would have for everyone, or if it reacted to you. I'm trying to figure out the rules of the magic, hoping that will help to send you home."

"Any great insights?"

"Not yet," she admitted with a sigh. "If you have your own ornaments, though, was there some reason you were looking at these? You said you bought new ones when you moved to a new home. Are you doing so again?"

"I'm not planning on it. It is a special occasion, though. My sister just had a child. She was so tired when she called to tell me that she didn't even say whether my nibling is a boy or girl. The ornament is for when they're old enough to appreciate it."

A nice thought. "We'll have to make sure you get home to give it to them." She changed tactics. "Did all the ornaments look similar to this one?"

He didn't answer. She was about to ask again when he finally replied. "A lot of them were painted on bits of wood. There were some that were made with thread or paper, others with beads. The other glass ones were swirls of glass and color. A variety, really. This one caught my eye because it was different. I don't remember seeing any others of a similar style."

"Different indeed." And if his recounting of the various types was accurate, he would have seen others like this.

"I did see…something. I'm not sure what, a bit of light reflecting off the ornament or something, that made me turn and look at it."

That wasn't enough to say where it came from, but it hinted at him catching the moment of magic, whether it was the ornament appearing or being enchanted. Had he been targeted? Or perhaps something about him made the magic more likely to happen, even if he had no magic of his own.

She knew what made magic work, of course. Every fey did. They were born connected to the world, tied by a string of light that shimmered with the color of the season in which they were born. As they grew, the string took on colors of others they interacted with. Parents first, playmates, then, as they got older, fey who worked with different seasons. As long as the string was present, the fey could do no magic.

When they reacted to a color, resonating so their skin flashed briefly the same color, the string vibrated. Eirlys still recalled the note she had heard, crisp and crystalline, before she absorbed the light into herself.

That didn't sound like what Bran had experienced, although there had been light.

"Did you hear anything when you saw the light?"

He shook his head. "There were people all around, talking, and carols on the radio. Anything less than a trumpet fanfare wasn't going to make much of an impression."

"Carols on the radio?"

"Songs, recorded songs, being played without the people present."

"And you say you have no magic!"

"It's not—well, it's not mine." He turned forward and walked once more. "The point is, I wouldn't notice other sounds. Sorry if that would have helped."

It would have, but he wouldn't appreciate her telling him that she thought he might have participated in the magic after all.

They kept going in silence until the path broke through the last of the brush, leaving them overlooking the pond and her home on the other side.

•

THE COTTAGE IN THE CLEARING was the homiest place Bran had ever seen, reminiscent of something from a Thomas Kinkade painting, but real, with warm light glowing from the windows and cool blue and white snow like frosting on the roof and ground. The mounds surrounding the home spoke of garden plots, plants that would spring back to life when the weather warmed again, an idea reinforced by the bushes underneath the windows, some bare of leaves and others evergreen. A flatter stretch of snow leading from the front door spoke of a path leading down to the pond and possibly around it as well, though that was harder to judge.

"This is where the echo came from?"

Instead of answering him with words, she flicked the ornament again. The answering chime was more akin to standing next to a large bell as it tolled, filling the clearing and resonating through his body. It faded but never quite disappeared, and he noticed a line of steady light in the middle of the pond, like a movie special effect. A return portal?

He could hope, but he wasn't looking forward to stepping onto the ice to find out. Just because Eirlys could float over the ice didn't mean her magic would let him do the same.

To stall, he said, "Do you think the person who lives here had anything to do with my arrival? Do

I need to worry about them trying to stop me from going back?

"No." Her voice was low. "It's my home, and I swear I had no hand in bringing you here."

Bran wanted to believe her, but the coincidence was a bit much. "It seems rather a stretch that you were there when I arrived *and* your home is right next to what might be my portal back home."

"I know." She sat down cross-legged on the snow, creating distance between them, and looked up at him with distress on her delicate features. "I don't understand it. I told you I am a frost fey. I add the nip to the air in the autumn. I turn the morning dew to ice to glitter in the sunrise. I craft whorls on windows. I coexist with the sun elves and the snow elves, but I have not as much power as either." She motioned to the light in the middle of the pond. "This is beyond me."

"Is it?" He sighed. "Not that it matters, I suppose, if this will take me home. It would have been nice to think I could come back and visit occasionally, though."

Her smile was shy, barely a movement of her lips with a hint of color on her cheeks. "It would."

With the portal, or what was probably the portal, right there, he didn't feel as much pressure to rush. "You said you wanted to learn more about this magic. Any chance you figured out how to reproduce it?"

"Not yet. I haven't had the chance to study it, and it might vanish when you leave."

He extended a hand to her. "Then why don't we both go take a closer look? I won't touch anything."

She stared at him for a minute, then changed her focus to his hand. After a minute, she reached up and took his hand, then let him pull her to her feet. She didn't say anything, but she kept hold of his hand as they walked down to the pond.

Bran hesitated before stepping out onto the ice, but there was no way for him to go through the portal if he wasn't willing to try. Gingerly, he set his right foot down, listening for the crisp sound of solidness underfoot, but it never came. Her spell *was* as effective on the ice as on the snow; he was in no danger of falling through the ice.

Reassured, he moved his left foot to join his right. He still expected the ice to be more slippery than the snow had been, but there was no change. Eirlys squeezed his hand reassuringly and walked forward. Bran took a deep breath and walked with her.

She dropped his hand a few steps before reaching the portal. He felt a twinge of regret, although he understood why she had done it. He couldn't keep his word about not touching anything if he was holding her hand when she examined it.

What a story this was going to make for his nibling some day, a bedtime story that no one would believe had actually happened. Of course, for that to happen, Bran would have to volunteer for babysitting duties, although Sherry was sure to ask what the catch was. He could hear her now saying that he never volunteered for anything, and him responding that it wasn't like he was fool enough to have kids of his own to watch, probably followed by her saying what a relief that was.

In front of him, Eirlys approached the portal, one hand outstretched but not touching it. Wisps of icy fog rose off her fingertips and drifted toward the vertical line of light. In response, the light glowed brighter, looking frayed around the edges, as though it was giving off its own wisps.

She took a step closer, and the wisps of light and frost coming off the portal became larger and clearer. She laughed with joy and turned to him. "It feeds on the magic here, but it feels stable. Anchored, permanent."

"Permanent?" That sounded promising.

This time, her words were more hesitant. "I think so. There's no way to know for sure until you go through, of course."

"What if you go through?" First? Instead? With? He wasn't sure what he was asking.

"I…I don't want to be trapped on the other side. You said there's no magic in your world. I might not be able to get back."

Whatever answer he'd hoped for, this wasn't it. His shoulders drooped as he sighed; he still needed to return to his family, to see his sister and nibling. "Hand me the ornament, then. I should take it with me."

"Oh." What was left of her happiness melted like frost in the midday sun. "Of course."

The ornament came out of her pocket with the same ease with which it had vanished, her hand diving in and then reappearing with the globe resting on her palm. Before she could move to hand it to him, however, it flared with the same light as the portal, and the portal irised open to show the shop on the other side, complete with the wall of ornaments he had been examining. At the same time, he heard again the chime that they had followed to find this place. He couldn't tell whether anyone in the shop saw the portal, so rather than take the ornament from Eirlys, he began circling the opening, keeping his eyes trained on it. He'd hoped that he could get a panoramic view to know whether anyone was watching and would see him step through, but when he completed his circuit, he had seen nothing except the ornaments and heard nothing other than the initial chime.

"We still don't know why the ornament brought me here. Or where the magic came from." He had a thought, but it was too presumptuous. Had he come here to meet her? He'd never believed in soulmates, and the thought that he could be yanked across worlds to meet someone was too close to that. But maybe there was something in each of them, a longing for more that had helped.

She continued holding it out to him. "Don't you want to go?"

"I do...and I do not. Magic doesn't exist in my world, the ability to not touch the snow, to create frost with a touch. Once I step through, I might never see any again."

Might never see her again.

"The magic reached you once. Surely it can do so again."

He forced a smile he didn't feel and plucked the globe from her hand. It was cold, as though it had been stored in a refrigerator—or, he supposed, as though it had been outside in a snowy landscape. "We'll have to see. If I can return, maybe that will help you learn more of how this magic works."

Without waiting for a response, he stepped toward the wall of ornaments. The music hit him as though someone had flipped a switch, and he knew he was back in his own world. He turned to look at her again but saw only the shop. So much for being able to return.

Disappointed, he went to pay for his purchase, stopping to grab a plush pair of cardinals on the way.

•

THE PORTAL DIDN'T VANISH WHEN Bran stepped through. Eirlys grinned at him, waiting for him to come back so they could learn more about this magic together, but instead he walked toward her and vanished. Crushed, she sat down on the ice and stared at the ornaments until the moon had risen.

Then she slowly got to her feet and walked to her cottage.

She had made the right decision. She *had*. She'd been worried that she wouldn't be able to get back from Bran's world, and that appeared to have been a well-founded fear. What good was it to be able to see the small piece of his world? What good was the portal if he could not return?

Just before she opened the door, Karre's voice came from behind her. "He wanted you to go with him."

She dropped her head but didn't turn around to face her friend. Of course Karre had been watching and listening through the rocks along the way. "And what if I couldn't come back? There is no magic in his world. He said so."

"There was enough to bring him here."

"Once! He didn't come back through to show he could."

"You...are not good about going places because others want to see you. Perhaps he thought you didn't go because you didn't want to be with him, so he made it easy for you."

At that she did turn, showing Karre her face covered in icy tears. "This. Is. Not. Easy."

They looked sympathetic. "He doesn't know that."

Eirlys stared longingly at the portal. Her voice was a whisper. "I don't know how to find him in his world."

"If you go now, he can't have gotten far."

Still she hesitated, afraid of losing everything she knew — her home, her best friend — for a man who, whatever Karre said, might not be interested in her.

"If I'm not back when the leaves start to turn, will you come find me?"

"I expect you to come back before that and bring your man with you for me to meet." Karre nudged her back toward the pond. "Now go."

Her steps were slow as she crossed the ice. What if her magic didn't work? What if she couldn't find him? What if this didn't work? What if it did?

The portal stood unchanged, wisps of frost and light still curling off the edges, magic in motion. She took a deep breath and stepped forward.

"Honey, you are going to catch your death of cold dressed like that!" An unfamiliar voice greeted her. She looked to see a sympathetic older woman shaking her head. The woman wore even heavier clothes than Bran had. Around her, coming from some unknown source, was music with someone singing about drums. Eirlys had made it across.

She glanced toward the ornaments and saw only a slight shimmer that quickly vanished. Panic threatened to take her over, and she took a deep breath, reminding herself that she had time to figure this out. First, though, she had to find — "Have you seen Bran?"

The woman blinked at her, then pointed to her right. "He went that way. There was a line at the register, so you should be able to catch him."

"Thank you." She didn't know what a register was, but the response was helpful.

241

There was so many things in this building that she didn't recognize, but she didn't have time to stop and stare. She had to find Bran. A display of wrapped bars caught her attention, and she paused to grab two before going forward. Ahead, she could hear his voice.

She sped up and turned a corner. He stood on one side of a table, talking to a woman on the other side. On the table rested the ornament along with a couple of fabric birds.

"Can you get these, too?" she called, holding up the bars.

He spun around, disbelief warring with delight on his face. The delight won, a huge grin breaking out. "As many as you want."

An equally wide smile on her face, she stood next to him and set the bars on the counter. Karre had been right. Bran did want her with him. She slid her hand into his and walked with him out of the store.

Outside, he stepped to one side of the door, then paused and took her other hand in his as well. "Walking away was the hardest thing I've ever done. I thought I'd never see you again."

"I was afraid to come with you, but then I realized I was more afraid not to." She gave him a lopsided smile. "Karre showed up and talked some sense into me."

Bran chuckled. "I'm really looking forward to meeting them and thanking them."

"They said I had to bring you to meet them."

"Did you figure it out, then? Do you know how to cross again?"

"I have time." She smiled. "Besides, I haven't looked at the magic from this side. Surely that's going to be important!"

242

"Surely," he agreed.

He let go of one of her hands and brought his own free hand up to flatten against her cheek. Then he pulled her closer, tilting her head. "I want to kiss you now. Do you mind?"

It took a moment for her to be able to speak. "I'd only mind if you didn't."

His smile was fleeting, vanishing as he moved closer, bringing their lips together, moving against her mouth and flicking her with his tongue. She opened her mouth in surprise and his tongue slid inside, gentle, probing, making her want to respond in kind. She grasped at his waist and pulled herself tight against him. She lost herself in the feel and scent of him.

Finally, he broke away. "I don't want to stop, but there are better places to do this. First, we'll go see my sister and her child. Mom will probably be with her, so I can tell her I'm bringing a guest for Christmas. She'll be thrilled. And so will Sherry, who keeps telling me I need some change in my life."

Change...that was what she brought. Transitions, one thing to another. Perhaps her magic had been part of the key for the ornament all along. She reached into the bag that Bran was carrying and pulled out the ornament, unwrapping it enough to touch. Frost wisped off it along with a soft chime. This would work out after all. Together, they had the magic.

•

KARRE WAS UNSURPRISED WHEN EIRLYS and Bran appeared over the pond in front of Eirlys's cottage in a flash of light, late the following summer. As

Eirlys's feet touched the water's surface, it froze, giving them a solid surface to walk from the portal to the garden path.

"I told you that you'd make it back," they said.

Eirlys laughed and hugged them. "I wasn't sure if I was returning too late. Some of the leaves are already starting to change in the other world, even though it's still hot as midsummer!"

"You're in plenty of time. Of course, if you want to get started working right away, I can amuse your friend while you chill the air."

"Tonight is plenty of time to add a hint of cold to the breeze." Eirlys blushed. "And Bran is more than a friend. We are planning to get married."

Karre looked over at Bran and held out their hand. Bran took it and gave a firm shake and nodded his head in greeting.

"I understand you're her best friend," Bran said. "We couldn't possibly have the wedding without you."

"You must be pretty confident about your portals," Karre teased Eirlys, "planning to take people across worlds with you."

"The magic was easy, once I figured out how it related to what I already do. I can't do this without Bran, though. He's my anchor."

"I'm happy for you." Karre nodded toward the cottage. "I've kept it clean and tidy for you. Why don't we have something warm to drink, and you can tell me about what you've been up to. There will be plenty of time for you to go tell your parents before you start work tonight."

"Oh." Eirlys stilled. "Did you tell them where I was?"

"Not on your life! I told them you were doing fine, just exploring more magic." They tilted their head to one side. "I do kind of wish I was going to be there when you tell them you're going to get married, though they're sure to like him. When's the wedding going to be?"

"Not until after I've finished my work for the year, of course."

They could tell Eirlys was avoiding giving a straight answer. "How much after?" Eirlys gave them a mischievous smile, and an answering smile tugged at Karre's lips. "That is one way to avoid the winter gala."

She nodded. "We're planning on the winter solstice."

ERIN M. HARTSHORN HAS MOVED states twice in the last two years and now lives in Nebraska with her husband, their teen, a ginger cat, and a blue roan English cocker spaniel. (Their older child has fled the nest.) A member of SFWA, Erin has had fiction published at *Clarkesworld Magazine* and *Daily Science Fiction* as well as in various anthologies.
Website: ERINMHARTSHORN.COM
Bluesky: ERINMHARTSHORN.BSKY.SOCIAL

Blackmont Bitters
Tracy Cooper-Posey

1.

THE NORTHERN LIGHT CAFÉ SOUNDED a lot more glamorous than it really was, but it was the only nightlife Blackmont offered, which was why Melina picked through a wilting salad, while the other five people at the table finished their steaks and fries. It was Friday night, which meant everyone who didn't want to sit at home at the end of the work week was here.

No one needed to be one of the Kine's precious prophets to know that.

Polly, on the other side of the table, pushed aside the remains of her T-Bone and curly fries and reached out a soft, round hand toward Melina, laying it flat on the plastic-coated fleece tablecloth. "Do you have your Tarot cards, Melina?"

Melina held in her dismay. "You want a reading here? Where everyone can hear it?" She didn't want to do readings *anywhere*. She only played around with the Tarot. Most of the time, she made up meanings, because she couldn't remember all the meanings the cards held.

When she did readings for herself, she used a well-tagged book to check the meanings. Lately, though, the spreads she'd laid out had been…disturbing.

"You don't need Tarot cards, Polly. What's to predict?" Buck Johnstone said. He put his fingertips to his greying temple. "I see Polly drinking too much tomorrow night and ending up in the back seat of Roger Dally's pickup. As usual."

The other three at the table laughed.

Polly wrinkled her nose. "You'll get drunk and go home and not be any use to Carol."

The laughter grew louder.

Buck pressed his fingers to his temple once more. "I see Melina bitching about wanting to resign, as she's overdue by a week for her monthly whine. Then, as usual, she'll decide there's nothing better to do in Blackmont."

Melina held her lips together, hurt trying to form in her chest. Only, Buck wasn't wrong.

"She's overdue by a week, because Christie is back home, visiting," Polly told Buck.

"Is that what Christie's doing here?" Dakota Walsh asked. "Visiting? I wouldn't have called it that, last night."

"What happened last night?" Polly asked curiously. She looked at Melina. "What did she do?"

Melina's appetite fled. She put her fork down. "I have no idea," she said truthfully. She hadn't seen Christie this morning, before leaving for work.

"Christie's staying with you, ain't she?" Buck asked.

"Where else would she stay?" Barbara asked. "Christie and Melina are roommates from way back."

"D'uh," Buck replied. "But Christie's mother is still in Blackmont." He winked at Melina. "So, what did our lovely Amica get up to last night?"

Melina shifted on her chair, as hot discomfort swirled in her belly. "Ask Dakota. He knows more than me."

"She was sloppy drunk, right here at this table," Dakota said. "I thought the Amica are trained to hold their drink?"

"They drink mead in Valhalla," Polly said, with the air of an expert. Polly devoured *any* information about the Kine. "You can't get mead outside the Kine halls, anymore. I'm guessing she wasn't drinking mead last night."

Dakota shook his head. "Martinis."

"But they train the Amica to go drink for drink with the Einherjar, and those dudes can *really* drink." Buck also sounded like he knew what he was talking about.

Barbara shook her head. "The Valkyrie can drink, too," she said firmly.

Melina sighed to herself. They'd only just finished their meal, and they were already onto their favourite subject. The Kine. Valhalla. Einherjar and Valkyrie and Amica and the whole Kine culture, which the rest of the world seemed to be obsessed with, these days.

Now Christie was back home for Christmas, the gossip was rocket-fueled. *Everyone* wanted a piece of Christie. She was the home-grown girl who had escaped to live a fairy-tale life. She had been chosen by the Kine to join their Amica training program, then take her place in the halls of the Kine, a privilege extended to only very beautiful, very talented or very intelligent women. It helped if one was all three, the gossips said, and Christie was certainly that.

Melina and Christie had gone to high school in Fairbanks together, then both had got jobs in the Blackmont Mining Company's railhead office and set up an apartment together. Then the Kine had found the lovely blonde, blue-eyed Christie and plucked her out of her cubicle and thrust her into legendary status.

Amica training, Christie had confided to Melina in a rare email, was difficult and exhausting. She was taught everything from how to stand, how to put on makeup, to how to sterilize a room, how to grow vegetables and make pharmaceuticals from those plants. Her wardrobe had been criticized and discarded and she had been supplied with a "better" wardrobe, that included the traditional apron dresses worn by the Amica.

She scrubbed and cleaned and cooked. She sewed and spun and wove. She read histories and was cross-examined upon them.

Eventually, Christie had been deemed sufficiently trained to take her place in the Kine halls. Not *the* Kine hall—which had upset most of Blackmont for three days, for everyone thought Christie was beautiful enough to deserve a posting in Valhalla itself—but a secondary hall in London, England.

Not that distance mattered a damn when one lived in the halls. The Kine used portals. A step through and they were thousands of miles away. You could cross the entire planet in a dozen steps, if you knew which portal connected which two halls.

Which was how the trains that hauled Blackmont Mining's rare earth elements worked. The Kine transported the rare earth for the mining company. But they also transported select passengers, those with Kine privileges.

Christie had used the train to come home for her first visit in five years. The whole town was lining up to quiz Christie about life among the Kine.

Melina was not one of them, even though Christie was right there in her apartment. Melina would be happy if she never heard another word about the Kine. The closer to Christmas the calendar got, the more talk about the Kine grated. She'd had a headache for two days already and it was only the 20th.

But Buck, Polly, Dakota and Barbara were in full swing. Einherjar training programs, selection process, how one had to die in battle to become an Einherjar or Valkyrie. How the Kine had lived among humans for centuries, completely unnoticed, until they had been forced to reveal themselves when the Alfar had invaded Earth. How the Kine had defeated the deadly elves. How the portals worked and why humans couldn't use them. Protocol. Customs. On and on and *on*.

Melina slid her hand into her handbag and found the pack of cards. As she unwrapped the silk scarf that contained them, Polly pressed her hands together in delight, then stacked dinner plates and cutlery to make room between her and Melina. Her softly rounded cheeks were touched with pink. Excitement.

Melina tuned out the conversation on the other end of the table and shuffled the cards. They were bigger than ordinary playing cards, so Melina moved slowly. A card jumped out of the pack and dropped onto the table, face down.

Polly knew that cards which dropped out while shuffling might have significance. "Oh, someone is trying to communicate," she cooed, and turned the card over.

The Queen of Wands.

Melina paused her shuffling, dismay touching her.

"Charlotte Rose!" Polly cried, pulling the attention of everyone at the table.

"The Queen!"

She's not the queen, she's the Regin, Melina thought.

"You're not meant to call her that," Buck said.

Polly waved him away, too excited to care. "You know what I mean! It's her. She's talking to us!"

"The Queen of Wands can represent many different people," Melina said. "Or it could be an idea. An emotion. Without other cards around it, it's just a symbol."

"Yeah, like the King of Wands is a symbol for Asher Strand, the Annarr," Buck said.

Shockingly loud, the opening chords of Mariah Carey's *All I Want for Christmas Is You* filled the restaurant.

Dakota straightened up, smiling, and withdrew his arm from behind the antique juke box. "Found it!"

"Turn it *down!*" Polly shouted, her hands over her ears.

"They're *Christmas* songs!" Dakota protested. "Get a little cheer, why don't you?"

"I want to hear what Melina says about my *cards!*"

Meline scooped up the cards and stacked them. "Doing a reading here won't work." She had to lift her voice. "I can't concentrate on the reading with this noise."

Polly pouted. "I'll buy you a drink."

Melina shook her head. "I'm going to go home."

"But you can't! It's Friday night!" Barbara sounded horrified.

Buck shook his head. "Let her go. It's Christmas." He couldn't say it softly.

Melina stood and zipped up her coat. Her hands were shaking, but that was nothing compared to the roiling and squeezing in her belly and chest.

Polly looked at Buck, puzzlement bringing her pale brows together.

Barbara flushed a deep red. "I'm sorry, Melina," she said quickly.

"Sorry?' Polly repeated. "What...? Oh. Oh! Oh shit...sorry, Melina. Yeah of course. I forgot. Please forgive me."

Melina pulled her bag strap over her shoulder. "No, it's fine. I'm fine. Really. I just have a headache and this noise isn't helping."

Buck came around the table and hugged her. "You okay to get home?"

Melina's eyes ached. Buck had been Axel's friend, but in the year since Axel had died fighting Alfar with a hockey stick, not even a hundred yards away from the restaurant, Buck had never said anything to her about Axel. Sometimes, though, she caught him watching her.

"I'm..." She stopped herself from repeating that she was fine, because they both knew that was a lie. "It's just...one year on Christmas Day...." She let out a breath that shook.

Buck nodded. "The town is going to do a thing, you know. On Christmas Day and everything. To commemorate the victory."

"Is that what it was? A victory?" It hadn't felt that way to her. It still didn't, even though the humans who had fought until the Kine arrived had kept the railway portal open. She had lost everything with meaning in her life, that day. Victorious was far from how she felt about it.

Buck grimaced. "I know what you mean. Listen, are you doing anything on Christmas…no, wait. Christie is here." He looked surprised. "Do you think that's why she came back? So, you wouldn't be alone on Christmas Day?"

Melina sighed. "Honestly, I don't think so, Buck. I don't know why she came back, but it wasn't for me, and it wasn't for Christmas, or for a vacation." All the conversations Melina had tried to start with Christie had been killed. "Dakota should pour more vodka down her throat. Maybe talking it out will help her."

Melina pulled out her gloves and put the fur-edged hood of her coat up over her head. It wasn't blowing out there, but it had been minus four when she had left the office. "Thanks, Buck."

Buck rubbed the back of his head. "Okay."

Melina gave him the best smile she could manage, then left before her aching eyes filled with tears and she made a fool of herself in front of friends who were already celebrating Christmas as hard as they could.

Just call me Scrooge, she thought, as the frigid air whistling down Blackmont's one snow-filled main street blasted her in the face. She put her head down and walked as fast as she could.

Her apartment was in one of Blackmont's oldest houses, that dated back to just after the Second World War. She had the top floor, Degataga and Jenny had the main floor, and Passang Iturburua had the basement all to himself. Passang was a train engineer, and Degataga ran the big trucks out at the Minehead. Jenny was the only one in the old house who *didn't* work for the mining company.

Blackmont was a mining town, through and through.

Melina climbed wearily to the top floor and dropped her bag on the tiny table by the kitchenette. More noise was assaulting her here, too. Every night Melina had returned home, some new band would be thudding its way through a song. Melina didn't know any of the songs, which showed how far Christie had moved on from Blackmont, which was wedded to classic rock 'n roll.

"Christie!" Melina called. She spotted Christie's phone, inserted into the speaker system, and switched it off.

The silence was nice, but now she could hear Jenny talking, below.

Christie had been sleeping on the couch. Her blankets and pillows were piled upon one end of it, and her suitcase with all her clothes was open on the floor next to it. Her handbag—no shoulder bag for Christie, anymore—sat beside the suitcase.

No Christie, although the apartment wasn't huge. It left only one other place where Christie might be. Melina moved through her bedroom to the bathroom door and knocked. "Christie?"

Silence.

Melina knocked harder. "Christie!! Are you in there? Say something."

In the few seconds that followed, Melina's heart squeezed and leapt, making her feel sick. She gripped the handle. "I'm coming in, Christie, okay?"

She opened the door and froze.

Christie *was* in there, but she hadn't heard Melina. She would never hear anyone, ever again.

2.

Pavlin Barr kept shooting Melina strange, penetrating stares when he moved around the big open office, while everyone else avoided her gaze.

Pavlin was the director of administration, and her boss and after she had flatly refused to go home this morning, he had reverted to this *I'm watching to see if you show the slightest sign of melt down* mode.

But he needed her here. They both knew from past experience that the office fell in a heap if she wasn't here to direct the work. A big enough snarl of schedules and data, and the mining came to a grinding halt, too, and *that* simply couldn't happen. They were already behind in tonnage for the month, and the holidays started in three days' time.

Melina couldn't stand the idea of sitting at home, anyway. Not in her apartment. She had got Pavlin's okay to send the mining company's cleaning service to the apartment, to clean it from top to bottom, especially the bathroom.

It was easier to work. All the little niggles and problems that she handled in a day took her mind off last night. She kept seeing Christie's body zipped up and rolled away.

Darryl, the State Trooper who served as the town's policeman, when needed, had not let Melina watch the two EMTs pull Christie from the bath. "You've seen enough. It's going to stick in your head," he'd told her. "You don't need to add to the reel."

Ben and Bosse, who ran the one ambulance in Blackmont, had patted her back. "We'll take her straight to the Memorial, Melina, 'kay?" Bosse has murmured, bending to look into her eyes.

Measuring me for shock, Melina realized. That had snapped her out of the frozen state she had been in since opening the bathroom door.

"Someone has to tell Christie's mom," Darryl had added. "She'll want to go to the hospital. Be with her."

"I'll do it," Melina said.

"Are you sure?" Darryl asked, and she realized he was measuring her, too.

"Sure. I can't sleep here. Not tonight. Miriam will let me sleep on her sofa...or I might go to the hospital with her."

In the end she had done neither, for Miriam had not answered her door. Like most of Blackmont, Miriam liked her Friday night dinner and drinks, but she usually did both with friends. Miriam knew everyone.

Melina had walked through the falling snow to Mohan's place, which sometimes operated as a bed and breakfast when strangers were in town who weren't part of the mining operations. Mining people stayed in the dormitories at the minehead. Mohan had given her a room, *gratis*, once he'd got over the shock of Melina's news.

This morning, Melina had skipped breakfast, even though Mohan had rustled up fresh bagels. She had headed for the office, getting there well before anyone else.

And working *had* helped. Work was normal. Even solving problems was routine. Every time

Melina thought of Christie, she reached for another problem or task and focused on getting it done. It also let her ignore Pavlin's scrutiny and the way everyone else was creeping around her and being super nice and polite and cooperative, as though normal behavior might jolt her into an emotional storm.

Melina still wasn't hungry when the noon whistle sounded, and told Carmilla, the receptionist, to take the early break. She settled herself behind the desk, instead, and was rattling off email replies when the company minibus pulled up outside, and three strangers stepped out.

The minibus regularly shuttled people from the train to different areas of the mining complex so it wasn't unusual for visitors to arrive at the administration building, but Melina usually knew about upcoming visits.

But these were *strange* strangers. They wore…it was impossible to catalogue what they wore, for all three had nothing in common. They were muffled to the brows with winter gear, which hid all but their eyes. One wore a puffy parka and snow pants, both dazzling white, with red gloves. His hat had a red pompom, and his scarf was red. He looked like he should be on a French ski slope, not here.

The tall one who had been in the front passenger seat of the minibus wore a black overcoat that was common as salt on New York's streets but was woefully inadequate for Blackmont. He'd added layers, though – a warm and wide woolen scarf that he'd wound around his head, so that everything up to his nose was muffled. He didn't have a hat, though.

Who came to Alaska in December and didn't bring a hat?

The third person looked to be the only sensibly dressed one among them. A fur lined coat, a thick wool scarf, a hat pulled down over his ears, proper gloves, and decent boots.

A fourth passenger got out, stood, and reached under their jacket to straighten up...Melina squinted through the scratched glass of the front doors.

A sword. She could see the tip of the naked blade jutting out underneath the person's thigh-length coat.

Then they flipped hair out of the neck of their coat, and it lay gleaming, black and straight, over her shoulder.

Melina got to her feet, her heart thudding. They were all strangers, but she knew exactly who they were. The sword told her.

They were Einherjar, from far away. There was only one Kine hall in Alaska, and that was in Juneau, far to the south.

She didn't think these Einherjar—and one Valkyrie, apparently—were from Juneau. The train didn't connect with Juneau.

The four of them shuffled through the still-falling snow toward the door. The sun was already heading for the horizon. It would be gone in an hour, and it sent long shadows across the snow as the four moved up to the door.

They were talking behind their scarves as they came in, and the talk sounded easy. Without strain.

The woman pulled down her scarf as she reached for the inner door and held it open for the other three. She had a square face that was handsome, rather than pretty, but there was a competent air about her that was oddly reassuring.

This was a Valkyrie, then?

Melina had no time to examine the woman closely, for two of the men were stripping off their outer gear. The one in the New York businessman's' attire took off his inadequate leather gloves and pulled the scarf away from his face.

"Hello." He didn't speak loudly, or in a hurry. He had dark hair, shorn short, and weathered flesh. His chin was thick with growth, as if he was in the beginning stages of growing out a beard. His eyes were blue and warm. "We're not expected, but we would like to speak to Pavlin Barr or Melina…" He looked at the Valkyrie and raised his brow. "Gone…" he said, sounding vexed. Then he raised his hand. "Richardson," he finished and smiled at Melina. "I was pulled out of a board meeting with twenty suits and shoved onto the train. *Their* names, I had down."

Melina pressed her lips together. She wanted to laugh, but didn't think it was a good idea to give in to the impulse. "I am Melina Richardson," she told the man. "What can I do for you?"

"Told you she wasn't a receptionist," the Valkyrie said, sounding pleased.

"It's just gone noon. I'm covering for the lunch hour," Melina explained.

"There. See?" The Valkyrie grinned, and the expression transformed her from a somewhat plain woman to a beauty. Her green eyes danced. Her smile made her face glow. "I'm Grace. This is Lucas Montgomery, the Earl of New York."

I know. The words rose to Melina's lips. She knew Lucas Montgomery's name, but he did not look like the few images she had seen of him. He looked both younger, and much older.

The man in the white suit finally got his parka unzipped and separated and shoved his gloves into his coat pocket. He appeared to be older than the other two by several decades, but Melina didn't let herself fall into that trap. The Einherjar didn't really *have* ages. There was the age they were turned from human to Einherjar, then the years they had lived as Einherjar, Some of the Einherjar, like Asher Strand, had lived for hundreds of years. While this man might have been made only a few years ago.

"That's Davor," Grace said.

"It's *cold*," Davor told Melina.

"It's Alaska," Melina replied, using the same tone.

Grace and Lucas both laughed, but the fourth person did not. He was unwinding his scarf, moving with an odd slowness.

Then the scarf pulled away and Melina knew why he had been moving slowly.

"You know Axel, of course," Grace said. Her voice was low.

Warm, copper-colored eyes, dark brown hair with copper highlights. Rough stubble around his jaw...

"Hello, Melina," Axel said. His voice hadn't changed. Not at all. It still had the low burr that once made her shiver when she heard it.

Sounds were muffled. Her heartbeat thudded in her ears. Her chest hurt.

Melina reached out weakly for the high reception counter. "I...uh..." Two almost-words, and neither sounded right.

Her throat was tight, and her mouth didn't want to work properly. She tried again. "I..." A high squeak.

She gripped the counter.

"She's turned white," Lucas said, his tone worried.

"Ooops, here we go," Grace said. She grabbed Melina's arms and moved her around the desk and propped her on the chair. "Take a few deep breaths."

She patted Melina's shoulder and stepped away. "I told you we shoulda phoned," she chided Lucas.

"No coverage on the train," Lucas replied, as if they were old friends, and he wasn't the Earl of New York. But then, Lucas Montgomery was the Regin's brother, and they had both been made at the same time, during the battle for New York, ten years ago, which had been the last battle in the Alfar war.

The facts flashed through Melina's mind, while she tried to breathe as directed. She realized she was trying to distract herself. Trying to avoid dealing with the fact that Axel was standing *right there*.

She wasn't ready for this.

But she lifted her chin anyway and looked at him once more.

Axel had moved over to the counter, watching her with a concerned expression. "I'm sorry," he said, when her gaze met his. "This wasn't planned. I would have…"

"Have what?" Melina asked.

"Let you know," he replied. "Warned you."

Melina took in another expansive breath. "Where is your sword?"

A tiny furrow formed between his brows. "What?"

"Einherjars have swords, given to them by Valhalla. Where is yours?"

Grace laughed softly. "It's a good question." Her hand settled on the hilt of her own sword.

A tinge of red touched Axel's cheeks, above the scruffy beard. "I…don't keep mine extended." And his hand dropped to the pocket of his coat.

It was in there, then, Melina realized. She had never seen an Einherjar extend their sword. Those who had rushed to Blackmont last year, to fight the Alfar, had all carried full-length swords. And TV and movies and documentaries always showed the Einherjar with normal swords. But she had heard that they could tuck the swords away, somehow. For all the centuries that the Kine had been hiding among humans, they had carried their swords that way.

This was the first hint she'd got that the swords were *extended*. Extended from what?

Her mind busily speculated about how that might happen. Then she realized she was once more avoiding the fact that Axel was right in front of her.

He looked alive. More than that. He looked *good*. He looked as though he was glowing with optimal health.

Melina clenched her fists. "Um…so, anyway, how can I help you?" And she deliberately turned her chin toward Lucas Montgomery. "Um…sir?"

He smiled. "Just Lucas is fine. I was just Lucas for forty years, when I wasn't 'hey, asshole'." One eye fluttered in a near wink. Then his expression sobered. "We're here to look into Christie's death."

"Oh…!" Her voice was back to pathetic again. Surprise took all the strength out of it. "You're from New York, though. Christie was in London…you really investigate when an Amica dies?"

Grace leaned over the counter. "She died by her own hand, Melina. She was unhappy. *That's* a concern for us. We want to know why."

263

"And I was the closest Earl," Lucas added.

"You mean, your sister dropped it on you because the other earls would have complained," Davor growled.

"That, too," Lucas agreed easily.

Axel wasn't joining in the banter. He was watching Melina, his eyes narrowed a little.

Melina got to her feet. "If you want to investigate, you'd best start at the Memorial Hospital in Fairbanks. That's where they took her."

"Fairbanks," Lucas repeated.

"It's only thirty minutes from here," Melina added. "Use the company bus you came in from the train. Jerry will take you where you need to go. Tell him I said he should."

Lucas rubbed his jaw. "Jerry is local?"

"Born and bred," Melina confirmed.

"That will be useful," Grace murmured, looking at her Earl.

Lucas turned to Axel. "Do you want to stay here?"

"No!" Melina said quickly, just as Axel did.

"I mean," Melina added, "I have an office to run. Sorry." She couldn't bring herself to look at Axel. Her heart was back to pounding once more.

Axel nodded. "You brought me along because I'm local, too, remember?" he said to Lucas Montgomery.

"Okay then. Everyone back to the bus. Davor, you need help zipping yourself shut?" Lucas asked.

"I got it," Davor muttered, fighting to clip the two zipper ends together on his coat.

Grace rolled her eyes. "He lives in Mumbai. It shows."

Melina couldn't bring herself to smile. Laughter was far away.

Axel wound the scarf back around his neck. This time, he left his face visible.

The four of them trooped back out into the last of the daylight and climbed back into the bus. Jerry swung the bus around and headed for the road that ran past the compound. It was the same road that would take them to Fairbanks.

Melina watched until the bus could no longer be seen, while her heart swooped and dipped.

With luck, she would never see them again.

Yes, that would be best.

His eyes hadn't changed. Not in the slightest.

Damn him.

3.

When he returned from his lunch break, Pavlin overcame his usual meekness and ordered Melina to go home. He wouldn't listen when she protested, so she had reluctantly walked home.

The apartment smelled faintly of cleaning solutions. The cleaning team had done a thorough job. Every surface gleamed, the carpet was vacuumed. They'd even made her bed and washed the few dishes that had been sitting in the sink.

She would have to praise their efficiency when she next spoke to Lovell Tran, the sanitation supervisor.

She settled on the sofa with a bundle of books from her shelves, all old favorites, and buried herself in non-existent worlds and stories that kept her from thinking too much or too deeply.

At six, even though she was still far from hungry, Melina set about making a small supper for herself. It gave her something to do and occupied her thoughts.

She chewed her way through the tuna salad sandwich, while wondering which TV show she should put on, and finding none of them appealing. But she was sick of reading for now.

It was almost a relief when someone buzzed the front door.

Melina reached up and tapped the intercom on the wall by the table. "Yes?"

"Melina, it's Axel. I have Grace with me. We need to talk."

Melina pulled her hand away from the intercom as though it had burned her. Her heart was abruptly back to bouncing around, and the sandwich solidified in her stomach.

"It's about Christie," Axel added. "We know why she killed herself."

•

The two Kine sat at her small table, while Melina made coffee. Neither of them had said they wanted coffee when she asked, but Melina couldn't stand the idea of sitting at the table with them.

She kept her hands moving, while Axel told her what they had discovered during the day.

"Christie was pregnant," Axel said. "The coroner says she lost the baby a day or two before she came back here."

Melina sank onto her chair. "*Pregnant.* Oh, poor Christie...." Then she shook her head. "Even losing the child...Christie never wanted children, not that she said."

Grace cleared her throat. "The thing you don't know, that puts it into perspective—"

"It does *not*," Axel said firmly, his voice low.

Grace glanced at him. "It does if you're a woman," she said simply. She turned her attention back to Melina. "The thing is, an Einherjar offered her a long-term contract."

"Davor," Axel added. "He's a fine man. A good Einherjar."

Davor, the rotund short man in the white snow suit and red scarf. With greying hair.

Melina pressed her lips together. "He was the father?"

"He can't be," Grace said, her voice gentle. "He's Einherjar."

"Of course," Melina said woodenly. "Oh, god, what a mess she was in!" She rubbed her cheeks. "Who was the father then? Do you know?"

"We're looking into that, but it doesn't really matter," Axel began.

"Of course it matters!" Melina cried. "He'll want to know Christie has gone, at least. And he might know about the baby, too."

Axel shook his head. "That's not why we're here, Melina."

"But you said..." She stared at him, her heart thudding.

"It's not the only reason we're here," Grace said. Her gaze was steady. "You read Tarot cards."

Melina grew still. "For fun. Half the time, I'm making it up."

"You did a reading for Buck Johnstone a few days ago. You told him there would be two deaths in the next week."

Melina flinched. She remembered the reading. The spread had been full of troubling cards. The Tower. Death. The Hanged Man. "I don't remember saying that." Her voice was strained. "You're not taking it seriously, are you?"

Grace glanced at Axel.

"You have moments, Melina," Axel said. "You call them ghost fingers, walking up your back. And you see things."

"You *told* her about that?" Melina asked, hurt. "That was...that is *private*."

Axel's gaze slid away from her. "You knew about the baby," he insisted.

"I *didn't!*" Her voice rose. "I just...it was...I don't remember telling him about people *dying!*"

"That's often how it happens," Grace said, her voice still lovely and calm. "The fates speak through you."

Melina lurched to her feet. "It's just fun. I can't even remember what the cards mean, most of the time."

"Most of the time, they mean nothing," Grace replied. "But sometimes, they speak through you. Prophesy is a serious business, Melina."

Melina recalled the spread. The horror that had touched her when she had seen the trouble swirling through it. She had lied to Buck, giving him a happy, positive reading. Or she thought she had.

Buck had thanked her, afterwards, as if nothing was wrong. If she really had told him two people would die soon, surely he would have been upset?

The Tower had laid right beside the Devil. The Ten of Swords, with all ten blades buried in a man's back, had been there, too. The Knight of Swords. And the Five of Cups, signifying loss....

Her belly cramped as the horror she'd felt, seeing that spread, seemed to descend upon her once more.

She gasped.

"Melina?" Axel said. His voice came from far away.

Then suddenly he was there. He took her arm. "Hey."

She shook her head. She didn't think she could speak. The cards were swirling in her mind. "Tower," she croaked.

"What did she say?" Grace demanded, from the table.

Axel walked her back to the chair. Melina sat without protest. She felt sick. Her breath came in small pants.

"What do you see, Melina?" Grace asked from right beside her.

Meline couldn't lift her head. "Fighting. Swords. They're dying."

"Who are?" Axel demanded.

"You are."

"The Kine? Where?" Grace's tone was sharp. "Look for a landmark."

Melina didn't have to. She could see in her mind as clearly as she would on a TV screen. "The Brandenburg Gate," she whispered. She heard the singing swish of the big blades. "The Myrakar are there."

4.

"Sit anywhere you want," Lucas told Melina, waving a hand along the short carriage.

All the seats were benches for two, and each had a table between them, like a diner.

Listlessly, Melina slid onto the bench closest to her. When Axel sat opposite her, she felt nothing.

"We'll be underway in a moment or two," Lucas added, as he sat on the bench across the aisle. "But you know how this works, I'm sure."

She did. The Kine had figured out that as long as any two of them were connected to each other via metal, they could put anything between them that was connected to that metal.

Which meant a train with a wire running from the front to the back, which two Kine held at either end, could pass through the portals, too.

And suddenly, the Kine were in the freight business, which had saved the world from hunger, because the seas were no longer safe for cargo ships—the Kraken that lived in them now destroyed ships with a wave of their tentacles. It also gave the Kine a legitimate income, too.

Special portals had been created by the Kine that had train tracks running through them, and freight trains now carried the loads that ships had once delivered around the world.

Blackmont's rare earth, which was needed for electronics and more, was delivered by train to normal freight trains in New York, or the same train could dive into another train portal to somewhere else.

There were almost daily announcements about new train portals being opened somewhere in the world.

But the trains could also carry passengers.

So far, the Kine had not set themselves up in opposition to air transport, despite most of the world demanding that they do so. Instant transport around the globe, instead of long-haul flights and jet lag? Everyone wanted it.

But only those who the Kine allowed on their trains got to experience instant travel. And now Melina was about to find out what it was like, even though it was the last place she wanted to be.

Axel pulled off his gloves and opened his coat, as the train rolled forward, picking up speed. "Do you want coffee? Something to eat?"

"No."

He gripped his hands together. "I'm sorry about this. It wasn't my idea."

"I know."

"But you prophesied, Melina. And you were right." His voice was low and insistent, as though he could *will* her to agree with him.

The battle at the Brandenburg Gate had happened exactly as she had seen it. Myrakar had poured through a temporary portal to attack the Einherjar guarding the train portal in Berlin, which emerged just to one side of the old archway.

Grace had called the Kine hall in New York to warn them, despite Melina's horrified protests. New York had warned the hall in Berlin, and had sent Einherjar through the portals to help fight off the Alfar.

Only twenty minutes later, both Grace and Axel's phones had rung with multiple calls, which they took with stoic calmness.

"About three hundred Alfar," Grace had reported to Axel.

"I heard four hundred." Axel had shrugged. "A significant number. The Kine in Berlin would have been overwhelmed."

"Yes."

And both had looked at Melina. Melina hunched in on herself, feeling something close to terror. It had just been images in her head. It hadn't been magical.

Someone who really, truly prophesied would feel something special when they did so, wouldn't they? A fever. Or light passing through them. Shock of some sort.

But she had merely felt like she was day-dreaming.

Except the images had been so *clear*.

Lucas Montgomery arrived at the apartment only a few minutes later, breathless, his phone in one hand. "Right, we've been called to the hall." He looked at Melina. "And you're coming with us."

Melina had refused. She cited work as her excuse. The office couldn't run without her. But Lucas had already spoken to Pavlin Barr, who had been almost eager for Melina to go with them.

"You'll be gone a day at the most. You don't have to pack anything," Grace said. "We'll have you back here before you know it. But you *must* speak to Charlotte Rose, Melina. She will know what to do with your talent."

Melina flinched. "I'm not talented."

Grace stared back. "Yes, you are. You just saved hundreds of lives, Melina. You can tell whatever lies you want about it, but nothing changes that fact. You're coming with us."

So now she sat on a Kine train, heading toward the Blackmont portal, which would put them in New York the instant they passed through it. And Axel, who had been essentially dead to her for a year, sat opposite her, his hands clenched together so the knuckles were white.

"You *were* right," he repeated, as if that justified her near-abduction. He hesitated, then added. "They won't hurt you."

Melina stirred herself. "No, but you are."

Axel's jaw flexed. "I *had* to come, Melina. It was an order. Lucas is my Earl. Grace is my Stallari. Asher ordered us to investigate."

She made herself meet his gaze. Yes, it hurt. Her whole body was aching, having him so near. "You wouldn't have come near me on your own, though."

"No. You know why."

She nodded. He had made it very clear, on the New Year's Eve after he had died, fighting the Alfar in the Blackmont battle. He had called her via Zoom, and while she had marvelled that he was alive again, he had said flatly, "I'm Einherjar now, Melina."

"Yes," she had breathed, fighting to not slide her finger down the image of his cheek. Oh, how she had wanted to kiss him! "You were a hero. Of course the Valkyrie would have picked you up from the field of battle. You saved people with just a hockey stick."

Axel shifted, looking uncomfortable. "That's not what I mean." He leaned forward. "I'm *Einherjar*, Melina. I didn't ask to be, but it happened."

"I don't care," she said honestly. The deeper truth was that she was proud of him in an intense way that made her warm when she thought about it.

It was good that he had been made an Einherjar. Axel was everything the Valkyrie looked for. Courageous. Brave. Strong.

"You *should* care, Melina," Axel replied. "You should hate this. You *must* hate it, because I do."

The warmth in her middle dissipated. "You...hate it?"

Axel rubbed his forehead. "Don't you understand, Melina? I now get to live forever."

"Yes." She smiled.

"But you don't."

Melina blinked. "I...well...yes, I know that."

Axel looked away, at something behind the computer he was using. "They're putting me through the most intense orientation and training I've ever had, Melina. And there's drinking and gossip at night. They say that Einherjar and humans...those relationships never work. Not for long."

Coldness gripped her. "They're telling you to break up with me?"

"No! But everyone is warning me, one way or the other." He hesitated. "I can't...there wouldn't be children, Melly."

That was when her heart started to break. "I don't understand," she whispered. But she *did* understand. At least, she understood what he was doing.

He was telling her goodbye. The why hardly mattered, after that.

"No children might not bother you now," Axel ground out. "But years from now, when you get older, it will matter. A lot. And you'll hate me for it.

And I'll hate you for not living forever with me...it can only end bitter."

So he had ended it right then.

Melina looked at Axel now. "It didn't work," she told him.

Axel looked puzzled.

"You said you didn't want us to end up bitter."

"I didn't," he muttered.

"But here we are. Bitter."

Axel drew in a breath. Let it out. "I'll get you a coffee." He rose and moved down the carriage before she could tell him that she didn't want coffee, that she wanted nothing from him at all.

Lucas was staring out the window of the fast moving train. It ran smoothly along the tracks and swayed not at all. "Portal," he warned, pointing.

Melina looked out her own window. The portal looked like a simple train tunnel, built into the side of a foothill, except the mouth was greyish white, not black. She watched the loaded freight trucks ahead of the passenger carriage roll through the grey curtain, as if they were passing through a mist.

Then the front of the carriage dived through, and she saw the grey curtain sweep up the carriage, then over her.

She felt nothing at all. Not even her body. Then, a second later, the blank sensation was gone. She was still on the train, but now the enormous spread of New York City lay on either side of the carriage, glittering with lights even at midnight.

The train braked and slowed, then stopped alongside a concrete platform that had none of the usual passenger signage or shelters. A frank iron roof spread over the track and the platform, hiding the city view.

"Now comes the slowest part of the journey," Lucas said, getting to his feet. "But it's midnight. We should be able to find a taxi quicker than normal, this time of night."

"In Queens?" Grace asked, her tone sarcastic. "Don't bet on it."

The three of them stepped off the train. Axel and Danor were already on the platform, waiting for them. They moved through a doorway guarded by Einherjar in full battle gear, out onto a perfectly normal New York street. At least, Melina presumed it was normal. She had never been to New York before, and the noise of the place, even at midnight, was astonishing. Everywhere, she could hear cars, horns, people talking or shouting, far away. Music, faint and far, but at least three different types, clashing with each other.

Blackmont was silent, in comparison. A moose bellowing outside the town would be heard by everyone.

Axel and Grace shepherded Melina into a cab when it pulled up beside them.

"Lucas and Davor are getting a second cab," Grace told Melina.

Melina wanted to shrug and ask who cared, but she realized she was turning her head, taking in everything, like a newbie tourist. She couldn't help it. This was *New York*. Five minutes ago, she had been in Alaska.

The cab shot through streets that seemed crowded with cars, to her. It crossed over a high bridge, the tires rumbling over the surface, onto what she could only assume was Manhattan. The New York hall was on Pearl Street, she remembered. That was far down the south end of Manhattan.

The buildings grew taller, and the streets felt narrower.

The cab stopped outside a new, modern apartment building, with a concierge out the front, and a canopy.

"This is the New York hall?" Melina asked, astonished.

"The new one," Grace said. "The Kine blew up the old one to stop the Alfar invading New York." She snorted. "Not that it stopped them for long."

"It's morning in the hall," Axel said, as if he was reminding Grace of something.

"Right." She moved over toward the door of the building. The concierge scurried to open it for her.

"Stallari." He touched the brim of his hat.

"But isn't it midnight?" Melina asked.

"Here, yes," Axel told her. "The hall runs on a different time zone."

"This hall, here?"

He glanced at her as they passed through the great glass and brass doors. "*The* hall," he said.

Valhalla.

It was only then she processed that of course they would have to go to Valhalla, as that was where the Regin and Annarr lived and worked.

She shivered.

There were tours to Valhalla. Polly was saving up for one. But otherwise, the mere human could not go there, not without an Einherjar escort. And they had to pass through a hall that connected directly to Valhalla via portals. New York was one. Geraldton, Western Australia, was the other. The Australian hall had been chosen because it was the closest to the opposite side of the world from New York.

They stepped onto an elevator, and Lucas and Davor hurried into the car after them. The elevator rose smoothly and swiftly and delivered them to a foyer that was lined with rough, old wood planks.

Ahead, enormous double doors stood open, and through them, Melina glimpsed a huge room.

Then she saw what was on the other side of the large foyer.

Two more, man-sized portals with grey mist curtains, with four Einherjar guarding them.

A woman—a Valkyrie—stepped through as Melina looked, nodded at the guards, and walked into the other portal.

"Hurry," Grace murmured, and moved over to the portals.

The Einherjar straightened up as they approached and looked ahead.

"Relax, fellows. I've had my morning coffee," Lucas said.

One of the guards grinned, then wiped the grin off his face.

Grace turned to Melina. "You have to hold someone's shoulder, to get through."

"Yours, please."

Grace laughed. "It won't do you any good, honey. I'm human."

Melina stared at her, her jaw sagging. "But...you're a Stallari."

"Best one in the world," Lucas said. "Almost worth all the fuss that was made when I picked a human over an Einherjar. But they've lived to eat their words since then." He turned and held his shoulder out to them.

Grace stepped up and gripped it firmly. "Almost?" she repeated.

Human. That explained why her sword was always extended. She didn't have the powers the Einherjar did to extend or...compact her sword?

Fold it? Put it away? It was why she needed Lucas to take her through the portal.

That left Davor or Axel to take Melina through.

With a sigh, she put her hand on Axel's shoulder. His hand rested over hers. It was warm, the way it always had been. "Don't let go," he warned her and moved toward the left-hand portal.

Lucas was already passing through, with Grace matching his pace right behind him.

The grey curtain passed over Melina, imparting the dead blank moment, then she stepped through into bright, warm sunshine.

Melina looked around and up...and up. Far overhead, a glass roof soared, coming together in an oval dome, supported by stone struts.

The hall was enormous, and many people were standing in it, or moving across it. More people passed through doorways and arches around the side of the rectangular hall. At the other end, though, were three pairs of giant doors, all standing open. Another room lay beyond, and it looked to be even larger than this one.

"Welcome to Valhalla," Grace told Melina.

She shivered.

"You're cold?" Axel asked, concern tinging his voice.

Melina shook her head.

Grace nodded. "It gets to you like that sometimes." Sympathy tinged her voice. "But you're entitled to be here."

"I am?" Melina asked, surprised.

"If Valhalla didn't want you here, you couldn't get here even if you were carried through the portals," Lucas said. "Valhalla has a way of deciding how it wants things to go and where people should be."

"Or what swords they get," Grace added, her hand curling around the hilt of her sword.

"Valhalla gave you a sword?" Melina asked, astonishment rippling through her.

"It's how I knew I'd picked right," Lucas said, bumping Grace's shoulder.

A chime sounded in the next room, a light sound that echoed in this hall.

People moved quickly, most of them heading for the other room.

No one had to tell Melina to hurry this time.

They passed through the doors into what Melina realized was the *actual* hall of Valhalla. At the far end—which was a long way away—a tall dais held two chairs. Thrones, more or less.

And Charlotte Rose and Asher sat in the chairs. Melina knew it was them because she had seen many photos and videos about them. From this far away, they looked just as they did in the photos. Charlotte Rose was a red head, and Asher was as blond as his name seemed to imply.

People were gathered on the floor at the foot of the dais, and in the small open space between them and the dais, a man stood speaking, while the Regin and Annarr listened.

Melina and the others were standing too far away to hear what the man was saying, but Lucas made no attempt to push through the crowd and get closer to the dais.

A woman came up to them. It was difficult to tell her age, for her hair was a light silver colour, fine and thin, and seemed to float around her chin. Her eyes, though, were young.

She had a terrible scar on her cheek, a red blotch that looked like a paint splat, and she walked with a limp.

She came right up to Melina, so that Melina could not see around her, and tilted her head. "So…hello."

And in her mind, Melina heard an echoing voice repeating the words.

"Hello…?" Melina replied.

"This is the one," the woman said to Lucas.

"Yes, this is Melina," Lucas said, as if the woman had asked a question, which she had not.

The woman smiled at Melina. "You know me."

Melina opened her mouth to say no. "You're Unnur," she said instead. She felt her eyes widen.

Unnur nodded. "Tell me about yourself."

"Um. I am Melina."

Unnur shook her head. "Tell me about yourself," she repeated.

Melina opened her mouth to ask what the woman wanted to know, but instead, she said, "My grandmother claimed she was a descendant of Noidola'an of the Koyukuk."

Unnur nodded. "It seems she might have been."

"I don't have magic," Melina said quickly. "The cards…I make things up."

"You *think* you do," Unnur said gently. "The cards speak to us in different ways."

Melina bit her lip.

"Your talent is just waking up," Unnur said. "It can happen that way. If we repress it, refuse to let it shine, it will stay dormant. Who scarred you?" The question was quick, startling her into another shocking response.

"My mother."

Unnur nodded. "She didn't believe in mystical nonsense. Said it was the devil's work, perhaps?"

Melina's mouth opened. She brought her teeth back together with a snap.

Unnur touched her arm. It was a light touch, but for a second, Melina *felt* the woman in her head and her chest.

"You're among friends here," Unnur said. She stirred and looked at Lucas. "It's the solstice, earl. You and yours must stay for the feast, for you won't get near Charlie and Asher today, not until this crowd has gone."

"Thank you, Unnur," Lucas said gravely, and nodded his head, almost like he was bowing.

Unnur moved away. The limp was distinct, making her hips swing.

"Who *is* she?" Melina whispered to Grace.

"Unnur?" Grace drew in a breath. "You haven't read about her before?"

"She's The Lady of the Lake," Axel said unexpectedly. "In Valhalla terms, anyway."

Melina understood instantly what he meant, for the King Arthur tales had been among her favourites as a child. Then she gasped. "I *have* heard of her! The Unnur Method. She's the Kine's prophet. The woman who was struck by lightning, and after that, she could see the future..." She turned to glimpse Unnur once more, but there were too many people craning to see the front of the hall.

"Well, we're going to be here a while, it seems," Grace said, stirring. "I'm going to visit a few people." She rested her hand against Lucas' arm. "Okay?"

"Knock yourself out. Find a pretty dress for the feast while you're visiting."

Grace rolled her eyes. "Is that an order?"

Lucas considered her for a moment.

"Yes, sir," Grace said with a sigh and stalked away, waving through people.

Lucas and Axel looked at each other.

Then Axel turned to Melina. "There is a drinking hall just off the foyer. I'll get you an early breakfast."

She wanted to protest that she wasn't hungry, but her belly cramped. "Do they serve coffee?" she asked hopefully.

"By the barrel," Lucas said. "I'll catch up with you at the feast. New York will have a table here tonight. I'm heading back to polish my shield." He nodded at Melina, and left, too.

Axel waved toward the big doors. "This way."

Fear and pleasure ran through her as Melina realized with a shiver that she would be alone with him.

5.

Through one of the many archways coming off the foyer was what Axel had called the drinking hall.

It looked, in fact, like any modern lounge bar, with sofas and armchairs with low tables, and dim lighting.

"The bistro doesn't open for a few hours yet," Axel said, "but you can get small meals here at any time, because Valhalla doesn't run to the same time as Earth does."

Melina halted just inside the door, astonishment running through her. "We're really in another world here, aren't we?"

"One that no one knows the location of," Axel assured her. "Including the Alfar. Charlotte Rose found Valhalla after it had been lost for centuries."

"I know the story," Melina said stiffly.

"Right. Of course. Here, there's a table over here." Axel made a fuss about getting them seated at the small table, which had only three chairs around it. There were few other people in the lounge, but two people were working behind the bar.

One of them came over. "Axel. Good to see you. Mead?"

"Francisque," Axel intoned. "Coffee, please. And a grilled cheese sandwich, and an apple."

Her favourite snack ever. Melina's eyes pricked hard and painfully with tears she refused to let fall. She blinked hard to disperse them.

But something must have shown on her face, for Axel frowned. "You don't want grilled cheese?"

"You know I love a good grilled cheese sandwich."

Her voice was husky, and she tried to clear her throat. "Why is there a feast today?"

"It's the solstice."

"Okay."

"They don't celebrate Christmas here. They celebrate the solstice, which is what the ancient world used to do, before the Christians came along and insisted that December 25 was the day for a mid-winter feast."

"Good," Melina said.

Axel considered her. "Good?"

"I don't want to celebrate Christmas this year." She looked away.

The silence stretched for too many heartbeats.

"Melina…"

She shook her head. "No. Let's not go over it again. It's all been said."

"It has," Axel agreed heavily. "But that doesn't mean I don't hate myself for it."

She looked back at him, startled. Her heart thudded.

Axel's warm copper-colored eyes were filled with some emotion she could not name. "I miss you, Melina." His voice was low.

"Don't *tell* me that." Her chest hurt and her eyes ached. "Don't tell me stuff like that. It makes you feel better, but it makes me *sick*."

"Sick?" He sounded shocked.

She gripped the center of her chest, pushing against her breastbone, to relieve the ache. "I used to cry myself to sleep, Axel."

He grimaced.

"I would cry until my eyes swelled, and I'd have to bathe them in ice water the next morning so no one would stare at me at work. And I'd work all day, then go home. But everything at home reminded me of you."

"So, you moved."

"I would have burned the house down if I could have got away with it," Melina replied.

Axel flinched. He put his face in his hands. "Okay. I get it." His voice was muffled.

"I don't think you do," Melina said. She reached over and gripped his thick wrist and pulled his hand away from his face. "It would have been easier if you'd died and *stayed* dead, Axel."

He closed his eyes. Nodded.

Francisque cleared his throat, bent and put two mugs of coffee on the table. He hurried away without comment.

Listlessly, Melina reached for a mug. It was a long while before Axel stirred and drank his.

The thought grew in her, building with each passing minute. *How can I get out of here?*

The coffee was bitter.

•

Melina's food came, and she ate it mechanically.

Another hour passed while they said nothing. It was safer that way.

But it wasn't boring, because it seemed that everyone knew Axel. A steady stream of them would sit in the third chair and swap quick news and catch up with Axel's doings.

Axel appeared to throw off his mood and respond with humor and easy charm—she remembered that charm all too well. He told nearly everyone about the apartment he'd found in Soho, that he was moving out of the hall itself. The Einherjar whom he shared this with would nod judiciously, then tell him that after a few years, he'd probably move back into the hall, that they had spent years shuttling between private residences and living at the hall and had never found a permanent compromise.

Some of the women were Valkyrie. Melina didn't know how she knew that for sure, only that as more and more people sat at the table, she developed a feeling for each of them that became a certainty. This one was a Valkyrie. This one was Amica, even without the apron dress uniform. This one was merely human. That man was Einherjar. And that one was human.

When Axel introduced them to her, Melina's guess was usually confirmed.

There were a surprising number of humans among the Kine, even though human access to Valhalla was highly restricted.

There was a great deal about Valhalla that didn't match with the reports, the bulletin boards, the images, the documentaries.

Axel laughed a lot while talking with his friends and associates.

"You like it here," she observed, between visitors.

Axel hesitated. "It hardly matters, does it?" he asked cautiously, his gaze steady upon her.

As he was Einherjar and would be one forever, this world was his whether he liked it or not.

"But you like it anyway," Melina pushed.

"Yes," he said flatly. "I do."

She nodded and looked away.

Sometime later—she didn't know how long, because she stopped looking at her watch—there was a stir and a murmur that seemed to wash over the room.

Even Axel stiffened and sat up straighter.

Melina looked around, wondering what had put everyone on high alert.

Charlotte Rose stood in the doorway of the lounge, a hand on one hip, scanning the room. Her gaze found Axel and she looked relieved and hurried up to the table.

Axel tried to rise to his feet.

"No, no, there's no time," Charlotte Rose said, and dropped into the third chair. "I only dare leave Asher alone with the wolves in the hall for a few minutes. He's listening to a friend right now, but if someone else stirs his temper..." She blew out a breath so that her hair lifted around her face. A pale pink scar ran down her face from the outer corner of her left eye, almost all the way down to her mouth. "I'm not the one who should have the red hair," she added with a smile.

Then she leaned forward.

"Regin..." Axel said. It was a formal acknowledgment.

"Einherjar," Charlotte Rose returned. "And you are Melina."

"You *know* that?" Melina asked.

The woman touched her temple. "I'm not at Unnur's level of skill but I have a touch of the power. It's what lets me make portals. So yes, I know who you are."

Her smile was warm, and her eyes danced with humor. "I don't have very much time, Melina, but I didn't want to leave you sitting in these uncomfortable chairs all day. I want you to stay here in the hall. Unnur feels you have powerful potential, and she needs an apprentice."

Melina blinked. "But…no, this can't be for real. I just play around with the Tarot."

"You saw the battle at Brandenburg before it began," Charlotte Rose said. "Tell me, since you've arrived here, have you noticed anything strange? I mean, beyond everything that is strange here compared to home. Have you felt anything?"

Melina jumped. She could tell if someone was Einherjar, or not.

Charlotte Rose nodded as if Melina had answered her. "There. You see?"

Melina shook her head. "With all due respect, ma'am, thank you, but no."

Charlotte Rose sat back. "I didn't come to you to hear a no. Tell me why."

Melina didn't look at Axel. She couldn't. It would be too telling. "I just…it's impossible. I'm just human."

Charlotte Rose considered her for a long moment. "There is a lot of impossible that happens here. You must have noticed. Lucas's second, Grace, came here with you. She's human, yet she's a Stallari, and a good one. We have another human, Darwin, who actually *married* a former Valkyrie. And Valhalla didn't implode over either impossibility. We have Einherjar living with humans all the time now, openly and committed for the long term."

"How *can* they commit for the long term?" Melina demanded. "They live forever, and humans…don't."

Charlotte Rose nodded again. "That *is* true, but just by being among us, and spending time here, something rubs off on humans. Darwin is over ninety, now, but he barely looks sixty. I suspect he will live quite a few decades more. There is something about keeping close company with the Kine that imparts this gift. You could have it, too."

Melina shook her head again. She could feel genuine anger building in her.

"You say no, but you have not explained why in a way that will let me accept your no," Charlotte Rose said.

"Regin, Melina is very tired…" Axel began, but Charlotte Rose held up her hand.

"Let her speak for herself, Axel," Charlotte Rose said gently.

Melina squeezed her hands between her knees, to stop the words from tumbling out. Her anger was driving them, and anger often erupted as cruelty.

But the emotion was too large, filling her chest and head and making it hard to breathe.

Desperately, Melina shoved the big ball of emotions and hazy thoughts away from her, everything that was swirling around in her mind right now.

How much she loved Axel still, but he did not want her in his life, where both of them must suffer through her aging and death. How much she resented the Kine for doing this to them, for saving Axel and taking him away from her at the same time.

That Melina's life would be terribly short, compared to Axel's, and besides, there would be no children.

And finally, to work here in these halls, among the people she had met, where she could see Axel day after day, and never be a part of his life…it would drive her mad. Every day would hurt.

The rest of her life would be filled with pain.

Charlotte Rose drew in a hard, heavy breath, drawing backwards, as if she had inhaled something noxious. She put her fingers to her mouth. "I see…" she said softly. "Oh…yes, I see."

Melina realized that she had not pushed the sensations away from her. She had pushed them *at* Charlotte Rose. She wrapped her arms around her middle, suddenly cold.

Charlotte Rose got to her feet. "I will have an Einherjar come and find you, and escort you home, Melina."

Axel stood. "Regin, I—"

"I'm not angry, Axel," Charlotte Rose said. Her tone was warm. "Melina has explained herself in a way I can accept." She gave Melina a small smile that seemed touched with bitterness. "For I was once in that very same place. I would never ask anyone to go through that themselves. I know how it hurts."

She nodded at Melina and left the lounge.

Five minutes later, an Einherjar who introduced himself as Yakov came to escort Melina back to Blackmont.

Axel's goodbye was stiff, and puzzlement married his forehead. But he let her leave without protest, which was just as well, because Melina could only hold it together long enough to step through the portal to New York, her hand on Yakov's shoulder.

After that, Yakov had to guide her, because her tears were blurring her vision.

6.

Melina had refused to put up a Christmas tree or any decorations. After returning from Valhalla, she also firmly refused every invitation to share Christmas day with friends. Even Pavlin Barr had suggested that she join his big family for the day, which was a first.

Instead, Melina made herself a grilled cheese sandwich for brunch, with three different types of cheeses and garlic juice brushed over the outer surface of the bread before grilling.

Then she sat at the table and ate it. Afterward, it sat like a rock in her stomach.

So she curled up in the corner of the sofa with all her favourite books around her, and read.

The tap on the door came a few hours later. It wasn't the downstairs buzzer, but the door to the apartment itself, and Melina held still.

No one had a key for the front door. No one who would tap on her door on Christmas day, at least.

The tap came again. "Melina!"

Axel's voice.

Her breath grew ragged. Melina pressed a hand to her chest.

"Melina, it's me. It's okay. I'm alone."

Moving like a marionette, Melina got up and opened the door.

Axel was taking off his gloves. "It must be fifteen below out there!"

"Eight below, actually," Melina said stiffly. "What are you doing here, Axel?"

"I'm here to speak to you. Why else would I be here?"

"There's no trains running," she pointed out. "It's Christmas Day."

"Which means it's safe to walk through a train portal." Axel shrugged and slipped past her. "I need to warm up."

"I need you to leave," Melina said. Finally, she felt something. Fear.

Axel turned to face her. "Shut the door."

"No."

"You want Degataga and Jenny, and Passang to hear every word."

"Degataga and Jenny are in Fairbanks for the holidays. Passang is with his cousin for the day." Melina shrugged.

"Everyone is with someone," Axel concluded. "That's why I'm here."

Melina closed the door.

"Lucas told me to get my ass here," Axel admitted. "But he's not the reason I'm here. He just gave me permission to leave the hall."

"I don't understand."

Axel pulled off the heavy winter overcoat and dropped it onto her chair beside the table. His scarf and gloves on top of it.

He pushed his hands into his pockets. He was wearing perfectly ordinary jeans, which might be fine in New York, but didn't cut it in Alaskan weather.

No wonder he was cold.

"Thing is," he said, then stopped.

Melina sank down onto the edge of the sofa, her hands between her knees, which hid their trembling. Her heart was making her chest vibrate.

"Thing is," Axel said again, then rubbed his jaw. The proto beard rasped.

"You never could say what is on your mind," Melina pointed out.

"I know, and it's driving me crazy right now because I *have…to…get…this…out.*" He pummeled his thigh with his fist, punctuating each word.

Then he moved over to the sofa with determined strides and sat on the edge, too, so they were facing each other. A foot of air separated their knees.

He rested his fists on his knees. "The thing is," he started again. "Asher came and drank at the New York table, during the feast. He told me a story."

"Asher…Strand. The *Annarr*?"

"Him. Yes. He told me about the time when he and Charlie were trapped under the Alfar shield in New York."

"When the Alfar were hunting both of them?"

Axel nodded. "He was Einherjar and Charlie was human, and nobody gave a damn, even though such relationships had been proscribed for centuries. He said it was the happiest time of his life. Up until then, at least."

Melina stared at Axel, wondering what it was he was trying to say, for he was coming to it from a very roundabout way.

"But here's the thing," Axel added. "That time ended. She died in the New York battle. And he thought she was gone forever."

Except that Charlotte Rose had returned as a Valkyrie, for she had found Valhalla. Melina didn't point that out, though, for she suspected it would push Axel even further away from what he was trying to say.

She waited.

"Things end," Axel said. "Everything ends. Asher lost Charlie. And I lost you."

Melina's heart swooped and fell. She felt giddy. "But—"

He held up his hand. It was trembling. "No. Let me finish."

She pressed her lips together.

"All anyone *really* gets is today, Melly. Everything ends. All relationships end, eventually. And no one knows how that will happen. Charlie didn't die of old age, the way Asher expected she would one day. She was killed in battle. And I don't know when your life will end either. It could be tomorrow. It could be a week from now. Or a hundred years from now. No one knows."

"No, they don't," Melina agreed, thinking of Christie, and her tragically short life.

"There's no certainty. There's just what is in front of you." Axel leaned forward and picked up her hand. His touch made her nerves tingle.

He tugged her closer and she slid across the sofa until their knees were almost touching. She didn't dare move closer. That would be much too tempting.

Axel looked down at her hand, laying in his. He stroked her palm, making her skin sizzle. "I love you." His voice was very low. "I always have, from the day we met in school at Fairbanks. For the last year, I thought it would be cruel to try to keep you in my life. That it could only end in misery."

His gaze met hers. "It *will* end that way," he added.

Melina drew in a breath that shook.

"Losing you will be the hardest thing I have to get through in this second life I've been given. But I would rather lose you at the end of thousands of days of having you in my life, than not have you near at all."

Her eyes ached as tears rose. Melina gripped his fingers. "Are you *sure*, Axel? I don't want you to end up hating me. You said we would be bitter, in the end."

"Not if we go into this knowing what we're facing. If we accept that we don't know what will happen."

"Only," Melina said, "Apparently, I can tell the future."

Axel's lips parted. Then he smiled and drew her even closer and wrapped his arm around her. "God, you're *warm*," he breathed, then touched his lips to her forehead. "It doesn't matter what happens. We take each day we get and be grateful. Yes?"

Melina stroked his cheek above the stubble. "Yes," she breathed and kissed him.

It was a heavenly kiss, one that seemed to make up for all the kisses they had missed. When it ended, they were both breathing hard.

"Let's ignore Christmas from now on," Axel suggested, his voice hoarse. "The Kine celebrate the solstice. We can make that our Christmas, instead."

Melina shook her head. "No. Christmas gave us a second chance. I think we should give it a second chance, too."

"Deal," Axel agreed. "Merry Christmas, Melina." And he kissed her again.

Tracy Cooper-Posey is the author of the popular Once and Future Hearts historical fantasy romance series, among others. She writes romantic suspense, historical, paranormal, fantasy and science fiction romance, plus women's fiction. She also writes under the pen names of Cameron Cooper (science fiction) and Taylen Carver (fantasy). She has published over 200 titles since 1999, been nominated for five CAPAs including Favourite Author, is an Aurealis Award Finalist, and has won the Emma Darcy Award.

She turned to indie publishing in 2011. Her indie titles have been nominated four times for Book Of The Year. Tracy won the award in 2012, a SFR Galaxy Award in 2016 and came fourth in Hugh Howey's SPSFC#2 in 2023. She is a city magazine editor and for a decade she taught romance writing at MacEwan University.

She is addicted to Irish Breakfast tea and chocolate, sometimes taken together. In her spare time she enjoys history, Sherlock Holmes, science fiction and ignoring her treadmill. An Australian Canadian, she lives in Edmonton, Canada with her husband, a former professional wrestler, where she moved in 1996 after meeting him on-line.

Other SRP Anthologies

A Gathering of Stories: Halloween

A Gathering of Stories: Valentine's Day

Thriller Digest 2022: Hunted

Space Opera Digest 2022: Have Ship, Will Travel

Christmas Romance Digest 2021: Home For The Holidays

Space Opera Digest 2021: Fight or Flight

This is a Stories Rule Press Title

STORIESRULEPRESS.COM